Praise for Susan Coll

"Coll ably juggles chaotic details, turning them into hilarious running gags while making it completely clear why Sophie wants to bury herself in the nook—though she can't, because the power went out. While this is full of nods to the publishing world that those in the know will appreciate, every reader who loves books will relish Coll's comedy of errors."

—*BOOKLIST* FOR *BOOKISH PEOPLE*

"As much fun as Coll has with vacuum cleaners—a truly surprising amount—it's literary humor where she slays."

—*KIRKUS* FOR *BOOKISH PEOPLE*

"Susan Coll's *Bookish People* is a delightful, hilarious, and utterly charming novel about a quirky bookstore and its motley crew—ridiculously lovable people who think way too much about words, writing, dead authors, customers' dogs, cats who torment birds, canceled author events, British ovens, readers, vacuum cleaners, and Russian tortoises. The perfect read for bookish people everywhere!"

—ANGIE KIM, INTERNATIONALLY
BESTSELLING AUTHOR OF *MIRACLE CREEK*

"A smart, original, laugh-out-loud novel that fans of Tom Perrotta will adore. If you sell, buy, or simply love books, *Bookish People* is for you. I wholeheartedly recommend this quirky gem."

—SARAH PEKKANEN, *NEW YORK TIMES* BESTSELLING
CO-AUTHOR OF *THE GOLDEN COUPLE*

"There's not a wittier, zanier, smarter book about books and the people who love them than *Bookish People*. After reading about this single screwball week in the book biz, you'll want to hug your closest bookseller (and maybe apply for a job)."

—LESLIE PIETRZYK, AUTHOR OF
ADMIT THIS TO NO ONE

"Take a bookstore owner who is sick of books, a pompous poet who has managed to get himself canceled, and a crew of overqualified millennial employees, then add a week of political upheaval and a rare celestial event. The result is *Bookish People*, a sharp yet tender comedy of bookstore manners. Susan Coll has written a love letter to bibliophiles everywhere with too many hilarious parts to list—though the tortoise named Kurt Vonnegut Jr. may be my all-time favorite literary pet."

—LISA ZEIDNER, AUTHOR OF *LOVE BOMB*

Real Life and Other Fictions

Real Life and Other Fictions

A Novel

SUSAN COLL

HARPER MUSE

Real Life and Other Fictions

Copyright © 2024 Susan Keselenko Coll

Published by Harper Muse, an imprint of HarperCollins Focus LLC.

Published in association with the literary agency of HG Literary.

This book is a work of fiction. The characters, incidents, and dialogue are drawn from the author's imagination and are not to be construed as real. Any resemblance to actual events or persons, living or dead, is entirely coincidental.

Any internet addresses (websites, blogs, etc.) in this book are offered as a resource. They are not intended in any way to be or imply an endorsement by HarperCollins Focus LLC, nor does HarperCollins Focus LLC vouch for the content of these sites for the life of this book.

Library of Congress Cataloging-in-Publication Data

Names: Coll, Susan, author.
Title: Real life and other fictions / Susan Coll.
Description: Nashville: Harper Muse, 2024. | Summary: "Susan Coll uses her experience as both an author and bookstore employee to deliver a big-hearted and dramatic comedy about myths, real life, and the overlap between them"-- Provided by publisher.
Identifiers: LCCN 2024003528 (print) | LCCN 2024003529 (ebook) | ISBN 9781400234141 (paperback) | ISBN 9781400234158 (epub) | ISBN 9781400234165
Subjects: LCSH: Self-realization in women--Fiction. | LCGFT: Road fiction. | Novels.
Classification: LCC PS3553.O474622 R43 2024 (print) | LCC PS3553.O474622 (ebook) | DDC 813/.54--dc23/eng/20240126
LC record available at https://lccn.loc.gov/2024003528
LC ebook record available at https://lccn.loc.gov/2024003529

Printed in the United States of America

24 25 26 27 28 LBC 5 4 3 2 1

For my mother, Marian Keselenko

There are more things in heaven and earth, Horatio,
Than are dreamt of in your philosophy.

—*Hamlet*, William Shakespeare

Part 1

CHAPTER I

The Incident on the Chesapeake Bay Bridge

A HEAVY GREY slush begins to fall from the sky, and the windshield wipers turn themselves on, startling me. Although the car is seven years old, it is new to me, and I'm still getting used to its high-tech features, many of which are already obsolete. It has none of the self-driving technology one reads about, for example, so it's entirely on me to stomp on the brakes to avoid hitting the car ahead as traffic comes to an abrupt stop.

The vehicle which I mercifully did not plow into is a green Honda CR-V with a University of Virginia sticker affixed to the top right corner of the rear windshield. The speed at which I am traveling is precisely one mile under the fifty-miles-per-hour limit.

I lock into these details because I am the sort of law-abiding-to-a-fault motorist who minds the rules of the road, always staying at or below the speed limit, and because my daughter, Vera, has only a few days ago completed her first semester at the University of Maryland. In front of me is presumably another student, or a former student, or the parent of a student, or an instructor, or someone student-adjacent in one form or another, albeit at a different public institution of higher learning.

But also, I lock into these details as a way to ground myself. I'm feeling light, without anchor, as if I might unbuckle my seatbelt and crack the window and slip through the slit like a puff of steam or a wisp of smoke. It's not simply that my daughter is away for the holidays for the first time in nineteen years; I have also just left my husband. I have brought to a conclusion a long, painful stalemate, taken my poorly behaved puppy, and walked out the door.

No harsh words were exchanged, although I had half-hoped for a provocation, or at least some display of emotion, when I told him I was leaving, that I was headed to my aunt and uncle's house on the Delaware shore. We were meant to go together—it was our family's long-standing tradition to spend the week between Christmas and New Year's at the beach— and I confess there was still a piece of me that hoped he would protest, that he would apologize and suggest we sort things out, bundle up and take some long walks along the sea and clarify our situation, maybe find a way to start anew.

Instead, he replied only with a warning: *"The last place you want to be in a weather event is on the Chesapeake Bay Bridge."*

Richard and I have been idling in an indeterminate state for some time now, and have more recently begun to trend in the direction of collapse. After a series of problems with which he has refused to engage—first professional, then personal—

Richard moved into the basement, where he now works and sleeps. This morning, as I departed, I told him I couldn't live like this anymore. But what, precisely, I hoped to achieve, I can't say for sure.

I suppose I would have welcomed any sort of reaction, anger included. At least it might have moved us toward the next place, wherever that might have been. But my formerly dynamic, rabble-rousing, storm-chasing meteorologist husband has imploded on so many different, spectacularly painful levels that there is little left of him, or of us. He is like a star that has collapsed under its own gravity, a black hole, a closed presence that spends most of its time and space crafting copy for the newspaper's weather desk, staring at a bank of screens.

⋈   ⋈   ⋈

Before slamming on my brakes, I had been singing along, loudly, to a catchy, infectiously upbeat song that included lyrics about a dog, sung—or rather hoarsely and charmingly croaked—by an oddly named band called Clap Your Hands Say Yeah. In the song, the dogs have quit their barking. In my car, as it came to its abrupt stop, my dog's barking had just begun.

Luna, my puppy, now barks and barks and barks. She stops for a moment and then begins to bark again. In the rearview mirror I glimpse something fluttering. An insect appears to have presented itself in the car. It flutters, it lurches, from one window to the other, flutter-lurching back and forth madly, which I believe is what prompted the puppy to bark. As my foot continues to press hard on the brake, I wonder idly whether it is odd to have an insect trapped in the car in winter. I catch another glimpse and realize it is a moth. At this point I feel a shift in my equilibrium, a minor anxious jolt.

To keep myself from thinking about the possibility of being stuck in a traffic jam on a four mile-long bridge nearly two hundred feet over the largest estuary in the country, I try to focus on practical matters: If the traffic does not ease, I should tell my aunt and uncle that I'll be arriving later than planned. Also, I am low on kibble for the puppy and make a mental note to order more for overnight delivery as soon as I get to their house. Entirely unrelated: I need, badly, to find a new hairdresser and do something about my too-long, nearly feral hair.

I try to take a few deep breaths, the sort a yoga teacher might recommend, but my thoughts continue to boomerang toward the end of my metastable marriage, then toward this steel and concrete structure, plus the open water, plus the possible moth. The need to tend to logistics about my late arrival, or kibble, or my wild hair, does not detract from so much as compound my anxiety.

This might or might not be a good place to mention that my parents died in a bridge collapse—an event that was presaged, some say, by the appearance of a giant moth. I was never sure what to make of this story, but I find myself obsessed with it, nonetheless.

⋈　　⋈　　⋈

Many minutes tick by, allowing me to further ponder and stew. Luna calms for a few moments, then lunges again at the trapped winged thing. In the vehicle in front of us, the head of a

passenger in the green CR-V emerges through the sunroof like
a periscope. He puts his hand to his forehead, forging a makeshift visor as if protecting his gaze from the sun's glare, even
though the sky is grey and emitting slush. He looks around in
all directions, and as he rotates his head to face me, I can see
that my assumptions about his collegiateness need some refine-
ment. He is a heavyset bearded man who appears to be in his
midthirties, skewing a little old for a student, a little young for a
parent, although admittedly neither possibility can be ruled out
conclusively. It is also the case that he might be an instructor,
or employed in some other aspect of university endeavor, or
that, as evidenced by the fact that he is a passenger, this might
not even be his car.

I don't know what the man sees in the distance, but his
posture inspires me to open my own sunroof as an invitation
to the insect to leave. Immediately Luna, possibly startled by
the rush of cold air, ceases to bark. I see no evidence of the
insect's departure but am unable to say with any certainty
that it remains.

Although I had not assigned much significance to them at
the time, I now re-reflect on my husband's parting words: *"The
last place you want to be in a weather event is on the Chesapeake
Bay Bridge."*

The content of his warning aside, I had latched on to this
comment like the rope I needed to pull me, finally, to the opposite shore of indecision. I'd had enough of the weather. It ruined
Richard's life. Now it is ruining my life.

Richard always loved the weather despite his complicated
relationship with it, which vacillated between an intellectual
fascination, the need to throw himself into the middle of it,

and animal fear. This had always been the case, according to his mother. Even as a child he fancied himself an amateur meteorologist. He had turned a closet in their basement in Silver Spring, Maryland, into a command center, outfitted with various weather-related gizmos, including a radio that tracked tornados, a barometer, and a large map of the Delmarva region—his self-proclaimed catchment area—that he taped to his wall. His mother had a collection of videos she recorded of him broadcasting against this backdrop, pretending to be a weatherman on TV. You could track his growth this way, not unlike the way I had ticked off Vera's height with a pencil on the wall of the closet each year. For Richard's fiftieth birthday, Vera and I took the many VHS tapes that had accumulated and had them digitized into a nearly hour-long montage of faux weathercasts about brewing, unavoidable, deadly storms.

We have not watched any of them since Richard made his mistake. I called it a mistake. He called it shame. His shame led to what he called his mistake. Nomenclature was part of the problem but not the whole problem.

There is, perhaps, some literary value to be mined from Richard's unraveling, from our general unraveling state—parallels to be drawn between the weather and our marriage and the emptying of our nest and whatever traffic situation is occurring here on the bridge. I am in a position to know of what I speak. I used to be a reporter, then aspired to write fiction but have thus far failed to put more than a few words on the page, and now I teach creative writing at the local community college. I tell my students that the DNA of the entire story is contained in its opening pages, and—this bit I see no reason to reveal to my students—the same is true in a marriage.

Richard postponed our first date, some twenty-three years ago, because of the possibility of rain. We were meant to meet at the zoo, so his concern was not entirely unreasonable, but it seemed a little much. When I suggested we brave it—wear ponchos, bring umbrellas, maybe just get wet—he gave an unqualified no. I proposed shifting to a coffee shop, but he raised the stakes, suggesting there might be thunderstorms. Thunderstorms, snow, sleet, hail—whatever the weather—I was game. I'm weather-oblivious to a fault, but I didn't want to seem pushy, so I let it drop and chose to view his extreme caution as a charming bit of eccentricity. But over the years, as his weather phobias waxed and waned and countless events were canceled due to forecasts that seemed uncatastrophic in potential, it began to seem less cute. Then, this morning, when he made no effort to accompany me, citing the weather as at least a partial excuse, I saw this as the story looping back to where it began, the end of our narrative arc.

That said, just because Richard is hyperfocused on the weather doesn't mean he is always wrong. The Chesapeake Bay Bridge is famously closed from time to time on account of storms. The thought of being stuck here, on a bridge, with a frantic dog and, of all things, a moth, was undesirable.

The moth now begins to flutter again, and it sets down on the passenger seat beside me. I look at it in astonishment. "My heart stopped," I might say, were I not a cliché-averse writing instructor. Or I might say that my heart began to race. Or that I froze, or stared at the moth, slack-jawed. In reality, every one of these anatomically incompatible things is true, paradoxically. Although tiny by comparison, this particular moth, with its silver body and bright red eyes, is familiar from images I have seen on the internet in connection with the giant moth that supposedly appeared before the disaster in which my parents died. I do not believe in giant moths, or in omens, and I am not a catastrophist, and yet I can't help but wonder if something very bad is afoot, aloft, or both.

More specifically, I wonder whether the bridge is about to collapse.

The moth looks at me imploringly, or at least I believe it does. We stare at each other for what seems a long time but in reality is probably only a nanosecond. The windshield wipers startle us all as they begin to bat from side to side again. Luna stares at me staring at the moth. Then Luna lunges once more at the creature and I let out a little scream.

An idea then occurs to me. Perhaps I can capture this moth, sneak it into my aunt and uncle's house, take a closer look at it, possibly identify it with some internet sleuthing. I look around the car for something I might use to contain it but see only my overstuffed purse and a tote bag packed with three times as many books as I can possibly read over the holiday. Then, as if the universe is speaking to me, I see out the window, by the side of the roadway on the bridge, a cooler that must have fallen off, or out of the back of, someone's vehicle. It has spilled open, and an odd assortment of pantry items is now strewn on the asphalt. I do a quick scan of the contents: a quart of 2 percent milk soaking in its own puddle, a box of Honey Nut Cheerios, a family-pack assortment of cold cuts, various condiments including a cracked jar of mayonnaise, several different flavors of potato chips, and a six-pack of Bud Light.

I zero in on the Cheerios. I could pour out the contents, poke tiny holes in the cardboard, and put the moth inside. The task of retrieving the box is the only thing standing between me and this plan. Also, I need to prevent Luna from eating the moth in the seconds it will take me to retrieve the box.

It is, admittedly, a slightly bananas plan on multiple levels. But I decide to stop trying to think. I've been doing too much of that over these past few years, and now it is time to act, as I have done already by simply getting in the car. Accordingly, I open the door to retrieve the box, failing to anticipate that Luna might follow me out. The swift, sleek creature, an unusually limber retriever, leaps over my shoulder and out the door in a move so elegant it might have been choreographed and practiced. I grab the Cheerios box and then give chase as Luna begins to prance along the deck of the Chesapeake Bay Bridge, heading east, toward the ocean.

She runs and runs and runs, then mercifully pauses to take in her surroundings, barking at a flock of seagulls overhead and sticking her snout through the cables to take in the foaming waters of the bay. I have nearly caught up to her when she begins to run again, as if this is a game. I follow as fast as I'm able given my inappropriate footwear. My clog boots are warm and cozy with their shearling lining, but highly impractical. Also, they are now very wet, as am I. A hard wind begins to blow off the Chesapeake, from the direction of Annapolis, and I have left my coat in the car. Nouns synapse through my brain: *Cheerios. Puppy. Moth. Bridge. Keys. Wallet. Phone.* As I run what seems about another half mile, even though this chase has nothing to do with Richard, another word begins to percolate: *divorce.*

The Chesapeake Bay Bridge has no shoulder to speak of, but fortunately traffic remains at a halt. Also, I now realize, the westbound lane is completely devoid of cars. Clearly something has happened ahead, causing traffic to stop.

Luna continues to run. I have the sense that she is not running *away* from me but rather *toward* something. Periodically she looks back to check on me, as if to be sure I'm still there, following along. It reminds me of a playground game Vera used to play called "kiss chase." The girls would run up to the boys and threaten to kiss them, and then the boys would run—hence the chase. It worked in reverse as well, when the boys would chase the girls. Whether any actual kisses were ever exchanged, I don't know.

A few motorists honk. A few motorists jeer. I must look a sight—a middle-aged woman with long, ropy hair running along the side of the bridge, chasing a puppy in the icy rain.

I entertain, briefly, the thought that I'm a superhero, running, running, running, about to take flight. But I am not a superhero, or if I am, I'm a particularly stupid one. You don't see a lot of superheroes clad in wet clogs. Wet Clog Woman to the rescue.

I hit a slick of ice, arc backward, and hit the asphalt hard.

Once a person begins to slip, I think to myself while slipping, *it is easy to slip a little more.*

Luna, startled to see me horizontal, runs back and licks my face. I have not lost consciousness, but it still takes me a moment to regain my bearings. Bridge, dog, rain, a box of Cheerios clamped to my chest. Now there is a police officer leaning over me.

"Ma'am?" he says. "Ma'am, are you all right?" He is shining a flashlight in my face, which makes it difficult to open my eyes, although through my squint I can see he has a chest full of badges and, strapped to his waist, some gadgetry that is beeping and lighting up.

I hear the sound of a helicopter overhead, and through the blur of my wet glasses, I see the flashing red lights of rescue vehicles.

"I'm fine!" I say, although I'm not sure that I'm fine. But the last thing I want is to be whisked away in a helicopter or stuffed into the back of an ambulance.

"You're bleeding," the police officer says to me.

I put my hand to my head, and it comes back sticky and red.

"Let's get you some help."

"No, really, I'm fine. I just need to get back to my car." Luna remains next to me, Lassie-like obedient, as if she is the savior, as opposed to the instigator, of my head-crack-on-the-asphalt event.

"I think we'd better take a look at that head. Stay here for a minute," he instructs. He removes his belt, which has me briefly puzzled and a tad alarmed, but he then affixes it to Luna's collar. A makeshift leash. He begins to lead her in the other direction.

"Hey! Come back! Where are you taking my dog?" I cry.

I am not going to lie supine on the bridge in the icy rain while he walks away with Luna. Plus, I want him to see that I am truly okay, so I quickly stand up. This does, in fact, make me a little dizzy.

He turns back toward me, and I notice that his badge says Officer Keel. The name seems familiar, but I can't think why.

I remove my glasses and wipe them on my shirt, then set them back on my face, half thinking that revisiting his name through clean lenses might jog my memory. Unfortunately, this doesn't help, and now my glasses are even more streaky, the landscape blurred further.

It is only then that I realize I have fallen a few feet away from the scene of an accident, and that this helicopter, still buzzing overhead, and these rescue vehicles with their screaming, bright swirling lights have nothing to do with me.

"What happened?" I ask.

I see, through the impressionistic fog of my lenses, mangled vehicles, a roadway strewn with shattered glass, a disturbing amount of blood on the road.

"An accident, ma'am," he replies.

Obviously there has been an accident. "But what happened?" I want, or rather need, specifics.

He retrieves from his pocket some sort of communication device that is emitting loud bursts of static. "Damn thing is still broken," he says apologetically, fiddling with its switches. "There was a collision, bad accident up ahead, and one of the vehicles went over."

"Over *the bridge*?" I inch over to the guardrail and peer down into the bay looking for evidence but find none. If a vehicle has in fact gone over, it is now submerged.

Given my family history, the thought of a vehicle plunging into water is almost more than I can process: A vehicle that was once here is now there, or somewhere not here. Even if there is a vehicle—and a presumed driver—beneath the frigid waters, the sight of the Chesapeake itself is strangely soothing and serene in its own grey-blue stillness.

I lean farther, trying to get a better look.

"Ma'am, take it easy," he says. "You are bleeding." It sounds somehow accusatory.

"Yes," I agree, looking at my hands. They are stained with blood, as is the fur of my dog, who I am now holding in my arms.

"You're soaking wet. You must be freezing," he says, softening.

"I am," I say. I am, in fact, shivering.

He ushers me into the back of his cruiser and stares at me some more. I get that I make no sense. On the one hand, I could be your garden-variety middle-aged, middle-class, mid-Atlantic woman, the sort who might splurge on overpriced clog boots. On the other hand, I am behaving strangely and am covered in blood, so I might well be a fugitive, perhaps a bank robber or a murderess.

Officer Keel retrieves a first aid kit and a plaid blanket from the trunk of his car. Grass and leaves and bits of something that might be pizza cling to the wool fabric, suggesting it was most recently used not to cover a bed or to warm a body but rather to sit on the ground, possibly at a picnic or a child's sporting event. It smells vaguely of mildew, but I am in no position to complain. Inside the metal kit I find some gauze and begin to blot the spot on the back of my head from which blood is issuing.

He then hands me a bottle of water and even produces, from where I am not sure, a plastic receptacle for Luna to use for her hydration.

After asking several questions—some friendly, some less so—he threatens, vaguely, to arrest me. It is illegal, apparently, to abandon one's car and walk, or in my case run, along the bridge. But he does not arrest me. I sense that he has bigger problems to deal with, other fish to fry—namely orchestrating four ambulances, three police cars, a flotilla of inflatable motorboats beneath us, and now several helicopters, including one *Eyewitness News* chopper buzzing overhead, as well as the submerged vehicle, if one indeed exists. Also, someone needs to tow these wrecked cars.

Instead of arresting me, Officer Keel gives me his cell phone and urges me to call someone who can meet me on the other side of the bridge once the accident scene clears. He seems eager to pass me on to the care of someone better able to ensure my "continued well-being," he explains, although I believe he is skeptical about this, possibly unsure that I have any well-being to ensure.

As if seeking to reassure himself of my being okay, he says these sorts of things happen on the bridge more often than one might think.

"What sorts of things?" I inquire.

"People have panic attacks on the bridge all the time," he replies.

I nod agreeably. I'm not sure that I've had a panic attack—that seems one thing not on my list of challenges—but tacitly agreeing to this theory is clearly, in this moment, the right thing to do. Better, at least, than explaining that I left my vehicle in order to retrieve a soggy box of Cheerios now clamped to my chest so I could capture a moth.

I stare blankly at the rectangular speaking device for a moment. Eventually I remember the number for Uncle Harry and, employing some muscle memory, place the call.

It occurs to me a beat too late that Officer Keel would not have known, or cared, if I only pretended to place the call, if I feigned the conversation. He's going through the motions, doing his due diligence, dispensing with me in a way he could later justify should I meet with harm. But I am already on the phone with Harry when I realize my mistake.

"I'm here with a police officer . . .

"I'm fine, please don't worry . . .

"No, Richard is not here . . .

"I'll explain later but I'm fine, please don't worry . . .

"Officer Keel is his name . . .

"Yes, he is going to have someone walk me and Luna back to my car . . .

"Luna is my puppy.

"MY PUPPY!

"Didn't I tell you about THE PUPPY!?

"No, really, I'm fine, please don't worry . . ."

I shout all of this into the phone.

Officer Keel kindly hands me off to a young woman whom he identifies as a police trainee and says she will escort me to my car. "Don't forget to give me back my belt," he tells her. "Once you get them to the car." He then turns his attention to the accident scene.

I shift the stupid cereal box to my other arm and begin to walk. As I look back out over the expanse of bay, I find myself wishing I could fly.

CHAPTER 2

PAW Patrol

LUNA IS AN eight-month-old rescue from a shelter in Northern Virginia, a white Lab with what might be a little husky thrown in, with one eye brown and one steely blue. Every dog in my life has looked more or less like this. I am frequently stopped by strangers who wish to inquire about her breed and those beautiful, mismatched eyes. They ask whether Luna can see properly, and if her condition is genetic, as if heterochromatic eyes are indicative of disease. One recent morning while on our walk, I was asked by a man in a business suit whether she was related to Max Scherzer, the former Nationals pitcher, who has since been traded. I feigned astonishment and said, *"Yes, she is actually Max's younger sister,"* hoping to see the look of confusion on his face. Instead he deadpanned: *"I thought so!"*

I have brushed up on my knowledge of Major League Baseball to be able to engage in this sort of banter, and admit to now being intrigued, maybe even a little infatuated, with Max Scherzer and his enigmatic eyes.

Luna's eyes are definitely striking, as is her luminous coat. She looks ethereal, like the goddess of the moon for whom she is named. And now, as she runs along the shoreline, venturing gently onto the pebbles, dashing from approaching waves, batting with curiosity at the foam they leave behind, she is practically aglow, her fur refracting the light of the setting sun.

⋈   ⋈   ⋈

I see Uncle Harry open the side door and begin to descend the steps that lead to the beach, where I sit beside the firepit. The flames are leaping bright and high. He is bundled in a puffy blue parka, a tasseled hat on his head, insulated gloves of the sort one might wear to scale Everest. His mind is sharp and his body hale, and he still sports a shock of grey Einsteinesque hair that grows straight up. But he is undeniably aging. Even with his new hearing aids, he doesn't always hear, and his movement is incrementally creakier each time I see him, which is not surprising as he approaches his eightieth year. Olivia appears behind him carrying a picnic basket. She is one year younger than Harry but aging at a different pace, still physically active and working full-time.

From the distance of some three hundred feet, I feel their worry. It's a physical, pulsing thing, a simmering perturbation I have unleashed, or maybe awoken, or intensified. It thrums like an icon on Google Maps, moving toward the crackling fire. Harry is bearing three plastic tumblers.

It's my fault, of course; the moment I heard Harry's voice on the phone I regretted calling him from the bridge, but at least I had successfully lobbied for him to stay put, to let me meet him and Olivia at their house as soon as the debris from the accident was cleared.

With hindsight it might have been better to omit mentioning, upon my arrival, that a strange-looking moth had been trapped in the car and that I had tried to capture it. I know better than to mention moths, especially in the context of bridges. I was, despite my better judgment, being deliberately provocative. Perhaps my walking out on Richard had emboldened me to stop pretending things away.

Olivia had let out a sound that is hard to describe but is frequently rendered in crossword puzzles as *gah*: a three-letter word for exasperation. And while I'd thought Harry would be interested—he is, after all, a scientist who ought to have been curious when I mentioned the creature's strange red eyes—he had ignored my anecdote entirely and said, *"You are bleeding."*

"I don't think I'm bleeding anymore."

"I know blood," he said. *"You are bleeding."*

A retired pathologist, he has the standing for this claim.

I put my hand to my head and determined he was not wrong.

Olivia instructed me to take a shower, and that had ended the conversation, at least for the moment.

ж ж ж

"What a day," Harry says now, settling his long-limbed self into the flimsy beach chair and adjusting it into a comfortable recline.

"Indeed!" I say. It really was quite a day, even though we are evidently not going to talk about it beyond superficial details.

"Look at the sky!" Olivia instructs us, and we all look up.

It is a striking atomic fuchsia, offset by the orange flames of the firepit Harry has dug in the sand.

I raise the plastic cup containing the gin and tonic Harry has handed to me. "Cheers!"

We clink our receptacles. I'm not much of a drinker, but gin and tonics are part of a family ritual, the welcoming night tradition when we visit Harry and Olivia at the beach, where, as of a few weeks ago, they now live full-time, and from where Olivia broadcasts her show remotely from a bedroom closet she converted into a studio.

"It's a little weak, Harry," I say. "I barely taste the gin."

"No gin for you, my dear," he says. "You might be concussed."

"I'm not concussed," I protest, but no one races to fill my glass from what I now see is a second thermos.

"Amazing how clear the sky is now, given the ferocity of that storm this morning," Harry says. "It came on so suddenly. I didn't hear anything about it until I started getting weather alerts on my phone. I'm surprised Richard didn't warn you. I tried to call you, but there was no answer."

I don't tell him that Richard warned me about the storm because (1) I don't want to discuss the subject of Richard, which will inevitably lead to a question about why he is not here, and (2) I don't want to acknowledge that Richard was right.

I stick to the empirical instead. "I didn't get a call."

"I definitely called. I left a long message."

"Maybe you called the landline again," I say. "No one answers that number anymore. You need to call my cell."

I have told Harry this many times, but he persists in calling our old line, the one the newspaper installed years ago at the height of Richard's storm-chasing days. He was among the last generation of newspaper reporters to be assigned an old-fashioned phone with an office extension, back before everyone had cell phones. We used to call it the Batphone. Whenever it rang, a hurricane was forming off the Texas Gulf Coast, or some other weather-equivalent of a three-alarm fire was about to alight, meaning we needed to put on hold whatever family dinner or birthday party was transpiring so Richard could suit up, get in the Batmobile, and speed off to report conditions from inside the eye of the storm.

That was back in the era—a period that lasted some fifteen years—when Richard's weather phobia was in remission. Before his bravado recapitulated to his terror. Now, after years of overcompensating by throwing himself headfirst and sometimes quite literally into the storm, Richard's fears— compounded by the latest addition to our marital problems in the form of the family friend with whom he had, or is having, an affair—have mutated into an entirely new condition: the basement barricade.

He has moved downstairs, and he rarely emerges. A couple of years ago we did a quick renovation, with the intention of turning the basement into his home office. While we were sprucing it up we updated the small bathroom and shower as well. It didn't occur to me at the time that he was perhaps already intending to make this his home. From this office, the only weather he interacts with now is on his screens. As for the Batphone, these days it rings only with telemarketers and Uncle Harry.

"Yeah, it caught me completely off guard," I lie. "Still, it was just a bit of precipitation, not any major winter storm."

"Regardless, that was some accident," Harry says. "I don't know if it was weather-related, but I heard the driver of the van that went over the side of the bridge died."

"Oh, jeez. That's terrible," I say, although I had pretty much assumed this much, given that it submerged.

"First it straddled the guardrail for a few minutes as they organized cranes or whatever they needed to secure the vehicle. They tried to get the driver out, but the van was in a precarious spot."

"Like in the *PAW Patrol* movie," Olivia volunteers. They have watched this movie multiple times with Eli, their three-year-old grandson, my nephew. "Remember how it begins with a truck stuck on the what-was-it?"

"Yes, except in this case there is no happy ending," Harry says. "The pups don't come to the rescue."

We absorb this grim news with a moment of silence.

"The police officer told me a vehicle had gone over," I say. "I didn't know that was even possible. The guardrail seems pretty high."

"Not high enough, evidently," says Harry.

"Were there other fatalities?" I ask.

"Three people were taken to the hospital," Harry says. "I think someone is in critical condition. The driver of the van is the only death. That I know of, that is."

"That's awful," I say. "Ugh. Very sorry to hear."

"Washington drivers . . ." Olivia says. "Famously inept."

About this subject there is not much more to say.

✄   ✄   ✄

We have been coming to this beach house for as long as I remember. It once belonged to my grandparents—Olivia and my late mother's parents. This is the rare parcel of land that remains relatively untouched in this tiny beachfront town in Delaware that is a mixture of large, old-money estates, white-gated mansions, American flags flying over multicar garages, and new condo developments that have spread like algae, flimsy and overpriced, in the proximity of water.

The developers knock on the door, but Harry and Olivia have no interest in selling, or renovating, even though this house has seen better days. It may be stuck in the last century—and not in the part with any design sensibility—but it's been kept up, and everything is functional and clean.

Harry raises his glass. Another toast.

"Cheers to Cassie's safe arrival!" he says.

I take a sip of my ginless drink and force a smile.

"So can I explain what happened this afternoon?" I try again.

"It's not a big deal," Olivia says. "We don't need to belabor the point. It's not unusual to have a panic attack on the bridge."

"I didn't have a panic attack," I protest.

"Clearly you did."

I'm pretty sure I did not have a panic attack, but if Olivia thinks I had a panic attack, then I had a panic attack—or at least that will become the narrative. She is formidable, the sort of person who appears to have never harbored a self-doubt in her life. A former book editor who worked at a handful of prestigious imprints in publishing, she now hosts one of the most successful radio programs in the universe called, uncreatively, *The Storyteller*. It airs weekday afternoons on NPR to an estimated audience of over five-and-a-half-million weekly listeners.

"It happens all the time," Harry says. "It's called gephyrophobia. Fear of bridges. And the Chesapeake Bay Bridge is especially famous for that."

I decide it's easier to give in to this theory than to continue protesting. "Everything you say is true, Uncle Harry. I don't know what happened today. But maybe I've developed a late-in-life phobia."

"Phobias are nothing to sneeze at. People condescend to phobias at their peril. But there are workarounds. Did you know there are now two different services that will provide drivers to get you across?" he asks.

Olivia is now silent, staring out at the sea.

"Great!" I say, feigning interest in this very old news.

"Do you know how many cars have actually fallen off the Chesapeake Bay Bridge?" Harry asks, unhelpfully.

I'm about to hazard a guess when we hear voices and a barking dog heading toward us. Luna runs to greet the approaching party, her tail wagging.

"Hey," I hear a male voice say. He's clad in a lime-green parka, accompanied by another man twice his size in an identical parka, and an overweight dachshund who is practically mopping up the sand with her low-hanging belly. They appear to be in their forties or so. "Sorry to interrupt. We just moved in, three houses down. This is my partner, Damian. I'm Leon. And this is Patrice," he says, pointing at the dog.

Small talk ensues. Olivia is especially chatty, probably relieved to have a normal, lighthearted conversation rather than one about cars plunging from the bridge. Damian and Leon also hail from DC; they just sold their condo in NoMa. There is a brief discussion of neighborhoods, of the hot real estate market, of how good it feels to be out of the city. There is mention of me, the visiting niece. I force a smile and wave.

I would point out to my writing students that, technically, I am a peripheral narrator in this scene, with nothing to contribute and no role in the arrangements being made as Olivia plugs their contact information into her phone and sets a tentative date to have them over for drinks.

I'm grateful for this brief reprieve, but as soon as they leave, Olivia picks up the thread of our earlier conversation without missing a beat.

"Do you mean, like, plunged over the side?"

"Yes," Harry says.

"Five hundred and fifty-two." OIivia pulls this number out of the air. "Ten a year, plus change, since it was built."

"Nine," says Harry.

"Really? Is that all? Where are you getting your facts?"

"Well, wait. Correction. That number evidently pertains to the Chesapeake Bay Bridge–Tunnel," he says, brandishing his phone. "This is very confusing."

"You're getting service out here? I can never get it this close to the water."

"I am. It's a miracle, but yes, three bars. Okay, here is an article about a woman whose car plunged over the side, but she managed to get out. She swam several hundred feet to a jetty. She survived!"

"And this is supposed to make Cassie feel better?"

"Well, actually, yes. That's a happy outcome!"

"Can I ask a question?" I say boldly.

I choose to interpret their silence as permission.

"I don't mean to be insensitive or disrespectful, but why is it we can have a casual conversation about bridge fatalities but we don't ever talk about what happened to my parents? And then, whenever I ask you what you think about the story of the moth, or so much as mention the word——"

"I don't know what you're saying, Cassie. We can talk about anything you'd like," Olivia says. "For example, let's talk about your hair!"

"My hair?" I ask, flustered. She has gone from the most important subject in my life to . . . my hair? Still, I put my hand to my head reflexively, and it comes back smeared with blood. "I must have opened the scab when I shampooed," I say, reaching for a napkin to blot the wound. "I need to get it cut," I quickly add, so as to change the subject from my fall. "My hairdresser moved to Florida. His girlfriend decided to go to law school. I need to find someone new."

This is not untrue, yet it is not the entire story. Once my hair reached a length some four inches longer than my norm, I decided that I liked the slightly unkempt look. I spent much of my life trying to tame it——dousing it in product, experimenting with a variety of cuts, straightening it with an iron——before choosing to embrace it. My hair has long been my antagonist, but now it has become my friend, even if I look a bit like Gorgo, the Greek figure who has snakes coming out of her head.

"I have someone here; I can make you an appointment."

"Two days before Christmas?"

"Well, no, good point."

I once heard an expert on linguistics say this is how mothers sometimes talk to daughters, that commenting on their appearance can be a form of love, so I have learned to let it go, infuriating as it is. Besides, as confusing or even irritating as this torrent of free association might be to an outsider, it has a comforting familiarity.

"I hope you don't mind, but it's been a long day. I think I'm going to head in."

"Keep an eye on your head," Harry says as I fold up my chair. "If you feel any throbbing, or experience dizziness or anything unusual, like seeing double or more, give a holler. It could be a concussion." After pausing to consider the range of clinical scenarios, he adds, "Or a bleed."

"I'm fine, Harry."

"Should we wake her up every hour to be sure?" Olivia asks.

"No, that's unnecessary. Just an old wives' tale."

"That's good, because I'm exhausted. See you in the morning!"

I summon Luna. She comes bounding from the shoreline, bits of algae in her fur and something thrashing in her mouth. She jumps on me and releases a wriggling creature at my feet. I let out a scream, then begin to laugh. It's a hermit crab. No big deal.

The crab is fine. I take him to the ocean.

I have no beef with crustaceans. It's only moths that set me off.

CHAPTER 3

Flight

AS A CHILD I would don wings—gauzy blue fairy things with elastic bands that slipped over the arms and sprouted fetchingly from the back, right below my shoulder blades, just above my scars—and I'd race through the house, wishing myself aloft.

Every child passes through a phase of this sort, wanting to be something *other*. My cousin Evan aspired to be a fireman and spent weeks, possibly months, wearing a red plastic helmet as he toddled around in a diaper and a pair of polka-dot snow boots, even in the summer months. He once spilled a glass of water on my head, insisting that I had smoke pouring from my ears. My cousin Samantha skewed heavily ballerina—taking lessons, twirling in tutus, and even wearing them to school—until one day, seemingly overnight, she transitioned, briefly, into a young goth.

You might think this makes us a traditional family, a mother and a father, an adorable trio of kids, but this conclusion might be somewhat misguided. Tolstoy, oft quoted as an expert on the subject of domestic harmony, may have gotten it wrong:

Not all happy families are alike. We are a happy family, and yet there are things about us, or at least about me, that do not fully align with the standard interpretation of what family happiness means—chiefly that I was orphaned at the age of two, and my aunt and uncle took me in.

Raised as the middle child, I was vaguely aware that something bad had transpired, that my parents were gone, but I was so quickly and lovingly absorbed into this family unit that I can't say I suffered. Samantha was five when I moved in, and Evan was still an infant, so I slipped between them seamlessly, and the fact that I was not a biological sibling rarely arose. We all got along well, and now Samantha is not just my cousin-sibling but one of my closest friends. Evan joined the State Department and moved with his family to Japan, so lately we are in less close touch.

I was too young to remember my parents, although over time it became difficult to separate what might have been early memories from what was recounted to me, even though that was not much.

It was one of the deadliest bridge collapses in US history. Although my aunt is a self-proclaimed storyteller, about this story we do not talk. When I was a child, my occasional queries were met with a quick change of subject. Most of what I know about the accident I have gleaned from overheard chatter, and later, when I was old enough to investigate, from the internet. Some of what I learned about the intersection of the bridge collapse and the moth seemed completely nuts. It wasn't merely a giant moth—it was said to be part man. The Mothman, it was called. I would look, then look away. I would later return, go down the weird rabbit hole, freak myself out, then vow never to look again.

This is part of the reason I aspired to fly. I never wanted to be a fairy. I was too young to understand it at the time, but what I wanted was to be a moth, to soar above the wreckage, to try to understand.

CHAPTER 4

Regression

WE HAVE BEEN coming to this stretch of the Eastern Shore for as long as I can remember. My mother and Aunt Olivia inherited this house from their parents, and now that Olivia and Harry have made it their primary residence, much of the family memorabilia lives here, too, such as it is. Even back in DC, I could find little to nothing that belonged to my parents. No high school yearbooks, old postcards, or journals moldering in boxes, not even a wedding album.

One of the few photos of me and my parents now sits atop the fireplace mantel in a silver frame. I found it in Olivia's dresser back in Washington many years ago, and after she scolded me for rummaging through her private things—the fact notwithstanding that she had sent me to retrieve a sweater from her drawer—I convinced her to put it on display.

On my way back upstairs, I stop in the living room and study it: There we are, on the same stretch of beach where I sipped my ginless tonic, the ocean behind us, my smiling parents on either side of me. My mother is tall and slim, wearing a big straw hat and oversized sunglasses. Glamorous and very retro—she reminds me of Jackie O, with long black hair pulled into a ponytail on the side. She wears a purple bikini and looks so young she could pass for a teenager, although I know she was twenty-five in this photograph. My handsome father squats on the sand, his hand on my back. His skin is olive, and he has the same dark, tightly coiled hair that I have inherited. I am a chubby pink Buddha, sitting on a towel, shrouded beneath a hat and lathered in sunscreen, about to tip over.

I sometimes commune with this photo, imagining that beneath my father's hand is my spray of scars. As a toddler, Olivia has told me, I was running to catch a ball when I backed into the wire mesh cage surrounding the tomatoes in the yard and fell. It had seen better days, the cage, with spiky bits of wire that tore into my back. Many stitches were required. I have no memory of this but have nonetheless always been guarded around tomatoes.

⋈   ⋈   ⋈

Whenever we'd visit the beach house, which used to be at least twice a year, Richard and I would sleep in the guest room at the top of the stairs to the right. This had once been Evan's room. As the only boy he got his own space, even in our progressive family run by a fiery feminist matriarch. Samantha and I shared the room on the other side of the hallway, which is still referred to as the children's room. Like nearly everything in this house, the rooms, and the objects they contain, remain frozen in time, but for the fact that the bunk beds have been disassembled and now sit side by side.

I have parked myself, this time, in the children's room. Perhaps this is because I am feeling a little childish myself, as though I've behaved badly, which I have in a way, with my ridiculous behavior on the bridge.

This is where Vera usually sleeps, and the thought makes me long to send her a text—or at least a heart emoji or a wave—but she is away with her roommate in Barcelona for the holidays, where it's the middle of the night. I don't want to startle her awake if she's left her phone's sound on.

It's a physical thing, like a toothache or a phantom limb, this emptiness I feel with her away at school, and now especially with her in Europe for the holidays. At home, her room is too clean, the house too quiet, the refrigerator too empty. There's no one to do silly holiday things with, to listen to loud, schlocky renditions of Christmas music with, the kind that would drive Richard out of the house if he were still leaving the house. Or to bake cookies with, not that I'm much of a baker, but still, we have our tradition of rolling out dough and making lopsided snowmen, dousing them in colorful, sugary doodads, then Instagramming our mess. But I don't begrudge her this trip. I'm glad she is a happy kid and that she has the opportunity to travel and improve her Spanish, although I suspect there's more to it. Traveling is also a way to avoid the tension in our home.

It's too quiet here as well. I don't know the last time I came to the beach without Richard or Vera. But at least Luna is here, and she's reading my mind as she bounds onto the bed and puts her paws on my shoulders and licks my face.

⋈　　⋈　　⋈

It's habit, I suppose, that causes me to text Richard. I may be done with him, yet I have known this man for twenty-five years and simply need to know that everyone in my life is okay, or at least not in imminent physical distress.

I arrived safely at the beach, I type on my phone.

Richard does not reply.

Luna says hi, I try.

No reply, not that I should have expected much from mentioning the dog—*my* dog.

It is conceivably true that my unilateral decision to acquire a puppy did not help our situation, but that was my response to our circumstances. Vera had gone off to college, Richard had moved to the basement, and I was lonely. Plus Ruth, our previous dog, had only recently passed away, and the year-long stretch before Luna's appearance was the longest I had ever been without canine companionship. Is it possible things might have turned out differently had the puppy not destroyed two pairs of Richard's shoes and eaten through the internet cord, disconnecting him from the weather for two days? I think not. Luna had nothing to do with Richard's troubles, yet that did not stop him from dragging her into our mess.

The longer Richard does not reply, the more I need him to reply, just for peace of mind. I try a foolproof approach.

You were right about the weather.

To this, he responds.

Yup. A narrow band on the cold side of the warm front moving in from Ohio = icy rain.

Whatever, I think. But I type: **Exactly.**

I wait a few minutes, but apparently that about sums it up weather-wise, and there is nothing else to say.

⋈   ⋈   ⋈

As a child, I liked to pretend that the large wardrobe in this room contained a Narnia-like portal to some other world. Once I came to understand that I was born to a different set of parents—a surreal concept at the time, given my comfort level in this family—I became obsessed with stories featuring orphans, or at least children who had been separated from their families. I found it fascinating that Olivia and Harry were not my birth mom and dad. For a while it was all I could think about, and I fantasized that if I could push behind the toys that occupied the shelves, I could reach some other dimension and find my biological parents, or at least wind up somewhere that would help me better understand what had happened to them. Even then, I was hoping to solve some mystery, to figure out my own murky plot points, although I'm not sure I understood, at the time, the degree to which they did not align.

⋈   ⋈   ⋈

Luna has made herself at home. Within minutes of her climbing onto one of the beds, her body begins to twitch and I hear gentle puppy snores. Maybe she is dreaming about catching one of those seagulls on the bridge.

I'm exhausted too, but before turning in for the night, I begin to poke around the room, which is booby-trapped with nostalgia. In the wardrobe I find an old Raggedy Ann, a Gumby, and a naked Barbie, also naked Ken. There is another naked plastic person of the same vintage, but she is impossible to identify other than by gender, as she has lost her head. Stuffed animals of various shapes and sizes, a mangled Slinky. I see a small plastic box. It looks vaguely familiar. I'm fishing for the memory as I shake it gently and hear something rattling inside. I open the case and see a bunch of mostly disintegrated pods, or seeds, or shells. It takes a moment, but then memory floods back, along with the words *Mexican jumping beans*. Did we actually amuse ourselves by playing with beans that jumped or jittered? Was that a real thing, or a product of my imagination? I'm so puzzled by this memory that I punch the words into my phone and indeed, it was, and is, a thing: frijoles saltarines in Spanish, seedpods native to Mexico.

I learn that they are not actually beans but rather *spurges*. These spurges sometimes become inhabited by moth larvae, which eat the seeds. They apparently eat and eat until they hollow out the inside of the bean, and as they are curling and uncurling, they hit the sides of the little walls and make the beans . . . jump.

I think of me and Samantha spilling the beans from the plastic case, watching them jump, the poor trapped larvae serving as our amusement. I continue to read and learn that the larvae sometimes go into a pupal stage and force their way out, becoming moths.

Moths and more moths. Does everything in my life involve moths of one sort or another, or am I simply viewing the world through this lens the way one learns a new word and then notices, suddenly, that it seems to be in constant use?

I put the small plastic case back inside the wardrobe and shut the door. On the other side of the wardrobe, nestled in the corner, I notice Hoppity, whom I haven't seen in years. Hoppity is a big blue inflatable rubber ball with the head of a horse. His once firm torso now sags, but his essence remains, and I am reminded of the good times we had. One is meant to sit on the ball and hold on to the handles that protrude from either side of his head, then use one's feet to bounce. Or, rather, hop. Hence the name. Hoppity Horse. Although apparently, adorably, I thought Hoppity was a dog. Because even as child I was dog obsessed. Hoppity Dog.

I take the ball and pick it up and let it drop. I don't know why I do this, since it is clearly not going to bounce without an infusion of air. Still, this offers a moment of levity after a long, lousy day. Luna wakes up and lunges playfully at the ball.

I pick it back up and hold it high in the air as a tease. If she were a child, she would be laughing, but she is a dog, so she barks.

Back on the bed Luna jumps. I throw the ball again, and the game amps up. This goes on awhile, me leaping onto the bed and then back off. I catch a glimpse of myself in the mirror—arms in the air, hair flying. This person with the wild hair reflected back at me, she looks not so bad. Surprisingly buff, for someone her age.

Even though walking out on Richard was not premeditated—I not only stuck with him through his troubles and his erratic moods, but I also forgave him for the affair—some quiet self-preservation instinct kicked in over the last couple of years. I began to exercise. I slept well. I became more mindful of my diet too. Nothing radical or punishing. I simply decided to eat less meat. Vera told me I was now technically what they call a flexitarian, which made me laugh. It was the first I'd heard of the word, but I decided to embrace it even though it sounded a bit loopy to me.

Richard's refusal to come with me to Olivia and Harry's for the holidays, his invocation of the weather—it was the final straw even though I was not aware I was about to break. And now, in the mirror, I reconsider myself. For a moment I'm not even sure who that person is. I put my hands in the air as if I'm going to fly, a thought that is never not there.

Luna studies the blue blob, her ears pricked straight up.

I toss Hoppity back in the air in the other direction to up the stakes, and she lunges playfully at the blue blob, sinking her teeth into the latex. This time, what is left of the air rushes out, reducing Hoppity to a sad mound of rubber. No great loss; one less piece of clutter in this house, in this room.

Now Luna stares at me as if anticipating a treat, which reminds me that she is nearly out of food. I log into my Pets! Pets! Pets! account and order a four-pound bag of kibble for overnight delivery to hold me over until I figure out next steps.

CHAPTER 5

Mojo

BEFORE HIS TROUBLES sent Richard into basement exile, marking the beginning of our descent, he had been a prize-winning journalist and meteorologist who was something of a legend in his field. After studying meteorology at MIT, he then walked straight into a position on the weather desk at the *Washington Post*. He has stayed there through his entire career. Through a collaborative weather arrangement with the local NPR affiliate, his broadcasts could often be heard on WAMU, as well as on the television network that the newspaper briefly owned.

Richard has—or had—a trifecta of endearing traits: brains, charisma, and dreamy good looks, with a charming crooked smile. He also had that jaunty weatherman delivery that is hard to describe, but you know it when you hear it: When Richard talked about a cyclone forming in the South Pacific, he sucked you right into the story regardless of where you lived. He gave the weather urgency—like if a cold front was crossing into the area, you'd better stop whatever you were doing and bring your begonias inside before the frost, even if you couldn't distinguish a begonia from a geranium in a police lineup.

During his first few months at the newspaper, he mostly had worked on generic weather news having to do with storm fallout: "Snowstorm Tangles Vehicles on Virginia Roads, Causing Long Delays," or "Scorching Heat Creates Dangerous Conditions for Elderly and Infirm." That sort of thing.

He also helped craft the daily weather squibs, or *ears*, as they are known in the trade, that run alongside the masthead on the front page. They may not look like much, but stylistically there are many rules. *Sun* is always spelled out to *sunshine*. *Showers* and *thunderstorms* are always plural. There are other idiosyncrasies of this nature, and Richard added his own thumbprint to these, which I doubt anyone besides me noticed.

Cloudy, chance of snow. High forty-one, low thirty. Tomorrow: some rain.

Five syllables, seven syllables, again, five. He created little weather haikus.

In our early days of dating, I liked to imagine these were coded messages meant for me.

Richard loved his job. Part of the attraction, at first, was that it allowed him to write about the weather without going anywhere—without getting wet, so to speak. It was the professional equivalent of his childhood broadcasts from the basement. But he was ambitious, and he could see that while his desk work was appreciated, it wasn't advancing his career. By chance, after Richard had spent a couple of years on the weather desk, a key reporter working on a team-reported climate series left for the *New York Times*. Richard was offered his job and assigned to the in-progress story regarding the global implications of deteriorating air quality around the world. He was sent to India to report. The series wound up winning multiple prizes.

That was where we met, me and Richard, at a dinner party on a rooftop in New Delhi, some twenty-five years ago, although it would take us two more years to reconnect.

He was, at the time, in his sweet spot. His weather phobia was contained, but also he was able to write weather-adjacent news without having to engage with the weather itself. His assignment in India was not easy. He was there for over a month and did some immersive reporting in challenging conditions that included getting stranded in the Calcutta airport for some thirty-six hours when his flight to Delhi was grounded because of fog. He was later laid flat with dysentery for nearly a week. But those weren't the sorts of things that threw him off.

After the air quality story broke big, the rest was history for Richard. His star rose, his first marriage imploded, and we serendipitously reconnected in DC at a dinner party at the home of a mutual friend. We dated, we married, Vera was born, and at some point early in our time together, I urged him to deal with his fears and helped him find a therapist to work through his weather anxiety, which had resurfaced by the time we began to formally date and had grown in intensity over the years.

He'd dealt with weather anxiety all his life. It came and it went and then it returned, often without discernable reason. As a kid his mother had to make special accommodations for him to stay indoors at recess if the weather looked like it might turn bad, and he was politely asked to resign from his Pop

Warner football team because his attendance had become unreliable. But at some point in college, determined not to let this phobia ruin his life, he coaxed himself into a more relaxed state. He didn't tell me much about how this had worked, other than to compare himself to my brother, Evan, who overcame allergies in order to marry his cat-loving wife. Then, a few years later, Evan's allergies returned, and the cats had to be rehoused.

Samantha, while in her midtwenties, had developed a fear of flying—aerophobia, it is called—and I remembered that she'd found a therapist who had helped. Some talk therapy was followed by instructions to buy six sets of round-trip tickets to Kansas City, which were, at the time, ridiculously cheap. She was told to lean into her fears and get on the flights and go back and forth. I remember she resisted at first, protesting that this was an absurd idea, but she eventually gave in and flew to Kansas City six times within the space of six weeks. It worked. As a bonus, she had a lot of time to kill in the airport and brought us all copious amounts of Chiefs paraphernalia. I still have a sweatshirt. I was pretty sure that Richard could do the same by (1) getting to the root of his problem through therapy and then (2) forcing himself out into the rain.

I know little about the conversations Richard had with the therapist. He didn't offer details, and I didn't pry. I was intensely curious, of course, but it was not something he was inclined to share, and I never learned whether he'd suffered some childhood weather trauma, such as being left outside in a storm, or whether this was a completely anomalous thing. We are always eager to assign blame, to trace a neat line from effect back to cause, but sometimes it can't be done.

Although I was not involved in the psychiatric aspects of Richard's weather recovery, I was a full participant in the exposure parts. We took it slow at first. We'd take walks in a light rain, bundled up in slickers and holding umbrellas. Once he was able to do this without trembling and hyperventilating, we worked up to leaving the umbrellas behind. Eventually we ventured out into downpours. From there he accelerated into all manner of weather events, and the next thing I knew he was quite literally chasing storms.

He was never one to share intimate thoughts—why I married such a private man, I cannot say. Perhaps it had to do with growing up with, and becoming accustomed to, Olivia's emotional reserve and her way of avoiding important topics, but it wasn't something I spent a lot of time thinking about. It was all I knew. It was what it was. Still, he did confide in me that his therapeutic breakthrough occurred when he realized that his mind quieted when he was experiencing weather at its extreme.

In other words, it was better to be somewhere more chaotic than inside his own head, and that better place was inside a storm. Or at least it was until his mistake, or his shame, or his Waterloo, or whatever you want to call it, sent him to the basement, where he set up a home office with banks of screens to track the weather. It seemed rich in symbolism—this was where he'd begun reporting as a kid. Now he was back where he began, and a sadness permeated our house like the terrible metaphor this was.

About his mistakes: The first one was straightforward and not hugely surprising with hindsight. He had miscalculated, albeit spectacularly. He had made a bad prediction. A less generous interpretation might be that his ego had grown so large it could no longer be contained. Or more sympathetically, perhaps: The storm that had been gathering inside his head was beginning to erupt.

There is always what's called a *cone of uncertainty* when predicting a hurricane, far more common than your average consumer of weather news understands. But on this occasion, Richard's forecast was spectacularly off. It happened two years ago, when he predicted that the deluge of rain on the West Coast was the precursor of an ARkStorm—that the Pacific jet streams would cause unending storms that would lead to catastrophic flooding and leave much of the West Coast underwater. There would be landslides, power lines down for months, property damage in the billions of dollars. This is the sort of thing that is said to occur every thousand years. The name derives from combining the first letters of *Atmospheric River*, which is the technical name, with the *k* for one thousand. But it also is, of course, synonymous with the story of Noah, who in preparation for the great flood corralled his pairs of animals onto an ark.

Richard said that everyone should prepare for the worst. This resulted in mass hysteria. Grocery stores were picked clean, gas stations had empty pumps, airports were jammed, the financial markets went haywire, and Home Depot stock shot up fifty-seven points.

Not everyone agreed with his prediction. Several other prominent meteorologists said the storm systems would both weaken and shift course. Richard called his colleagues out on air and on Twitter, labeling them fools—and worse—for disagreeing with his prediction.

As it happened, the rains were bad, but not biblically so.

No lives were lost; property damage was minimal. Home Depot stock stabilized, and the financial markets recovered within days.

The only lasting damage was to Richard, who became—and still is—a meme. Clips of his prediction went viral. They continue to pop up on Instagram: Richard in front of a giant weather map, his mouth open midsentence, his finger hovering over Oregon. This is now synonymous with the head-slap emoji. This is what he calls his *shame*, or at least the beginning of his shame.

It got worse. In an effort to be taken seriously again, once hurricane season began a few months later, he raced to North Carolina to report on the progress of a storm forming in the Atlantic. There is footage of him clinging to a telephone pole, reporting breathlessly, supposedly braving gale-force winds. The only problem was that behind him, as the camera rolled, people were walking by, seemingly oblivious to the weather. One man could be seen in flip-flops, talking on his cell phone, an ice cream cone in hand.

This, too, became a meme, the meaning subtly different from the first. Instead of a head-slap, his face was now synonymous with LOL.

Richard wasn't fired—no. But he never appeared on air again. Also—surely not a coincidence—his weather phobia returned. He ceased chasing storms and went back to editing stories and crafting weather ears. It was around that time that he moved into the basement. It wasn't an official move, at least not at first; he went down there to work, and some nights he then collapsed on the couch. For a few months, he still emerged on occasion. He'd go with me and Vera to dinner sometimes, and he traveled with us, albeit reluctantly, to Harry and Olivia's for our traditional holiday visit as recently as last year.

But after that, he stopped coming upstairs, or slipping into our bed, at all. At the time, I chose to view it as a phase. Through this I stuck with him, bringing him meals, talking with him patiently and at length, coming down in the evenings to keep him company, sometimes even sleeping beside him on the couch. This became our new normal, a concept that is almost endlessly elastic until it is not.

With hindsight, I can't say which version of Richard was easier to live with. When we first began to date, he'd been a head case with his weather phobias. Every activity, even going to dinner, required multiple checks of his screens and apps. But once he was freed of his fears after therapy and exposure, he moved into a sort of weather-chasing mania. He'd not only frequently put himself in danger, but he was often gone.

So perhaps this time he spent in the basement was not the worst of it, as terrible as that might sound. At least we talked— at first—even if we mostly talked about him and the weather. He spoke nostalgically of the adrenaline rush of reporting amid a tornado chase, standing on top of the car with his camera pointed at the funnel, rasping into the mic. In the short time that it lasted, being one with the weather had been a wonder, a near religious experience, he said. And now he had screwed up big. Even if he could coax himself back out there, he didn't think he could ever get it back.

"Get what back?" I'd asked. His mojo, his charisma—the thing that had made him a star. No one would ever listen to him again, he said. No one would take him seriously. His reputation was ruined.

He wasn't entirely wrong, but then, people rise above all sorts of difficult circumstances. He hadn't said anything sexist or racist. He hadn't harassed anyone. He hadn't masturbated on Zoom. People tend to forget. Life goes on.

Nothing I said helped. I tried to be patient, but I sometimes failed. I didn't need Richard to be a star. I just wanted Richard to get over himself. To see that the world still existed in all its beauty and amazement, even if he was not at its center. The weather too: the hot, the cold, the storms, the wind—none of this was about him.

Also, ironically, even though he was now home all the time, he was for all intents and purposes gone. I wound up single parenting, in a sense, coaxing Vera through the tensions of her last two years of high school, teaching her to drive, taking her to look at colleges, helping her navigate applications. Even then, I continued to try. I urged him to return to the therapist. I suggested he go back into the newsroom. Anything to get him out of his head, out of the basement, even just to see a movie or take a walk.

CHAPTER 6

Uncle Harry, Phenomenologist

IN THE MORNING I find Harry at the kitchen table, a knotty farmhouse pine, squinting through his thick lenses as he studies the newspaper. The sunlight is streaming in bright.

"Do you mind?" I ask as I walk behind him and pull the blinds.

He looks up at me, startled.

"I don't know how you can see. The sun is blinding!"

"How are you feeling?" he asks.

"I'm fine. Although, now that you mention it, I do have a bit of a headache. Nothing terrible though."

"See?"

"See what?"

"Light sensitivity. Headache. Classic signs of concussion. You should take it easy today. Drink plenty of fluids. Rest."

"Rest? I'm not sure that's possible. I have to leave today."

This announcement is not premeditated. I have no plan. Something has evidently been triggered by my walking out on Richard. I am now in flight, even if I don't know where I'm headed.

"But you can't go. Christmas is tomorrow!"

"No, Christmas is the day after tomorrow. Tomorrow is Christmas Eve." Harry is neither confused nor showing signs of dementia; it's just that while we have our sacred Christmas rituals—Chinese food for dinner, multiple viewings of *Elf*, long walks on the beach—our family celebrates Chanukah, so Harry is not paying close attention to the Advent calendar.

"Still," he says. "I don't understand. Wherever it is you are going, it can wait a day or two, especially given your headache. Are you feeling at all nauseous?"

"No."

"Seeing double?"

"Not."

"Ringing in the ears?"

"Nope," I reply perhaps too enthusiastically, but I'm eager to demonstrate my hale state.

"Any confusion, like you are in a fog? Or forgetfulness?"

"No more than usual," I joke.

Harry leans in closer and looks at me, concerned.

"I'm kidding, Harry! I'm fine. You're making too much of a little thing. All I said was that it was too bright in here."

"No two people experience things the same way," he responds. He takes a sip of his coffee and returns his attention to the newspaper.

"Look! There's a little squib here about the accident

yesterday." He lifts the paper closer as he reads: "'Traffic was stalled for over two hours Wednesday on the outer span of the Chesapeake Bay Bridge when a Toyota Corolla veered out of the westbound lane and slammed into a UPS truck, which then spun into a tractor trailer, which then . . .'"

I look over his shoulder at the story, but my eye catches on a glossy insert that drops from the paper and falls to the floor. I walk over and pick it up.

West Virginia, it says on the cover. The words *Explore Mountaineer Country* are overlaid on a spray of clouds that have settled between the mountains. *Almost Heaven* reads the tagline. I pick it up and flip it open and begin to leaf through.

"Are you listening?" Harry asks.

"I am. I heard every word. It's truly awful." I feel implicated in this tragedy, as if the too-loud music I was playing, Luna barking, my moth distraction, contributed to this collision, even though it was more than a mile away and had likely already occurred when I slammed on my brakes.

But my attention has now shifted to this advertising supplement, which I'm perusing as Luna nips at my ankle, asking to be fed. I walk over to the counter, where I have left the nearly empty bag of dog food, and scoop the second-to-last cup of kibble into a bowl. The order I placed last night is scheduled to be delivered by 5:00 p.m. today, but that won't do me much good given my sudden decision to leave.

Harry is still reading aloud. "'Two others were transported by helicopter to the hospital and were evaluated and released.' I wonder why it doesn't mention which hospital. Did they take them to Shock Trauma in Baltimore, I wonder? Or—"

"Oh boy," I say, wishing he would stop already. I understand that it was bad, and I feel bad, and this is only making me feel more bad, even though I get that this is not about me, and that my selfishness in not wanting to hear more details is the most bad thing of all.

"It's fascinating," he continues. "The different ways different people experienced the accident."

"Yes," I say. "Definitely. Some experienced a mere inconvenience, a traffic jam. And one person is . . . dead." I am now rummaging through the refrigerator, looking for something to eat, and wondering what level of insensitive it would be, given that we are talking about death, to ask if there are any eggs.

"And then you . . ." he says.

"Me what?"

"Well, it led to your panic attack, or at least contributed," he says, looking up from the paper. "I'm thinking about experience. The experience of experience. The way one person experiences something differently from another."

I can't believe he is still going on about this. Perhaps he is the one who has been concussed.

"I mean, yes, we all experience things differently. That's painfully obvious, is it not?"

"You might think so, but it's also painfully obvious that it's not as obvious as it seems."

"For example?" This conversation is doing very little to improve the state of my headache.

"Even in my work, or my former line of work, which you might think is pure science—how did the patient die, for example—the answer is colored by multiple factors, right?

Perhaps it looks like a clear-cut heart attack, and perhaps it was, but that determination is also going to be affected by my own mood as I go about my examination of the body. Maybe the outcome has been somewhat predetermined by what is written on his chart, the presumption that he had a heart attack, and that I am, as the pathologist performing the autopsy, being asked to confirm. That injects bias, obviously. And maybe he had a heart attack, but were I in a different mood I might be curious enough to probe deeper. Perhaps there are other factors, maybe an overdose contributed to the heart attack, or even caused the heart attack, but let's say I had a rough morning—your school bus didn't show up and Olivia was already at work and I had to run you to school, and then I hit traffic, and I have a meeting at eleven, and a backlog of cases and . . . You see where I'm going with this? My own experience is going to impact this particular experience of determining the cause of death of this particular patient."

"Well, sure, but . . ." I begin, not at all sure which part of this I am attempting to refute, apart from the obviousness of the assertion.

"Please don't tell me he's going on about phenomenology again," says Olivia. I hadn't noticed her slip into the room; she's wrapped in a blue striped terry-cloth robe with her hair, presumably just washed, enshrined in a towel on top of her head. She looks radiant, confident, somehow regal even. Not unlike a woman with a syndicated radio broadcast that has five-and-a-half-million-plus weekly listeners, and who has just signed a contract to write a book with the eponymous name: *The Storyteller*. Her presence makes me want to self-improve; I pull my hair into a ponytail using the elastic band around my wrist. It's not much, but on the spot, it's the best I can do.

She pours a coffee and settles into a chair at the table, then readjusts her position, looks around, walks over to the window, and opens the blinds.

Clearly I am alone in this too-bright experience of the morning sun.

"Phenomenology, Uncle Harry? Pray tell."

"It's a class I'm taking. Online. An introduction to phenomenology."

"That sounds very you," I say, which I mean in a good way. He is always trying to broaden his horizons. He has taken continuing education classes in both figurative and still-life drawing—as I helped them move this summer, I unearthed about twenty canvases chronicling his largely failed attempts to capture, in acrylic, a bowl of pears. Also, he is now an amateur astronomer, and he recently took a one-day deep dive into the life of Alexander the Great. The last time I saw him, right before the move, he had completed a class in Peruvian coastal cuisine, and he cooked for us Parihuela, which we spooned politely. He has never been to Peru, as far as I know, and has no particular connection to the country. I'm not sure he'd ever even eaten at a Peruvian restaurant prior to enrolling in this class.

"Phenomenology is one of those topics I don't really know anything about," I say. "I mean I know, and I don't know, what it's about."

"Like I just said, it's about experience. About how everyone experiences things differently. Like you on the bridge . . .

overcome probably because of whatever it is that's going on with you and Richard, preoccupied with that experience and reality, while the experience of the ambulance driver was . . . well, who can say, a million other things . . ."

I stifle, with some difficulty, a response. We spent the better part of last night not mentioning Richard, devising alternate theories for my behavior, even diagnosing me with a panic attack and a sudden case of gephyrophobia, when he evidently thinks the whole episode had something to do with my husband. This upsets me more than it should.

"You were saying, the experience of experience," I repeat through gritted teeth.

"Exactly. I will never experience my coffee in silence again," says Olivia.

"Silence is overrated," Harry replies.

"In this house, obviously. Let's change the subject. You are not helping Cassie one bit."

We experiment with this concept of silence, briefly. I continue to rummage through the refrigerator and find, finally, some berries and a small container of yogurt, which I bring to the table. I then continue to peruse this faux editorial product from the West Virginia Department of Tourism, turning the pages, reflecting about how I have never paused to consider the state's physical beauty. I have only thought of it as the place where my parents died. A place I have deliberately avoided for that reason. That it might have anything to offer as a destination—a place to vacation or recreate—had not occurred to me. There are stunning pictures of mountains, a feature about a historic village, a list of superb dining options, a story about the tradition of sports at West Virginia University, accompanied with hotel suggestions and restaurants in which to dine.

I then see a feature about—of all the subjects in the world—bridges.

The headline reads "If Bridges Could Talk."

"If only," I concur.

"If only what?" Olivia asks.

"Sorry . . . I'm talking to myself. That's not a sign of concussion!" I quickly add. "There's a story here, in this piece of West Virginia tourist propaganda," I say, holding the magazine aloft. "The headline is, 'If Bridges Could Talk.'"

Do Harry and Olivia lock eyes, or am I being paranoid? My parents died in a bridge collapse. My aunt and uncle will not talk about said bridge collapse. *If only the bridge could talk about its collapse, how helpful that would be*, I think.

Whatever response they might be contemplating is interrupted by the sound of something crashing above where we sit. Then a scampering sound makes me think of the family of squirrels recently discovered and expensively removed from our attic at home. But this situation does not involve squirrels. It's Luna, who appears with a blue piece of plastic dangling from her mouth.

"What does she have?" Olivia asks.

"Oh no! I think it's Hoppity!" I say, laughing with relief. "Or a piece of Hoppity. Thank God it's not the internet cord."

It takes Olivia a moment to register what I've said. "Wait, that's Hoppity? The *horse*?" she says, clearly upset.

"Well, he's not an *actual* horse," I say absurdly. "It was an accident. I mean, it hardly had any air left inside. We were goofing around with it last night and she sank her teeth into it."

Olivia's public-facing persona is even-keeled, almost rabbinical. She sees both sides of every argument and rarely takes a position, which is arguably a good quality for someone who has made a career in public broadcasting. But on the family front it's a different story. She has no shortage of opinions, and she generally prevails. While she rarely loses her temper, it's best to stay in her good graces.

Why in the world would Olivia care about this ancient piece of deflated rubber that is just taking up space, collecting dust? Probably best not to mention that when I woke this morning, I noticed Luna was gnawing on Gumby, and while he survived the assault, he is now riddled with teeth marks.

"I'm really sorry," I say. "I can buy a new one . . . if you want it for some reason."

"It had sentimental value," she says. "I don't know that you can even buy one anymore."

"I'm pretty sure you can."

"Not like this one."

I'm waiting for her to step in to correct herself, to apologize for overreacting, but she's not backing down.

"I'm really so sorry," I say. "Let me look around. I can probably get another on eBay. You can find pretty much anything these days. If I'd known it was special, I wouldn't have let her near it. I used to play with that thing when I was a kid, right? So it's got to be, like, fifty years old."

"It's fifty-three years old," Olivia says. A strangely precise number. "What were you doing in that room anyway?" Olivia asks.

"I'm sorry. I didn't think it mattered. I don't know why I slept there. A change of pace, I suppose?"

This is strangely unsettling. I have always considered this to be my house too. I've been coming here all my life. But I get that on a practical level, even family members become houseguests who require clean towels and sheets and need to be fed.

"You should have asked," Olivia says.

"Honey, let it go," says Harry.

"Don't tell me to let it go."

It's rare that they exchange harsh words. I'm not sure why Hoppity has become this sudden flashpoint.

"Can someone tell me what is happening here?"

"Olivia is fond of that toy," Harry says.

Olivia is looking at him with daggers in her eyes.

"But it's been sitting there in the corner for fifty, sorry, *fifty-three* years. What's the big deal?"

"It wasn't sitting there in the corner," Olivia says. "It was in the storage closet back in DC until the move. I put it in the children's room only last week when I unpacked those boxes."

"Okay," I say, wondering what that has to do with anything. "Still. Can you fill me in?"

"Fine," Olivia says. "If you must know. Your mother bought it for you, shortly before she died."

"She did?" I ask. This small disclosure makes me feel like I might cry. Olivia speaks so rarely about the past that I'm a little stunned, and I want to prod her for more information. Once I was old enough to ask questions about my parents, Olivia told me they died in a bridge collapse in West Virginia, but it was always hard to get her to elaborate. I wanted to know what my parents had been like, how they had interacted with me.

Had they read me stories, bought me toys, sung songs to me at bedtime? I have a hard time imagining myself as the child of anyone other than my aunt and uncle, which is part of why I spend so much time staring at that photo in the living room.

It wasn't just that Olivia talked very little about my parents, but the whole subject of the bridge collapse seemed taboo—and she and Uncle Harry most definitely did not want to talk about the moth. They said that was a lot of crazy talk, a distraction, which had nothing to do with the tragedy our family had endured.

"Where did she get it? Do you know? And when did she give it to me? And if it's of such great sentimental value, why was it lying around when we were kids? I mean, I played with it all the time." I don't mean for that to sound accusatory. I'm genuinely puzzled.

"I don't know. Don't put me on the spot. It probably made some sort of logical sense at the time, that your mother would have wanted you to have it. She certainly wouldn't have wanted your dog to destroy it though."

"I know very little about my mother, but I know she loved dogs, so I'm guessing she wouldn't be making so much of this," I say boldly. I don't mean to sound angry. Or maybe I do.

"What is it that you want from me, Cassie?"

"I want to know more!"

"About what? What more is there to say?"

"Why were my parents even on that bridge? You told me they were going to a wedding in Toledo, but Point Pleasant is not on the way. It's like there's some big secret. And whenever I even mention the moth, you completely shut down."

"There's no big secret, Cassie. Maybe they were lost. What

is it you want to know about this moth nonsense? I don't understand what you're asking. I'm not sure you know yourself. Some questions are so completely off base that they make no sense. It's like you are asking me to tell you 'How blue is a mile?'"

"Maybe tell me more about Hoppity. It doesn't need to be anything profound. Just . . . anything."

"They picked it up for you at a toy store in West Virginia," Harry says. "Or maybe Ohio. One or the other. But it was while they were on that trip."

"Seriously?" This small detail astonishes. "So . . . was it in the car? Did it *survive*? Obviously it did. How did we get it?"

"Enough," Olivia demands.

Every bone in my now extremely tense body tells me that I need to get out of here, that I need to hit the road, that I need to go, at last, to West Virginia. Olivia may be right: I don't know what I'm asking, what my "blue mile" question is. But I know that I need to confront this place I've been avoiding all my life, the place where my parents died. Maybe I can find a way to make the loss—of something I don't even know, no less—feel less forbidden, less unsettled, less like there's something jagged inside that is tearing me up all the time.

"Let's see what the paper has to say about the weather today," Harry says as if we are not in the middle of one of the most potentially explosive exchanges in our family history. This is typical. Every time we get to an important emotional juncture, we take a step back and change the subject and pretend it never happened. This has become my modus operandi too—I'm a rule follower, an obeyer of speed limits, a person slow to act, as evidenced by the slow burn of my marriage's end, or by the fact that I'm ready to hit the road, and yet I'm sitting here listening to Harry talk about the weather.

He flips back to the front page and reads the description: "Rain. Light snow. Cloudy. Sun emerging after noon. High 45. Low 31."

"Sounds like it will be the same tomorrow."

"Something is off," I say. Something is off about pretty much everything right now, but I am referring, specifically, to the weather ear.

"What do you mean?"

"He's got an extra syllable."

"Who does?"

"Richard. In his ear."

"I'm sorry, he has an extra syllable in his *ear*?"

Harry is squinting, examining me like I have just confirmed his theory: most definitely concussed.

"No, that's a newspaper term, *ear*, remember? That's what Richard used to write when he first started out at the paper. Now he's writing the ears again. That's the information that goes at the top of the front page."

"Where is Richard anyway?" Olivia finally asks.

"He had to work," is all I say. I love Olivia and Harry like the warm, loving family they are, but I've kept from them my marital woes, and I don't want to have this conversation right now.

"I was about to tell you, something just came up," I lie. "I was just telling Harry . . . I have to leave a little earlier than planned."

"What? Why?" Olivia asks.

"I've got a job interview," I lie again, somewhat to my astonishment.

"You have a job interview on a holiday weekend?" Olivia asks.

"Oddly, yes. They said it's nice and quiet—that it's counter-intuitively the best time to come."

"Strange. But wow! That's big news! Congrats!" Olivia says. "I thought you loved your job though."

"I do. But still, a friend told me about an opening where she works, and it sounds intriguing."

"An opening where? Doing what? Teaching in an MFA program somewhere, I hope?" My perceived underachieve-ment has always bothered Olivia. I had a promising journalism career that I drove into a wall. Then I got an MFA and began to work on a novel. Or I tried to work on a novel. I never got anywhere. I mean that quite literally. It's not that I tried and failed, or that I wrote awhile and hit a wall. I simply couldn't write. To call it writer's block seems reductive, but that might be me being averse to the cliché.

My MFA was not a waste; I put it to use teaching aspiring fiction writers at a local community college. It's a job that I take quite seriously, the only problem being that I tend to become overly involved with my students. Not with them personally but with their stories, hundreds of which are stuck in my head. I'm haunted by their narratives, most of which I read before they reach completion, given that my intro creative writing class is only one semester long. I fret about those characters and their stories, many of which seem autobiographical—true stories that were too painful to tell, turned instead into fictions. One story involved a single mother from Nigeria who worked as a nanny for a wealthy family in Bethesda. The employer would not help her out as she teetered on the verge of eviction from her apartment. Another story was about a high school soccer goalie with Hodgkin's lymphoma. When the class ended, she was left suspended on the page, waiting to learn whether her treatment was working, as well as whether she would be awarded a college scholarship. I wake up at night sometimes, wondering what became of them. It troubles me not to know.

"Exactly!" I lie some more. "An MFA program in . . . Ohio."

"Wonderful!" says Olivia, a little too excitedly. "Is it tenure-track?"

"Yes!"

"Where in Ohio?" Harry asks.

"Columbus." It's the first city that springs to mind.

"Buckeyes!" he says excitedly.

I can't believe we are all cheerfully leaning into this story, too polite to acknowledge that obviously something is going on in my marriage, not to mention that moments ago, we had a tense and unsettling exchange.

"But what about your own writing?" Olivia asks. Now she is fanning the flames, needling me with my least favorite subject. Just because my aunt is a writer, and my cousin Samantha, a reporter for the *Pittsburgh Post-Gazette*, is writing a book on infrastructure, doesn't mean I have to write too. I am aware that I am protesting too much, presumably because the opposite is true. Maybe I do need to write. Still, I don't think Olivia understands how much it pains me each time she brings this up. Or perhaps she does.

I decide to ignore the question and to continue embellishing, which is kind of fun, imagining this entire alternative future. "I just got an email saying they want me to meet the department head, and she's leaving for vacation next week, which means I to have to hit the road this morning, unfortunately."

"Can't you do that on Zoom?" Harry asks, not unreasonably.

"No, they want this to be in person. You'll have to come out, Uncle Harry. We can go to a game. If I get the job, that is."

"But you only just got here," Harry says.

"I know. I'm disappointed too."

"I have a thought," Olivia says. "Why don't we get you across the bridge? Harry can drive your car, and I'll follow, and then when we get to the other side, we can pull over and switch vehicles and you can be on your way."

"I did not have a panic attack on the bridge," I say. "I do not have gephyrophobia! Anyway, I'm not driving back over the bridge. I'll head out the other way." I don't know why I say this.

"That makes no sense," Harry says, appearing concerned.

"Don't worry about it. I've mapped it out."

It's fascinating, the way one lie slides so easily into the next. It's as though I've awakened some sort of recessive lying gene and am now making up for lost time, piling on the fabrications like accelerants to my departure.

"Luna!" Harry snaps and then laughs. I look over and she has jumped into his lap and is licking his face.

"She loves you," Olivia says. "Speaking of which, wait . . . You're driving to Ohio for a job interview with the puppy?"

"Yes. She's my copilot," I joke, although it is not much of a joke.

"Have you identified pet-friendly hotels along the way?"

"Not yet, but I'll figure it out."

"Leave Luna here," Olivia says. "She clearly loves Harry, and she is learning to love the water, and I'll shut the door to the bedrooms to keep her out of trouble. The last thing you need is to be worrying about a puppy when you are preparing to interview for a job."

There is a rustle and a gasp as Luna tears the newspaper out of Harry's hands and begins to lick his neck.

"I appreciate that, I really do, but I think I'll take her." I can't imagine leaving her behind. Right now, I need her more than she needs me. There is, however, one small glitch: The food I ordered will not arrive until tonight, and I have enough for only one more meal. But this great country is lousy with Pets! Pets! Pets! stores that carry her precious overpriced organic food, and once I hit the road, I figure I'll pick up a bag.

"Are you sure you're okay to drive with that head?" Harry asks.

"Good grief! You two please stop! I am completely fine!"

Let it never be said that I am orphaned. Aunt Olivia and Uncle Harry are enough parents for all three of us kids, with enough hovering left over to spare.

CHAPTER 7

Flight, Cont.

FOR MANY YEARS I did fly, so much so that I was awarded elite status on two different airlines. Also, I wrote.

Before I met Richard, in a brief pocket of my life that I don't talk much about, I contributed to a number of prominent publications that included two well-known international newspapers, a handful of US-based news magazines, and a couple of glossy travel outlets that were, back in the day, quite flush. I loved my work and was, in fact, quite successful for a time, one story leading to the next and then the next until I was getting what most would consider plum assignments, which began to skew in the direction of disaster coverage.

All that time, my real dream was to write fiction. It wasn't that I preferred to make things up, but rather, the story I most wanted to tell was not always possible to pin down factually, which is part of what finally got me derailed.

I had no formal training, but I was ambitious and took pleasure in perfecting even the lightest of features, in finding an arc, in bringing a thing around to a poetic conclusion, even if I was, at first, only writing about the christening by the mayor of a new shopping center in Rockville, Maryland—the subject of my first published story. I didn't mind cobbling together what others might consider to be puff pieces. Covering the opening of a museum exhibition, or interviewing an author, or writing a workaday piece about how the recession was affecting the restaurant business—there was always a story to be found in any of these, and I was game. A story well told is a good story in my opinion, and I felt, at the time, that being paid even a paltry amount to work with words was a privilege. I would have been happy to proofread crossword puzzle clues. Even now, when I teach, I am as happy to work with a student on a novella about zombies as I am on a piece of literary fiction.

I turned my reporting for the county newspaper, where I first began, into magazine work, accumulating clips and eventually getting asked to write long, expository pieces that took me around the world.

My troubles began to quietly percolate in Ukraine, where I was sent by the *New York Times Magazine* to write about the lingering effects of radiation on victims in Chernobyl ten years after the disaster. The piece turned out well—eight thousand words with a three-page photo spread—but I had some issues with my translator. It would have come to nothing had I not returned, some three years later, to write about the apartment bombings in Moscow in 1999—an event that triggered the war in Chechnya, and which set the tone for Putin's career. A different translator this time, of course, given the different language, but the same problem occurred: She was refusing to ask one of my questions.

We went back and forth about this a bit. I am a nonconfrontational person and generally not impulsive, but I found this frustrating. I was, after all, the reporter. I was driving the story. She was being paid by the hour to turn my questions into Russian, not to tell me what was and was not appropriate to ask. In the end I had no power over the situation. I wrote my story, it turned out well, and had it ended there, I'd probably still be hopping on planes, a reporter's notebook in my pocket. But I couldn't let it rest. I figured I'd give it one more try.

A few months later, I had a hunch about something, and I needed to get myself to India to follow it through. Also, I had been looking for a reason to go to India. My great-grandfather, my father's grandfather, emigrated to the US in the early 1900s from India, part of the Bene Israel community of Jews, and I was eager to see what I could learn about that side of the family, about which I knew very little.

I managed to get an assignment from *Rolling Stone* to write another retrospective, this time about families in Bhopal who were still seeking compensation for the family members who had died in the toxic gas leak in 1984. While there, I interviewed dozens of survivors.

Their narratives were horrific. More than a half-million people were exposed to toxic gas. The number of reported deaths varies widely but is in the thousands.

It was harrowing—the deaths, the disfigurements, the long-term effects. One of the families I profiled had lost four of their five children, and the one who remained had become blind.

On a personal level it was a journey of beginnings and endings, although I didn't know that at the time. I met Richard on this trip, at a dinner party thrown by a mutual acquaintance the day after I arrived back in Delhi from Bhopal. Richard had been there working on the series to do with the global implications of deteriorating air quality to which he had just been assigned.

We had been seated next to each other by the hostess. Whether this was random or deliberate I don't know, but the attraction was fierce. Instantaneous and unexpected. I hadn't been looking for anything, yet there he was.

A sweet, smoky fog enveloped the rooftop that night. Part incense, part dung, part diesel—it could have been part toxic, for all I knew. It was nevertheless intoxicating, whatever effect it might've had on the lungs. I was under a spell from the moment I arrived, saw Richard, and took my seat next to him at the long banquet table shimmering with tea lights.

Servants began to tend to us, fussing, and I remember telling Richard that it was awkward to be waited on like this, and he said something about how this was the way expatriates lived, still, in India, which led to a conversation about travel, life abroad, cultures not our own.

I remember trying to keep the conversation moving in this poetic vein and told Richard that among the things I loved about cities not my own were the sounds. How I found it a comfort that the noises outside my window were always the same, even if they were of a completely different nature, or in a different language. It's a not an especially profound observation, admittedly. It's like saying there is darkness and there is light. Also, it's not true. One doesn't hear the call to prayer, for example, broadcast from speakers in Washington DC. I had trouble articulating this thought, but that didn't stop me from trying. I told him I liked to sleep with the windows open so I could hear children playing, music in the distance, the honking of horns. I was babbling, trying to make too much of nothing, when what I really meant was that I liked to hear proof of life outside my window, to remind myself that I am not alone.

Richard indulged me. He said he agreed and refilled my wineglass. We talked all night, as if we were the only ones at this table around which some fifteen people were seated.

It was as we parted that I learned he was married. He told me this when I suggested we exchange contact information. He said things had been deteriorating for some time, that his wife was a generally unhappy person with an aversion to travel. He had convinced her to come with him on the reporting trip, he said, after which they would take a restorative trip to Goa, just the two of them, to try to set things right. But after three days in India she had been unable to abide the chaos, the heat, the food, and had gone home.

I had taken this at face value, her possible depressive state, her dislike of travel, or at least of traveling on the subcontinent. But now, as the years have worn on with Richard's neurotic weather behavior and refusal to communicate, I have begun to wonder if this first wife, whom I have never met, knew something I did not.

Still, the memory of that night on the rooftop kept me going through many a challenging moment in the following difficult years.

It was my Bhopal translator who finally did me in. He spoke to my editor about a certain line of questioning that I wished to pursue. It turned out that my other two translators, the Ukrainian and the Russian, had also released my questions into the rumor mill. There is an adage: One is an accident. Two is a coincidence. Three is a trend. We now had a trend.

Word spread that I was less interested in learning about the injuries in Bhopal, or the effects of radiation in Chernobyl, or the political ramifications of the apartment bombings outside Moscow, than in whether the people I interviewed, in the days prior to these catastrophes, had seen a giant moth.

CHAPTER 8

The Long Goodbye

LUNA PRANCES BESIDE me, lanky like a baby deer. Olivia and Harry follow behind her, out the front door and along the path that leads to the driveway, their arms full of random provisions.

"Do you want a blanket?" my aunt asks, putting an old floral quilt in the back of my car without waiting for an answer.

"I can't think why I'd need it."

"How about some extra water? And snacks?"

"Really, I'm fine!"

"Who says no to snacks?"

"Please, no snacks!" I insist. "I'm trying to lose a few pounds." I don't know why I say this. It's true, a few pounds could be lost, but it's not a priority, especially during the holiday season. Plus it wouldn't kill me to indulge Olivia, let her do some mothering, and pressing stuff on me is part of how she shows her love. She has never been one for deep conversation, unless it's with the guests on her radio program, where she gives the impression she's fully emotionally in touch.

This is how Olivia has always been, and I've accepted that; she is who she is and she has been very good to me. But right now I'm incensed by her willingness to play along with this charade of a job interview. She's barely inquired about Vera. And she's asked me very little about *me*, now that I think about it. All we've really talked about is the incident on the bridge. But then I ask myself, *Do I really want to go deep with Olivia right now?* I do not.

"The car still holding up okay?" she asks, surveying my old—*her* old—silver Audi with what might be interpreted as affection as I open the back door and place my bag in the rear compartment.

"It's great," I say. "Thank you again!"

I'm not sure that it's great, really. The car has a few more scratches than it did when Olivia gave it to me last year so she could upgrade to an electric. Since we live in the city, it was inevitably going to get a little dinged up, and so it has. I try not to care, which is not difficult because a few imperfections on the car are extremely low on my list of concerns.

"Really great," I repeat as if to convince myself. The scratches are not the problem; it's the expensive maintenance that sometimes makes me question whether I should have accepted this gift or whether I would have been better off keeping my six-year-old Corolla, which Vera now drives. I had not been looking to get a new car when Olivia's offer came along, and although it did not occur to me then, I now wonder if the gift was related to Richard's on-air gaffes. She must have suspected he was in some sort of decline—assumed, perhaps, that we were on the verge of financial ruin.

She gifted the car so subtly that she made it seem I was the one doing *her* the favor, taking it off her hands, sparing her the hassle of having to sell it. It was generous, though the car has been a money pit: I recently had to replace the brakes, and only two months after that not insubstantial expense, an issue involving crossed circuitry, or possibly it was wet circuitry, caused the driver's seat to cease moving back and forth. Vera is significantly taller than I am—she inherited her father's height but is otherwise the spitting image of me—and when she borrowed the car over her fall break while the Toyota was in the shop, it froze in a position such that my foot could no longer reach the pedals. They fixed that, only to tell me they'd found a nail in one of my tires, and that it was probably time to get all four of them replaced.

The vehicle has required some rethinking of who I am: Behind the wheel I feel like an impostress. I'm not a German-luxury-vehicle sort of person. I'm a writing instructor at a community college, a former journalist, a would-be novelist, with a daughter who attends a state university.

Each time I settle into the driver's seat, I think of a manuscript I helped a student revise about a woman who donated nearly all of her money to charity—every penny she did not need to subsist. She never ate out, or bought new clothes, or went to the theater. She kept her heat low in the winter, and in the summer did not use the air conditioner, even though she lived on the top floor of a walk-up in a converted townhouse on Capitol Hill. She didn't even allow herself small indulgences like trips to the local public swimming pool, even though it was free, lest she might be taking the place of someone who needed to recreate more urgently than her. My mind sometimes drifts to this fictional woman when I am behind the Audi's steering wheel, and I feel a pang of guilt.

⋈ ⋈ ⋈

This car may not be me, but I don't know who I am right now, untethered from my husband and child, about to hit the road. And besides, traveling incognito is strangely liberating. A magnet on the rear bumper boosts the lacrosse team at the exclusive private school that Parker, my niece, attends in Pittsburgh, and there is also a bumper sticker for the campaign of a city councilwoman whom I did not support. I suppose the fact that I do not strip the car of these statements is a statement of its own.

Olivia approaches and envelops me in her lovely fleshy arms. She smells like gardenia and a touch of something familiar that takes a moment to register. Might it be rosin? It's a smell I remember from my days of cello lessons, of the terrifying instructor who had been a cellist in the Moscow Philharmonic before defecting and accepting the fate of having to teach indifferent children like me. I resisted practicing and had trouble keeping up with the school orchestra, which Harry and Olivia insisted I join. Everything to do with those days of enforced music instruction was a struggle, yet the smell still inspires a pleasant nostalgia.

"Be safe," Olivia says. "Please call when you arrive." She holds me a little too long. It makes me nervous. Perhaps our tense exchange in the kitchen was portentous. Maybe I am heading off into some danger zone. Maybe she knows something I do not.

Harry then pulls me in for a hug, releases me, and begins

ticking off directions, along with a traffic and weather update. He's like my personal WTOP news station, weather and traffic on the eights.

"I just checked and it looks like there's a pileup on I-70, but it will surely be clear by the time you get there. Also, there might be snow in Pennsylvania this afternoon," he says.

"Am I going through Pennsylvania?" I ask.

"I thought you already mapped this out," says Olivia.

Ignoring her, Harry continues, "I suppose you can avoid it, but that will add time to your travel. Do you not want to go through Pennsylvania?"

"I have no problem with Pennsylvania. It was only a question."

"Okay, you can stay on 68 if you want to avoid the turnoff . . ."

"Truly, I am not Pennsylvania-averse."

"It's true that weather-wise, it might be better to veer south."

I am no longer listening, but I nod.

"Then again, if you don't mind Pennsylvania, you will be close to Pittsburgh, and you can stop for the night at Samantha's," Olivia volunteers. "I already asked her, and she said it would be fine."

"But I think she doesn't want to go to Pennsylvania," Harry says.

"Sure, I understand, but it's a free place to stay. Plus, a chance to see family."

Good grief. I announced my fake plan to go to Ohio only thirty minutes ago, and they have already arranged my accommodations. I suppose that some time with Samantha might be restorative, but she's on a book deadline—on top of which, even though she is family, I do not want to present myself to her in my current messy state.

"Thanks, Olivia. I think I'll power through to Cleveland," I say. "But maybe I'll catch her on the way back."

"I thought you were going to Columbus," Harry says.

"Yes. Columbus. That's what I mean." I don't really know what I mean. All I can tell you is that they are both in Ohio and begin with the letter *C*.

"Good, because that's what I mapped. Columbus. So if you really do want to avoid the bridge, even though it's out of your way, you'd better head out to DE 1 north, but it's going to add a lot of time and it might be worth it to take a deep breath and—"

"I've got it, Harry," I interrupt. "Don't forget I also have a phone. With a navigation system!"

"Nevertheless, you might want to write it down," says Olivia. "What if you lose service?"

She's not wrong. I do, in fact, have a famously bad sense of direction, and even with a voice in the speaker guiding me, I manage to get lost.

"I'll be fine!" I say. "I'll figure it out!"

I settle into the driver's seat. The steering wheel is cold, as are the leather seats. I turn on the ignition to let the heat run.

"Turn on the seat warmers," Olivia suggests.

"There are seat warmers?" How have I been driving this car for six months without knowing this?

Olivia opens the passenger side door to show me. Then I watch her gaze land on the warped box of Cheerios on the seat. "Want me to take any trash?" she asks.

"No, I'm good." I have no idea what happened to that moth,

which seemed to have disappeared by the time I returned to the car with the police escort. Yet for all I know, it might still be in the car, assuming it was really here to begin with. I'm not sure I could even rehabilitate the crushed box, but I'm not ready to part with it.

As she shows me the switch that activates this sublime seat-warming feature, I can't help but think of the overly altruistic woman and wonder if she would want me, in this moment, to self-deprive, to send the heat to someone more in need—someone who does not own a puffy winter coat.

"I'll tell Samantha maybe you'll come, in case you change your mind," Olivia says.

That I have already decisively dismissed this idea, that it is still under discussion, is another Oliver family trait. Even when we have arrived at a restaurant where we have a reservation, alternative options are still actively discussed. No decision is ever final. No discussion is ever finished, except for the discussion I would like to have.

"I'll give her a call," I say.

I strap on my seatbelt. Luna, from the passenger seat behind me, leans in and puts her head on my shoulder. It is so incredibly cute that we all pause for a minute and laugh. Olivia snaps a picture. She is very active on social media, my seventy-nine-year-old storytelling aunt, and I know that within moments my road trip departure will be broadcast to the world. Hopefully, once pixelated, I will look less frazzled than I feel.

Harry leans in to plant a kiss on my cheek. I close the door at last, pull out of the driveway, and feel instantly relieved at the prospect of time away from the lovely if oppressive concern of my family, this family of long Jewish goodbyes, where you think you are leaving and thirty minutes later you are still standing there talking, hugging for the tenth time, a new story about to launch.

In the rearview mirror I see Harry and Olivia waving and blowing kisses theatrically.

"Don't forget to keep an eye on your head!" Harry shouts to me.

I smile, wave, and catch a glimpse of myself in the rearview mirror. My head is still there, as far as my eyes can see.

CHAPTER 9

Obfuscation

THE E-ZPASS READER that serves as the gateway to the westbound span of the bridge looks like a giant metal centipede—some techno AI nightmare with an electronic eye that is programmed to fire lasers at vehicles with delinquent accounts.

I keep my eyes trained on the road. There's no reason to be nervous; there's nothing to worry about here, no sign of the moth in the car. And I do not have gephyrophobia, not even a little bit. Still, some distracting music would be helpful to break the silence in the car, to get me over this expanse of water into which a vehicle plunged less than twenty-four hours ago. My fingers punch blindly at the music app on my phone. I wish for something raucous, punk, or maybe death metal, with a heavy screaming bass. Instead, I land on an instrumental number. Discordant sounds of cold grey steel begin to pour through the speakers. It's a cello, I believe, but it's being plucked and pounded and abused to a strangely beautiful musical effect that echoes my mood.

I'm running away. I'm lying and fleeing, possibly still bleeding. My life has been reduced to what sounds like a country-western refrain, which makes a strange kind of sense: It's not just that I have finally snapped on the Richard front, which was a long time coming, but this Hoppity episode has set me on fire. This is the first time I can recall Olivia telling me something meaningful about my mother—that she bought me a gift shortly before she died. It's a blue plastic blob that is now as precious to me as the diamond band on my finger once was. I make a mental note to take it off.

My phone rings, interrupting the music, and the familiar voice of my sister-cousin pours through the car's sound system. "I hear you are coming to town!" she says.

"Ha ha, no, that's just Olivia unable to take no for an answer. I told her I was going the other way."

"You have a job interview?"

"Well, sort of," I say. I don't want to lie to Samantha, but Olivia is her mother, and I don't want to put her in the middle of any drama. "I've got a lot going on."

"What does that even mean?"

"Nothing . . . I just needed to leave." To leave and then leave again, I do not say.

"Did something happen?"

"Nothing important. I'm dealing with some Richard stuff. Plus, Olivia kind of lost it because my puppy bit into Hoppity."

"You have *a puppy*?"

I don't know why everyone seems so shocked by this.

"She's a sweetheart. Her name is Luna."

"And what, or who, is Hoppity?"

"Remember that blue bouncing thing? With the handles?

We used to play with it as kids. It turns out to have tremendous sentimental value."

"Oh, *that*. I know what you're talking about. I tried to throw it away when I helped them pack up for the move, but she freaked out. It's probably a thing that happens with age—you get attached to all of these objects from the past."

"I guess I do that, too, with some of Vera's things," I say, downplaying the fact that in this case there must be some historical significance to the blue plastic blob. "Like her soccer cleats from senior year. Don't ask me why I still have them in the back of my car. The ball is back there too." This is not untrue, but it is also not the point.

"Um, okay, so—backing up—where are you going? Mom said Ohio?"

"Yes. Ohio."

"Okay, road trip to Ohio with a puppy for a *sort of* job interview two days before Christmas. Totally normal thing to do," she says.

My silence is an answer of sorts, and she doesn't push.

"Please know I'm here if you need anything or if you change your mind."

"Thanks, Sam. That means a lot. I'll be in touch. Meantime, have a good holiday!"

It is only now sinking in that I'm about to spend Christmas alone. Even if we don't celebrate Christmas, our deranged snowman cookies, our Chinese food, and our movie ritual are so ingrained, so much a part of who we are and what we do, that it *is* Christmas, just done a different way.

We say another round of goodbyes and disconnect, and the music begins to pour through the speakers again. One cello riff responds to the one that came before. They are conversing. I don't know what they are saying, but they are so clearly talking to each other that I can see the punctuation—the quotation and exclamation marks, the periods, commas, and colons. I understand that there is a story here, one so fully realized in all its senses that I can even smell the rosin, which sends me back to my locker, to the hallways at school. To the battered cello case I used to lug, under protest, through the hallways. If only I'd continued to practice, perhaps I would have found my way to a life more musical, to stories less cluttered with words I can't seem to write.

I'm about a quarter of the way across the bridge, with the Chesapeake glistening on either side of this narrow, open conveyance. A snow drop falls, the clouds part cinematically, the sun comes out—all within the span of minutes. There's a joke about this, about the way in which the weather so rapidly shifts. If you don't like the weather in Vermont, the saying goes, wait fifteen minutes. I've heard versions of this in Kansas, in every part of New England, and in Michigan. And now, as I watch the weather change so radically as I cross from east to west, I might amend the joke to include a bit about crossing the Chesapeake Bay Bridge.

My instinct is to pick up the phone and share this thought with Richard, but I do not.

⋈   ⋈   ⋈

I have in my possession a set of retainers that are meant to keep me from grinding my teeth, but I haven't worn them in a couple of years. Around the time Richard's troubles began,

which coincided with my commitment to regular exercise, I seemed to have stopped clamping my jaw tight at night and gnashing molars. I put the retainers in my bedside drawer and nearly forgot about them until one night, last April, I noticed them on the nightstand.

I had just returned from a trip to California with Vera, taking one last look at colleges before she made her final decision to go to UMD. I should have given it more thought, but for whatever reason, I popped the retainers into my mouth. I figured it was a sign of some sort, the universe reminding me to wear them, even if only prophylactically.

But something wasn't right, probably on account of my not having worn them in a while. My bite seemed to have shifted an alarming amount. I truly could not get them to fit over my teeth. I made a mental note to call the dentist and then went to sleep.

When I mentioned this to Richard the next morning, he said Elaine had just called, wondering if she had left her retainers there. "Mystery solved," he said nonchalantly.

"Elaine?"

I tried to give what he was telling me the benefit of the doubt. Maybe she'd needed a place to crash for whatever reason, and since I had been away, Richard had suggested our room. But that made no sense. Not only was Vera's bed empty, but we also have a guest room. And Richard was living in the basement, so why . . . How . . . ? I stopped trying to make excuses for this. Elaine could only have been in our bedroom for one reason.

Elaine was a family friend. She was always at our house, often at our dinner table, sometimes even on the sidelines of Vera's games. She was single—chronically so, the way she described it, a condition she was always trying to fix, to no avail. She'd show us prospects she was considering on the apps and regale us with anecdotes about dates, both good but mostly bad: the sad-sack unemployed man who still lived with his mother and sister, the men who seemed great but then became ghosts, the men who looked nothing like their profiles, or had unbearably bad breath, or turned out to be married.

Evidently the latter was not as much of a nonstarter as she'd made it sound.

⋈   ⋈   ⋈

The windshield wipers turn themselves on and bat this unproductive memory away. A few rhythmic swipes that keep time with the music. Before I know it, I am on the other side of the bridge, merging without incident onto the highway.

Luna yawns, then stretches across the back seat. Within minutes, I again hear her gentle puppy snores. She is so long, this puppy, her limbs so flexible, that she reminds me of Gumby. Intact Gumby, that is, not the mutilated, gnawed-on Gumby whom I took and stashed in my bag to avoid another withering look from Olivia.

CHAPTER 10

The Richards

ALTHOUGH WE'D HAD our cinematic rooftop encounter in New Delhi some two years earlier, Richard and I did not have any communication until we met a second time, again serendipitously at the dinner party of a different mutual friend. (Washington is a shtetl, and journalism circles are a shtetl within a shtetl.) We wasted no time. Now that we had a clear path forward, we quickly became a couple.

His wife had taken nearly all the furniture, so what little he had in the way of possessions, including the air mattress on which he slept and the ratty sofa in the living room of his Capitol Hill apartment, had been hand-me-downs from friends. Bedsheets, and in one room a shower curtain, covered the windows, tacked to the moldings above the sills. It seemed amusing at the time, or at least Richard made light of it, joking about being reduced to living like a college student at the age of thirty-seven, his shabby domicile a reminder of the way a broken marriage can diminish the finances and flatten the soul.

I may have had a respectable apartment in Woodley Park, replete with blinds on the windows and store-bought furniture, but I was depleted in my own way, and professionally at sea. After the Bhopal trip, I felt I had little choice but to give up reporting and set aside my journalistic ambitions. It was hard to imagine anyone hiring me or giving me worthy assignments. Perhaps I might have still had a future, but I didn't have the courage to find out.

That I walked away from my profession, that I was embarrassed about the way things played out, was not indicative of any larger self-doubt about the story I'd been trying to report. I still believed I was on the right track. There had, in fact, been sightings of a creature—a gigantic moth that appeared to be part human—prior to Chernobyl and the Moscow apartment bombings. Regarding Bhopal, I was, admittedly, merely speculating. I'd heard a rumor or two, but nothing substantiated, inasmuch as a sighting of a giant Mothman can be substantiated. And as it happened, being shut down on this line of inquiry—having an enforced silence on the subject— fit neatly into the story of my life. Around Harry and Olivia, I was not encouraged to ask such questions. Now my inquiries had been deemed out-of-bounds professionally as well. In in my embarrassment, I left India before I had the chance to do any exploration of my family roots.

Not sure what else to do, I decided to try turning my story, such as it was, into fiction, but without an intuitive sense of how to go about that, I applied to writing programs and wound up getting an MFA. I was able to turn out the short prose required for applications, and later for assignments, and I even received encouragement from my professors—but everything

I wrote felt disingenuous, made-up. I got that the point of fiction is to make things up; yet I wanted to be writing from a place I understood, and I couldn't get any real traction.

I was still working on my degree when Richard and I reconnected. I had just begun teaching at the community college, and I was later offered adjunct positions at American University and at Maryland, but by then I was already in love with my students, many of them recent immigrants with interesting stories to tell, so I stayed where I was.

⋊   ⋊   ⋊

I don't know if Richard had heard about my derailment. He didn't ask, and I didn't mention it. As far as I knew, he thought I had simply switched careers. Perhaps one might say this means that I, too, had pieces of my history that I chose not to discuss.

Still, had he asked, I would have told him about my translator debacle. It would have been cathartic to discuss this and might have better laid the foundation for a happy, or at least functional, marriage. Perhaps he would have said the things I needed to hear—that I hadn't truly done anything wrong, that my behavior was understandable given the context. But after those first two enchanted dinners, it seemed Richard was never again especially curious about me.

Maybe in some Freudian sense this was what I needed. We didn't do a lot of sharing of emotions in my family, and we didn't discuss anything related to accidents *or* moths. Therefore, I had tried to report this professionally, and it kicked me in the teeth. Now, with Richard, I had tacit permission to keep the messy parts to myself, and it gave me a certain amount of freedom: Richard was never going to ask me why I had just spent an hour on the internet researching sightings of the Mothman. On the other hand, with hindsight, it might have been better to have had a partner who wanted to know.

⋈　⋈　⋈

A few months after we began dating, Richard and I went to dinner in Cleveland Park. We ate at an Asian fusion restaurant, which I remember because he commented on the aromatics; the earthy, nutty, salty smells of soy sauce and sake and tea hung in the air, and he said it reminded him of Hong Kong, where he had recently been on a reporting trip. I liked that. It made me think we were other, somehow. We had met on a rooftop in Delhi, and now we were sitting in a restaurant in Washington DC, smelling Asia.

After dinner, we emerged from the restaurant and noticed that the brightly illuminated marquee of the Uptown Theater across the street advertised a film called *The Mothman Prophecies*.

I drew in my breath.

I have reflected on these circumstances many times in the intervening years. If pressed, I would say it was sheer coincidence that the movie, a brand-new major motion picture, was playing, and that we left the restaurant a few moments before the film was about to start. I doubt Richard knew of my obsession with the circumstances depicted in that film.

It may seem surprising that I had not heard about this movie prior to that night, but my internet searches on the subject of the moth came in waves. I knew it was not healthy for me to spend time mucking around in the weirdness of my confusing past. I was able to abstain for weeks, months, and sometimes even years at a time. But once I began staring at the computer screen, I would want more. It was addictive and unproductive—on top of which, the more I learned about the Mothman, the further away I seemed to get from understanding what this had to do with my parents.

But back to that night. Across the street I noticed the word *Mothman* in the title, and I felt a wave of shock—but it was not until we drew closer to the theater and I found myself eye to eye with the movie poster that I became truly spooked. When I saw the ink-stain Rorschach-like rendition of a moth with a pair of eyes peeking through each wing, and when I caught a glimpse of the actor in the movie, it was like an out-of-body experience, or like I was in the middle of a dream. He looked like the man I was with.

We bought tickets and went inside without much deliberation. We were there, and a new feature film was about to start, so why not?

The number of coincidences in that film is itself a coincidence. Some overlap was to be expected, given that the movie is about the same incident—the same bridge collapse that claimed my parents, the same moth who is said to have appeared in the weeks and months prior to the event.

What I had not expected was the coincidence of the Richards, and for this, I'm not sure there is anything to be said apart from *holy shit*.

My Richard looks very much like the main character in the movie.

This in itself is no big deal: We all know people who resemble movie stars, and were this the extent of the coincidence, I would not bring it up.

The character in the movie is named John. The name of the actor who plays John is Richard. The last name of the fictional character who looks like my real-life Richard is Klein. My husband's full name is Richard Klein.

One last thing to share about the coincidence of the Richards: In the movie, John Klein is a fictional reporter at the *Washington Post*. My husband's name is Richard Klein, and his employer is the same.

I am neither the first, nor the last, to comment on this coincidence.

CHAPTER 11

The Wondering

BECAUSE NO ONE will talk about the accident, I have come to rely on a slim book called *The Silver Bridge Disaster of 1967* that I purchased on the internet many years ago. It is filled with photographs of victims and survivors, of items dredged from the waters, of statistics and minutiae of bridge construction, of what went wrong with the eyebar suspension, of how the undetected corrosion led to collapse, of the weather, generally, in the region at that time of year.

It's a little strange, I know, to have become so reliant on this book, to regard it, almost, like a family album. I have memorized the names of some of the victims, and sometimes I say them aloud, like I am reciting Kaddish for people I have never met and know nothing about, apart from that they died in proximity to my parents. But it is from the book that I at least know this much, even though some of the specifics vary in other reports:

- The Silver Bridge collapsed on December 15, 1967, at 4:58 p.m.

- Thirty-eight vehicles were on the bridge at the time, thirty-one of which fell into the river or landed in shoreline debris.
- Sixty-four people fell into the river, forty-six of whom died.
- Two people were never found.
- My parents were among the victims, and I can see them in the book, standing side by side in front of their Pontiac Bonneville. Although the picture is reprinted in black-and-white, I have seen a different version of this photo and know the car was powder blue, as was my mother's dress. My father wears a suit and tie. From what I can tell, the picture was taken a few months before the accident, although I am only guessing at this; the one time I tried to ask Olivia, she took the book away and scolded me. There were so many better books in the world to be reading, she said, she couldn't imagine why I was wasting my time on this. It had been a library book, and Olivia had not returned it, which put me in the awkward position of having to explain to the librarian that I had lost it. I could sense her disappointment and worried she might consider me a person not worth lending library books to. It took over a year to get the replacement copy that the librarian agreed to order for me, since it came by way of a loan from Ohio. When I was old enough, I finally purchased a copy for myself.
- That Pontiac, according to the book, was dredged from the river and sold for scrap.

Here is what I do not know about the accident, and what the book, even with its footnotes, is unable to illuminate:

- Were my parents crossing from Point Pleasant, West Virginia, to Gallipolis, Ohio, on December 15, 1967, at 4:58 p.m., or were they going the other way, from Gallipolis, Ohio, to Point Pleasant, West Virginia?
- Why were my parents there at all, when Olivia has told me they were going to a cousin's wedding in Toledo? Even with my poor sense of direction, I know the bridge would not have been part of their route.
- Do we even have cousins in Toledo?
- Winters in the region are often severe; during the coldest periods, thick ice can form on the Ohio River. Yet even Richard has seemed oddly disinterested in exploring this line of inquiry: How might the weather in Point Pleasant, on the day of the accident, have related to the bridge collapse?

Another thing no one seems interested in discussing, not even the book, is the matter of the moth.

CHAPTER 12

Maryland?

SOMETIMES I WONDER if I am anyone at all, or just a composite of the people I know and the stories I've read. I can't seem to let go of any of those hundreds of characters trapped in my head, particularly those with narratives left unresolved. The single mother on the verge of eviction, the philanthropist who would not allow herself to indulge in a swim at a public pool, the high school soccer goalie with Hodgkin's lymphoma. There are so many other stories, such as the one set during the Spanish Inquisition, where, in the last installment I read, a Marrano was left writhing on the torture rack. This student dropped the class—said she had a sick child and a sick mother and needed to pick up more hours at work since they were behind on medical expenses. In my mind, the victim is still imprisoned, writhing in pain. Although I encourage my students to keep in touch, and many of them do, I never heard from that particular student again. Ditto for the author of a story about an escaped slave, lost in the woods, who still has an iron collar with spikes affixed to his neck. I could go on and on. The refugee from Guatemala who lost his whole family when they died of dehydration in the back of a coyote's van. I've been walking around with some of these characters for so long that they course through my bloodstream and have possibly become part of my DNA.

⋈　　⋈　　⋈

The Maryland landscape is more variegated than most people think, assuming that the landscape of Maryland is something anyone spares the time to ponder. Generally speaking, the Old Line State presents a cheerfully crab- and Oriole-centric persona, and this is not untrue—yet it belies the fact that heading west the terrain turns ominously rugged. Luna and I wind through mountains; the stripe of asphalt road, my exhaust-spewing vessel, my blaring sound system, all incongruous assaults on the landscape.

Am I heading into something bad, or simply moving out of my comfort zone? I've always lived in the city. Those rusted-out barges, abandoned factories, and refineries along certain stretches of I-95 are blights on the landscape, yet they are so familiar they make my dystopian spirit soar. The curve in the highway that hugs Newark Airport is, to me, a turnpike poem, and I sometimes wish for the traffic to slow so I can stop and watch the planes take off and land. But there is nothing of that familiar wreckage here in western Maryland. Instead, there are charcoal mountains and a wild beauty that frightens me. It occurs to me that I might look over to the shoulder of the road and spot a mountain lion or a bear.

I do a quick mental scan of my assets: I have my phone, my

bag, my wallet, my dog, a mutilated Gumby, Olivia's blanket, two bottles of water, and, rattling around in the rear compartment, Vera's still muddy cleats and soccer ball.

What I do not have is food. My stomach rumbles. It is asking for a snack, mocking me for refusing Olivia's provisions. Also, what I do not have is a whole lot of gas in the tank. I have stopped twice to let Luna out, but for a long stretch it looks as if we are in the middle of nowhere—either that, or I just keep choosing the wrong spots. While generally not a catastrophist, I now imagine myself running out of gas, starving to death, and then being eaten by a wild animal on the side of the road.

One disquieting thought leads to another, and the next thing I know I am clenching my jaw, chewing on Elaine.

When Richard had mentioned her name—signaling with a surprising nonchalance that she had been in our house, in our *bedroom*, that she had left this particular personal item behind— I was, at first, confused. My brain went to autopilot, sifting through this information, trying to locate a rational explanation. When that failed—or rather, when the only explanation was the one most shocking—instead of pondering the existential nature of the Elaine situation and what this meant for my marriage, not to mention my friendship with her, I instead homed in on the visceral. Gross! I had put another person's nightguard in my mouth. I ran to the bathroom and threw up.

Next came a jumble of things. What the hell? Had Elaine been spending the night in our bed every time I took Vera on a college visit? And backing up, every time I had been away, or Richard had been away, over the course of twenty years? Elaine was always around. She was practically part of our family.

And another question: Why, on an illicit liaison, did she bring along her nightguard? More to the point, why did she leave it behind? Was she marking her territory, like a dog? There was something even more sordid, or at least more depressing, about this being such a prosaic item. A black thong, a garter belt, silk stockings, or a lacy bra might have at least signaled passion. This felt like her letting me know she was moving in.

Richard had apologized, but his penance lacked oomph. He waffled when I pressed him on how long this had been going on, refusing to give a satisfying answer. He said he had been in a bad place—but then, in some sense, he had been in a bad place since the day we married, so it was not clear what he meant when invoking this timeline. He went on to say that he needed comfort I was unable to provide. To that I was too flabbergasted to respond, given how much time I had spent trying to coax him through his woes, from getting him into therapy to providing basement catering services. He didn't really have feelings for Elaine, he assured me. She had just been around. It was what he'd needed for a time. It was over, he'd said. I tried to believe him but sensed it was not, and besides, she was only part of problem, or maybe she was the final indicator. Richard and I had endured years of dark clouds, changes in wind direction, drops in temperature, shifts in atmospheric pressure, and here she was at last, telling me it was time to take cover. Or in my case, hit the road.

I keep wondering how I missed it. Have I mentioned she was nearly always around? We'd have brunch, go to the farmers' market together, take walks, back when Richard left the house and when weather conditions—and forecasts—allowed. Vera even referred to Elaine as an aunt, and we never bothered to correct her—how we designed our family relations was deliberately jumbled anyway. Sometimes Samantha and Evan were introduced as my cousins, sometimes as my siblings. Both were true. Ditto for Harry and Olivia. My uncle and aunt, my adoptive parents. These labels didn't matter much at the end of the day.

Why did I make such an effort to include Elaine? I wonder now. Some of it, I think, was that I felt so rich in family and so hyperaware of the *need* for family, given my history, that I wanted to share, albeit not to that degree. Whereas Elaine had never married, her parents had passed away, and she had only one sibling from whom she was estranged. But another part of it was that I enjoyed her company. She was someone to talk to. She was fun. She was an antidote to Richard's remoteness.

Why did I not leave immediately upon discovering the affair? Vera is the only answer I can articulate. I didn't want to throw her off emotionally during her first semester of college. But that wasn't the only reason. I was, I confess, worried about Richard. He didn't seem to be doing so well down there in the basement, and after more than twenty years together, emotional ties still bind.

⋈   ⋈   ⋈

Another hour passes. Now the gas tank is dangerously low, on top of which I have bathroom needs. I'm grateful when a sign appears indicating an approaching exit. I put on my blinker and begin to shift right, easing gracefully between cars. I'm still riding high on the cold, rosin-inflected strings that are playing in a loop, until they are interrupted by the sound of my phone.

I push the button on the steering wheel, and Vera's voice bursts statically through the speaker.

"Hola!" she says from Spain.

"Sweetheart! How are you?" I am so warmed by the sound of her voice I could cry, and I can't imagine how I'm going to tell her what I've done—walking out on her father, during the holidays no less.

"I've decided to come home a few days early," she says. "I've already looked and I can change my flight and make it back in time to get to Delaware for Christmas dinner. But what's the best way for me to get out to the beach? Should I fly into Baltimore? I don't know if I'm old enough to rent a car, but there are all these new apps that don't care if I'm only nineteen. Or is that too expensive anyway? Is Wilmington closer? Or is that too complicated? I could also fly into Dulles and go home and get my car."

"Why are you leaving early? Is something wrong?" I ask, stalling for time before answering her questions. This is entirely unexpected. And I'm . . . I don't know exactly where I am, but I'm certainly not in Delaware, nor is her father.

"Sort of. I mean, nothing terrible. Spain is great It's just weird being here with Anna's family at the holidays, and I miss you and Luna. Oh, and I miss Dad of course!"

"Of course!" I add, perhaps too enthusiastically. Her dad has been missing in some sense of the word for a couple of years, maybe longer, so I assume "there isn't much to miss" is the subtle implication of her afterthought.

"Plus all of my high school friends are hanging out. So I thought after Christmas I'd go back to DC. Rachel is having a big New Year's party. There's no change fee on the ticket, so if it's okay, I'm going to go ahead and rebook."

"Sure, but I'm not there . . . I mean, I can be there. I will turn around."

"It's only Thursday, Mom. I'll be there Saturday." Clearly she is not focusing on what I've said. But then, we have a bad connection, and it's a little hard to hear.

"Right. Great. Send me the flight info."

"I can barely hear you, Mom. Where are you?"

"I'm in the car," I say. I'm not at the beach with her father, but the part about being in the car happens to be true. "I'm using the Bluetooth and . . . you know me, not so good with tech. I can't really hear you so well either."

"Hello? Mom?"

"I'm here," I say. "I'm in the car."

"I can't hear you, Mom. I'm going to hang up and try again to see if we can get a better connection."

I hear more static, much louder this time. The line goes dead as I exit, spilling me onto a ramp that loops and loops and loops until I am dizzy. The phone rings again. Again, nothing but loud white noise.

Now I am in a valley with mountains on either side, which must be blocking the signal. Off in the distance, peeking between ranges, I see a sign for Pets! Pets! Pets! A small miracle, it seems, given my need for dog food. My music ceases to stream. I turn on the radio, but even that emits static.

I cease looping and arrive at a stop sign. A graphic depiction of a knife and fork indicates that a person might procure food by turning right. There is also a pictograph of a gas pump with an arrow pointing left. A riddle of sorts. I am ravenously hungry, need to find a restroom, and am close to running out of gas. Logic dictates that fuel is the priority. I turn accordingly and head some two miles down a twisty road that is devoid of any retail. Where is this elusive gas station, and why, of all the possible exits off the highway, have I taken the one that seems to lead nowhere? I debate turning around and heading back the other way, but I've already made this two-mile investment and decide to give it a little longer.

An elementary school appears, an encouraging sign that I am approaching some sort of community, but as I get closer, I see plywood on the windows and not a single vehicle in the parking lot. On the next block is a small row of boarded-up shops.

I'm fighting off a sense of panic, but then I tell myself there is always more fuel in the tank than it appears. I guesstimate that I must have some twenty miles left before I am stranded here, wherever this is, with no gas, no cell signal, no bathroom, and a poorly behaved puppy.

Just as I'm about to turn around and take my chances in the other direction, I see a small station with two pumps, like something out of a movie set. I fill up, use the facilities, and then, as I head back the other way, my phone rings again. I have at least enough connectivity this time to see Richard's number appear on the screen, but the call drops before I hear his voice. Presumably he is calling to tell me Vera's news. Or maybe he wants to give me some warning about the weather—a light rain has begun to fall, possibly the precursor of a storm, the only problem being that he doesn't know where I am.

Vera and the weather: the only two things we have left. I will tell him I'll be back by the weekend, should we manage to connect. I figure I can still get to Point Pleasant, spend a day, and then turn around and get to Delaware, or to DC, depending on where Vera winds up. We can pretend to be a happy family until she goes back to college, and then figure out the rest in the new year.

This lucid thought clears the way for more lucidity and, like a miracle, a small town appears on the gloomy horizon ahead.

CHAPTER 13

Buffalo Plaid

THE STREETS IN this town appear to be empty, and I don't know where all the people have gone, but eventually I stumble onto the location of their many cars and pull into a vacant spot.

Luna's tail begins to wag with anticipation—or maybe she catches the smell of food before I do. I grab my umbrella and let her lead me along a cobbled walkway toward what quickly clarifies as some potent combination of sizzling onions, greasy patties, and burnt toast.

There must be something nearby, or at least someone cooking aggressively, yet we have walked a block and all I see are more shuttered things: a bookstore, an art gallery, a drugstore, all defunct. In the window of a men's outfitters called G. Rothberg, a couple of mannequins in the window clad in western gear look as though they last changed outfits back in the early 1970s, around the time the final episode of *Bonanza* aired.

Some deadly virus has ravaged this town, I muse. Then I remember that this is quite possibly what has happened. The pandemic might have been the last straw for this already economically teetering place. Yet someone, somewhere, is cooking, and Luna continues to tug us toward the source of the smell until finally, one more block away, we find a crowded café.

Something about this scene looks artificial in its merriment. It makes me think of a game Vera used to play called *The Sims*. It's as though these patrons are life-size avatars, cut and pasted from some other metaverse, one with a holiday theme. A plastic Santa grins beside the open door, his arm outstretched, his palm perpendicular to the ground in a frozen, perpetual wave. The dining room twinkles with strings of fairy lights.

The light rain turns into a more confident downpour, and I open the umbrella and pull up the hood of my jacket. Outside, peering in, observing these happy and chattering Sims feasting on their burgers and tuna melts and chicken Caesar salads, sipping milkshakes and iced teas, I am rendered, again, peripheral, as I had been at the beach, watching Harry and Olivia talk to the new neighbors. Who am I and what am I doing here? The same existential questions always, the human condition. Or perhaps this is merely me adjusting my mindset. It's been a long time since I've been a woman traveling on my own. Harry would probably say that any incongruity and alienation I feel right now is the result of the head injury, the one I do not have.

Whatever the explanation, I'm watching this holiday pageantry from the back row, standing in the cold rain. It's a state familiar from my days of frequent travel, when I would gaze through the window from the back of a taxi having just arrived in a new city. Bleary from a long overnight flight and feeling displaced, I would envy those who seemed to belong where they were, rushing about on commutes, reading newspapers in cafés, chatting with one another on street corners, often in languages I couldn't understand. They all seemed to know where they were going and had others anticipating their arrivals. They belonged in a way I never have. Even in my family I have always been other. I was loved unconditionally; I have no complaints, yet it was not where I was supposed to be.

At a long rectangular table flanking the door, practically abutting Santa, is a family of eight: a pair of toddlers in wooden highchairs, presumably twins, the others probably middle and elementary school age. A mom and a dad. Everyone blindingly blond and outfitted in identical red-and-black flannel shirts.

The proximity, now, to these delicious aromas results in a sharp tug on the leash. It's all I can do to prevent Luna from bounding in and jumping into the laps—or onto the table—of the members of this happy or possibly unhappy family outfitted in their buffalo check plaids.

I pause, unsure how to place my order without tying Luna to a pole, which I am hesitant to do given that I am a hovering dog mom. I briefly consider trying to pass her off as a comfort animal—one trained to swipe french fries out of the hands of children, perhaps, or lick clean customers' ears.

I decide on a different tactic: I stand outside and wave frantically until the waitress notices me and approaches the door. I order the first thing that comes to mind: a grilled cheese sandwich. I don't know why I order a grilled cheese sandwich. I cannot remember the last time I ate a grilled cheese sandwich, and lately I have been finding myself moving toward a mild intolerance of lactose, but such is apparently the olfactory sum of the equation of this variety of smells—the desire for greasy slabs of cheese slapped between bread.

"Cheddar on wheat bread," I say. I ask if she can make it to go.

As the young woman with a purple streak in her short, spiky, bleached-white hair scribbles the order on a pad, I notice that from her ears dangle tiny silver candy canes, which inspires the thought to indulge.

"Can you add a vanilla milkshake?"

As long as I'm at it, I ask for some onion rings and a second grilled cheese sandwich for later, because . . . who knows.

Waiting for the order, I settle onto a rock in the middle of the pedestrian walkway and pour some water from a bottle into the portable dog bowl I carry in my tote. Luna regards it for a moment and then decides, instead, to drink from a puddle.

All I need to do is get to West Virginia, and I will figure out what to do with the rest of my life, I assure myself, fighting off a sudden, urgent wave of angst. I can't say why I think getting to West Virginia is going to provide answers, but I've spent a lifetime *not* going to West Virginia, and now I feel that getting there may finally make sense of the holes in my life that I don't understand.

I try to return Vera's call, but it won't go through. I send her a text, but my phone informs me that it is unable to deliver the message. I check Instagram to see whether Olivia has posted footage of our departure, but it is unable to load new content. The weather app is also a no go, and Google Maps cannot locate me even though I am definitely here.

Luna loses interest in her puddle and bolts upright. Her ears prick. She is staring at the Buffalo Plaid Family, perhaps on some sort of spooky canine frequency that is one step ahead, anticipating whatever is about to transpire. A few seconds later, a glass of what looks like Coke spills, the liquid rushing across the place setting and into the lap of one of the younger kids. There are squeals and screams, a sudden pushing back of chairs. Napkins are produced, accusations exchanged, the eight plaid shirts a flurry of motion.

I stare and stare and my stomach grumbles and my mind sticks for a minute. What is it with this buffalo plaid? Why is it a Christmas thing, I wonder? It has always seemed to me more of a lumberjack thing. Or at least a rustic thing. It is nevertheless inspiring some sort of déjà vu. The waitress rushes over with a roll of paper towels. The child is now very wet in the lap. Her brother, or presumed brother, must say something rude because she gives him a push that is not of a friendly sort, and the mother scolds, and the memory suddenly retrieves.

It was a pillow. A buffalo plaid pillow, and it lived in the study of Harry and Olivia's home in Cleveland Park, nestled on the couch. Next to it was a misshapen owl pillow that I had made in sewing class—part of the study of home economics, as it was so quaintly called, having been required of girls at the time. Samantha's project, a replica of a ray of sunshine, sat beside mine, a superior pillow specimen with no stitches out of place, the yellow felt a perfect orb. I don't know where the red-and-black-checked pillow came from; it had simply been there, until all those pillows were purged when the room was overrun by moths.

It took a long while for us to figure this out. First there was one moth, then there were two moths, then there were what one might call several moths in the house. Still, we went on with our lives. We were busy people—three children with the usual overscheduled slate of sports and music lessons and too much homework, much of it requiring parental supervision as well as transportation, all while Olivia and Harry were both working demanding full-time jobs. A few moths in the house, then a few more, did not rise to the level of an emergency, until it did.

Eventually we could no longer pretend we were living in a house that happened to have a few stray moths. It reached such a level that we would walk into the study and have to wave our hands to part the curtain of moths. After a week of this, Harry went to the hardware store and returned with a can of spray. MOTHSLAY, it said on the canister. The can of MOTHSLAY was adorned with a picture of a large moth covered with an *X*. Harry sprayed and slayed, sprayed and slayed. It took a while to see the results, but eventually we began finding moth carcasses on the rug.

The success was short-lived. While it got better at first, it then got much worse. Many moths perished, but others must have developed an immunity to MOTHSLAY. Harry gave in to the realization that it was no longer a DIY job, and a professional exterminator was summoned. He instructed us to put the pillows in plastic bags and stick them, and the ravaged rug, in the trash bins out back. He then pumped some noxious spray into the room. For months we found the flaky bits of wings, and other unidentifiable moth remnants, scattered around the house, reminiscent of the way Washington becomes littered with cherry blossom bits long after the season has passed.

This particular piece of moth nostalgia was retrieved, however, only as a means of remembering why the Buffalo Plaids have sent my mind careening back in time, and not because of moths themselves. The infestation in this story might as easily have been of bedbugs, or stink bugs, or lice.

⋈   ⋈   ⋈

I devour my grilled cheese sandwich, then drink half the milkshake while Luna gnaws contentedly on what is left of Gumby, whom I retrieved from my bag to keep her occupied. Sated, then mildly ill moments later from ingesting this gluttonous lunch too fast, I ask a passerby if he knows how to get to the Pets! Pets! Pets! I had glimpsed in the distance.

"That store's long gone," he tells me. "It was a big local story. They couldn't find enough employees. Place went belly-up."

"Do you know where I can buy some dog food around here?" I ask.

"How about the grocery store? There's a Giant up the road."

"I suppose, but my dog eats . . . well, she's on a special diet," I say, too embarrassed to admit that she eats some fancy, small batch dog food I learned about from a woman in the dog park as she struggled to keep her two-hundred-pound mastiff puppy from humping a schnauzer.

"Try the feedstore up the road. I don't remember the exact name . . . something like Bobby's Farm and Yard. I can tell you how to get there."

I write down what he says, or at least some aspects of what he says, on a napkin.

Right then left then follow rd. 1 mile bear left @ fork, left @ the church, rt. @ high school, fire station on left and

*a DD on rt, bear rt up hill 1 mile rt. then left then grocery
store.*

We make our way back to the car, then attempt to decipher
these notes. I goof right off the bat. Right on which road? The
one that leads out of the parking lot, which leads to what looks
like a major thoroughfare, or do I turn right once I get to the
road parallel to where I'm parked? I choose incorrectly, of
course, or at least I think I do. I make a U-turn and head, with
little confidence, the other way. It takes another ten minutes,
but there it is at last, a large wooden edifice that looks more like
a farm stand than a pet store, situated at the edge of a pasture
down a long gravel road.

I ask the man who I assume to be Bobby—a large, stocky
man with a ruddy face—whether he carries White Fang Polar
Circle High Prairie Puppy Chow.

Bobby has a look that is hard to interpret. He turns and
shouts to someone in the back. "Hey, Harold, there's a lady
here asking for White Fang Polar Circle High Prairie Puppy
Chow . . ."

"Tell her no, we've only got the Low Prairie Chow."

I wonder, for a moment, if this is a viable alternative. And
then I understand this is a joke, and I, with my bourgeois dog
food and my Audi parked out front, am the butt of it.

"We don't have dog food here, lady," he says. "Not your
fancy stuff, and not your regular stuff. But there's a Giant up
the road."

CHAPTER 14

The Storyteller

WHETHER IT'S A function of poor cell service, the power of Olivia's suggestion, or my own ineptitude, my navigation system is not working. I try not to panic. How lost could I really be, here on a busy interstate that is crowded with holiday travelers, with ample road signs providing a general sense of place? Even without them, all I need to do is continue to move west, toward the setting sun.

I try not to panic when I hear, from behind me, the unmistakable sound of a vomiting dog. Amid the brief moment that I left her in the car to run into the supermarket and buy a bag of dog food, Luna ate the second grilled cheese sandwich. And who can blame her? The smell of my—or rather her—regurgitated lunch is nauseating. Being nauseated makes me think of Elaine, of putting her nightguard in my mouth, and then I fear *I* am going to be sick. I crack all the windows and let the cold air blow in at sixty-five miles an hour.

My phone rings once, then stops.

At least the radio comes in loud and clear, a helpful indication that I am *somewhere*. I locate the local NPR station, and the familiar voice of Terry Gross comes as a relief. It's a weekday afternoon, and life goes on as usual, even if I am veering off my own grid. Terry is conversing with a popular science writer about her book on amusing animal behaviors. Terry and the author chat amiably about bears who break into homes and go straight to the refrigerators, where they open the doors and help themselves to snacks. Sometimes they even take things out of the cupboard to inspect, then put them back where they belong. The author says that in one community she studied, the bears demonstrated a preference for a particular brand of high-end ice cream, leaving containers of the lesser brands untouched. She says that years ago, animals that broke the law were put on trial, assigned legal representation.

Luna begins to retch again, and I wonder which one of us would be on trial—the dog for eating the grilled cheese sandwich, or me for stupidly leaving it in the car?

Fresh Air ends, and there is an update on the local weather and sports. For a split second I expect to hear my husband's voice, but then I remember I am outside his region and he is no longer doing live broadcasts.

"We are experiencing unusually bright sunshine this afternoon," a cheerful male voice informs. "You might want to grab those shades! But bundle up tonight, when temperatures will drop below freezing. And it is almost certainly going to be a white Christmas here in the greater Charleston area. A storm front moving in from the north . . ."

The voice of the meteorologist goes in one ear and out the other. It's as if the trauma of my marriage has resulted in a weather allergy.

The sun is so bright I can barely see, and my head begins to throb again.

News headlines come next. Virus. War. Dow Jones up, S&P 500 down. The road veers in a slightly different direction. I begin to scan the road for a rest stop: I could use some coffee, Luna probably ought to pee, and I need to clean out the car.

Then I hear the smoky, throaty, sexy voice of my aunt burst through the speakers of what was once her car. She is doing a promo spot, evidently, for the next installment of her program, which will air tomorrow.

The subject is delicate, she confides. It involves someone with whom she is close. Generally, she continues explaining, she tries to avoid mixing the personal and the professional, but in this case, she needs some listener advice.

My need for caffeine evaporates; I am suddenly wide-awake. I turn the volume up even though I sense I should probably turn it off.

"What if someone you love refuses to let go of the past? To stop asking questions that make no sense? To acknowledge that these constant, nonsensical questions are creating problems in the present?" Olivia asks her millions of listeners.

Wait, *what?* I want to scream these words back at the radio. I want to flip these questions around. *What is the line between refusing to answer my questions and stonewalling? And more to the point, what are the ethics of talking about this on air, instead of in the kitchen?*

I don't know whether she threw this episode together quickly in response to our visit, or whether she has had this in the works for a while. And what is the point of this exercise? Is she trying to gaslight me? Am I really obsessing about something I ought to be able to let go of, or is she the one with an issue, refusing to talk to me, to share details she knows I want to know? She has me so confused, generally, that I'm not even sure which part of the story about my parents and the bridge collapse is taboo. Regardless of the answer, NPR does not seem like the appropriate place to hash out this intimate family matter.

⋈   ⋈   ⋈

The road curves again, and the already too-bright sun gets so bright that I miss the rest stop. Even the clip-on sun visors that are affixed to my prescription glasses do little to help. It is beyond blinding. It is a sun apocalypse. I put my blinker on and prepare to switch lanes, to inch over to the right, and suddenly there is a creature in the car, fluttering again. Luna darts at it, then tries to bat it with her paw. I let out a scream.

My navigation seems to hear me, and suddenly it is working and on full alert. It even begins to speak.

"Make a U-turn if possible," it instructs quite forcefully.

A U-turn? On the highway?

I shift right and nearly collide with a pickup truck as the creature darts to the front, skimming my head. The driver honks at me and I wave apologetically. Without realizing what I have done, I have successfully entered the off-ramp and exited the interstate. The sun now behind me, the landscape quickly changes from yellow to grey.

The moth settles on the dashboard and appears to be staring at me with those red eyes. I will it to stay put until I can pull over, maybe resurrect the Cheerios box and contain it. In the distance I see the billowing smoke from a coal mine, and as I drive toward it, I can taste something sulphureous in the air. When I look back at the dashboard, the moth is gone.

The road again bends, the sun again blinds, NPR cuts out, then back in. Olivia finishes speaking, and the announcer repeats the weather forecast: This evening it will be below freezing, with a 30 percent chance of snow.

Now my head is truly pounding, surely just dehydration and all that blinding sun. I think of the character left writhing on the torture rack in fifteenth-century Spain. I think of the woman in the fourth-floor walkup who will not allow herself air-conditioning or even the most minor of pleasures. Of the soccer player with lymphoma, of the single mom on the verge of eviction. I channel these characters the way some people must channel angels or patron saints.

Depending on what I am looking for, this channeling possibly works. The next thing I see is a sign that tells me I am in Point Pleasant, West Virginia, the place that has haunted me all my life.

Part 2

CHAPTER 15

No Dogs

JUST AFTER MIDNIGHT a couple of years ago, I was walking past Vera's room when something caught my attention. Generally, I'm an early-to-bed sort, but that night, as I recall, Ruth was having trouble settling. She was more than twelve years old, and she'd been having stomach troubles the last few days.

It was on my way back, as I walked through the upstairs hallway, that I heard a familiar sentence fragment issuing from Vera's room. I stood in the hallway, wrapped in my bathrobe, puzzling over this for a moment. It was like hearing a refrain but being unable to remember the song from which it came.

"Something's very wrong here. I don't know these people. I have never been here before. I'm from DC," said an agitated man. The voice, too, was familiar.

I knocked on Vera's door, then waited until she responded. She was propped up in bed, her lovely wild hair spraying in all directions from the ponytail atop her head, reminding me of the tails of the My Little Ponies she used to play with. She was too polite to say as much, but I could tell she was annoyed by the interruption, and she quickly shut her laptop. I wondered for a moment if I had caught her in the act of something subversive, like buying drugs or watching porn. But she wasn't doing either of these things, I knew. She was watching a movie or a television show. One I clearly must have seen before.

"What are you up to?" I tried to make it sound like this was a casual check-in, which it sort of was.

"Nothing. Just watching some stupid movie. But I'm about to go to sleep."

"What movie?" I did not mean to interrogate her, but I needed to know. It was going to drive me nuts.

"It's so dumb, it's really not worth talking about," she said. "It's just a pseudo horror movie. You know, a bunch of attractive people in peril. The usual stupid Hollywood fare."

Now I was even more curious. I didn't push it, but when I wished her a good night and bid her sweet dreams, I lingered a moment outside her door to see if she would continue watching the movie. And sure enough, she did.

I heard some indeterminate chatter and then, that same voice again. "I'm from DC," the man said again. "My name is John Klein . . ."

Then, of course, I knew what it was, unmistakably. It was dialogue from the movie *The Mothman Prophecies*. The movie Richard and I saw on our first date, the movie that has haunted me ever since. But what could Vera possibly have known of this movie? Why would she be watching this film? Perhaps it was random. Something that simply popped up in her algorithm and that she happened to click on. Like she said, it was just a dumb bit of Hollywood fare.

I was aware, at the time, of the calculation I chose to make on the spot. I could decide to assign this significance or dismiss this as meaningless. I chose to do the latter.

⚹   ⚹   ⚹

Now, as I arrive in this place that I've spent a lifetime considering, when I see the river glistening in the middle distance and the bridge stretching across the vast waters to Ohio, the moment is so surreal it's as if I'm in a dream. It's newly reconstructed, of course, now called the Silver Memorial Bridge, but nevertheless this is the spot, more or less, where my parents drew their last breaths.

I know I ought to think deeper, or at least more spiritual, thoughts, but instead I am drawn back to this moment in the film. John Klein, the character played by the actor who looks like my husband, Richard Klein, winds up in Point Pleasant, West Virginia, entirely by mistake. Though he is heading to Richmond, Virginia, he is sucked into some strange time-place vortex and winds up here when his car breaks down on the bridge. He begins to walk toward the town, and a few moments later, finds himself with a gun pointed to his head.

"Something's very wrong here. I don't know these people. I have never been here before. I'm from DC," is what he says to the man who is accusing him of trespassing for the third night in a row.

My own arrival in Point Pleasant is decidedly less dramatic. As I take in this startling, cinematic view, I also see, more prosaically, a hibachi steakhouse, a liquor store, a Piggly Wiggly supermarket, a pizza parlor, and a LibertyX Bitcoin ATM. I then spot a sign indicating that the historic district of this town is a block away, and I put on my turn signal. I don't know what I'm looking for, exactly, but whatever is in that direction has got to be more interesting than here.

I arrive at an intersection that appears to lead to the main road of a little town. It's not quite dusk, but everything is illuminated by cheery displays of twinkling holiday lights, strung from awnings and wrapped around trees. It's not personal, I know, these holiday displays that seem to track me everywhere, yet it's hard not to read them as a rebuke. What sort of woman leaves her family to go on a solo road trip the day before Christmas Eve? I self-flagellate for a moment about my human shadiness, then remind myself of Richard's behavior and of my need to figure out how blue is a mile, to put it in Olivia's dismissive words. I am finally, after all these years, taking some measure of control, even if I don't yet know fully what that means.

⋈　　⋈　　⋈

The first establishment I see, by some miracle, is a hotel: the Point Pleasant Inn. Some four stories high and boxy, the place has a certain turn-of-the-last-century grandeur. It is built in what I think might be called a Federalist style, or perhaps I simply think that because, although my language of architecture is not extensive, I can see that it shares a few details with our DC home, namely the distinctive brick masonry that features rectangular white dentil molding above the windows and the doors.

This could be ramshackle, and it could be the Ritz. I don't particularly care as long as there is a shower and a bed inside.

My relief is somewhat tempered by the fact that I don't see any lights, but I lean in, hopeful, and choose to interpret this as serendipity, especially since there is a parking spot right in front.

Whether the hotel is open or long since abandoned, I can't wait another moment to get out of this car, and neither can Luna. I quickly assess the vomit situation and determine it is not that bad—I'm able to clean it up using some tissues and the bottle of hand sanitizer that I have stuffed in my bag. I then snap the leash onto her collar and we set out on a quick walk. A brisk wind whips off the river, which stretches behind the hotel, and I let Luna lead. She pulls me past a storefront filled with tourist paraphernalia, and for a moment I wonder whether I have fallen into some moth fever dream. Every single item in this window has something to do with the moth—moth coffee mugs, moth finger puppets, moth sweatshirts and moth tote bags, moth shot glasses, moth pillowcases—and on each item the moth is depicted in a comically different way. There are the cartoon versions: smiling, cute, happy moths, including a stuffed moth so plush and cuddly in appearance you might think to put it in a toddler's arms. And then there are the villain moths, more than a little menacing with bulging red eyes and wings pointed high, making the shape of the creature's body form the letter *M*.

Those eyes make me wonder about the moth in the car. Was it there to begin with, or have I imagined the whole thing? Is Harry right about the concussion? But then, I saw it the first time before I was even possibly concussed. I've felt so *other* since walking out on Richard that I don't even know how to assess my own state of mind.

Luna does the needful and we reverse direction, back toward the center of town where, across from the hotel, I spot a life-size statue of the moth. Someone has popped a Santa hat on its head and strung a lime-green glow stick around its neck. I don't know what to make of any of this, that this thing that has haunted me all my life is now a bit of Instagram camp. But more urgent than the meaning of what I'm seeing is the question of whether I have a plastic bag in my coat pocket, because Luna has just, unceremoniously, done another thing. Fortunately, I do.

On the off chance that this hotel is open, I figure it's better to walk in without Luna in case dogs are not welcome. What I'll do in that case, I don't know—but I'll cross that bridge when I come to it, which in my case, feels like the setup for a joke I can't land. I coax her back into the car, then take another quick look around for the moth. In the process I smack my head on the frame of the door and let out a little curse. Another bang on the head is not what I need.

Peering into the hotel, I see an expansive, once-elegant lobby backlit by a pendant hanging over the registration desk. There are heavy yellow drapes on the windows, elaborate chandeliers, old Queen Anne armchairs. I can't tell if it's open for business or has gone bust, like half of the other businesses I've encountered today. It's also possible, I suppose, that they are taking a break, this town presumably not being much of a Christmas destination.

The adrenaline that has fueled my journey is quickly dissipating, as is the certainty that led me here. I ought to be with Harry and Olivia, taking long walks along the chilly beach. Or perhaps I should be home, trying to repair my marriage. Instead, I'm here. It's cold. I'm exhausted, the hotel appears closed, and the moth has been reduced to kitsch. I'm so tired, emotionally and physically, that I think I might just lean here a moment with my face pressed up to the hotel's façade.

I run through my options: I could find a place to get a meal, down a large cup of coffee, and power my way back home, or I could look for another hotel. But before I can continue processing these thoughts, the lights flick on, and the place is suddenly so brightly illuminated that it looks like a cruise ship.

A woman who appears to be in her midsixties appears at the door, turns the lock, smiles warmly, and invites me inside. She wears a cheery green sweater with a red-nosed Rudolph embroidered on the front.

Now that I have a full view of the lobby, I see a white-bearded man tucked in the far corner of the room. He jumps up and rushes toward me, offering, prematurely, to take my bags, which are still in the car. He appears spry despite his age, which is possibly close to seventy, although his left leg drags, as if from an injury or a stroke. He, too, is clad in a holiday sweater—this one red, with a smiling snowman and a long carrot nose.

Then I spot another man who looks just like him in the opposite corner of the room. *They must be twins*, I think. They are wearing identical sweaters, and even their white beards are trimmed in a similar fashion. Then I see a third man in a chair at the opposite side of the room, a newspaper spread open in his lap. He, too, sports the beard and the sweater, although this one has a wreath. They are triplets? Or is the fact that one has a different sweater meaningful somehow? Three brothers, but two are twins?

"Whoa, don't you look a sight!" says the first man. "Can I get you something for your head?"

"No, but you can get me a bed," I say, confused.

"Sure, Alma can do that." He shrugs toward the woman in the Rudolph sweater. "But let me first get you a cloth or something."

"For what?" I think of the state of my car, the dog vomit I just cleaned up, but how would he know?

He rummages behind the desk, tells me to wait a minute, then disappears through the door behind the registration desk. He returns with a washcloth.

I stare at him blankly.

"Your head," he says. "It's bleeding."

"Oh, that! It's no big deal. I took a fall on the bridge. It's a long story. Maybe I reopened the wound just now, when I banged my head getting out of the car."

He studies me for a moment, then seems to lock eyes with each of his doppelgängers before speaking again. *Why does this keep happening?* I wonder. *Does everyone in the world think I'm nuts?*

"Let's get you to a room," the woman who is Alma finally says. "We've got plenty. What kind are you looking for?"

I'm so happy to hear this that I want to throw my arms around her and rest my bloody head on her shoulder.

"Anything will do," I say. But then I think about Luna and her need for a bath. "Although I suppose a room with a tub would be good."

"We've got some rooms with tubs. How about a view?"

I don't particularly care about a view. I just need to clean up, find some dinner, and get some sleep.

"For fifteen dollars extra, I can upgrade you from a single room to a suite that looks onto the Ohio River."

This question is too challenging for me in my current state.

Real Life and Other Fictions

"I don't need anything fancy. Fifteen dollars on top of what?" I think to ask.

I look around the hotel lobby again and see that the three men are staring at me. Perhaps they think my question tacky. Perhaps I am meant to simply hand over my credit card and pay without asking, whatever they charge. I remember a salesman in a children's shoe store in the tony suburb of Bethesda once telling me "not to worry about it" when I inquired about the price of a tiny pair of Nikes for Vera's tiny toddler feet.

"You know, what the heck," says Alma. "It's almost Christmas and the suite is empty anyway, so merry Christmas. I'm going to upgrade you for free. So the room rate remains $180 per night."

This seems a bit steep but also frighteningly cheap. In New York, I'd be paying something like $500 for a suite with a river view—possibly even twice that much—but I'm not in New York, and I'm in no mood to question her, so I begin to fill out the requisite forms.

I am afraid to ask the next question, but I don't have much choice. "Dogs?" I ask, somehow believing that the less I say on the subject the better.

"You've come to the right person! Do you need a dog?"

"No, I've *got* a dog. In the car. Is she allowed?"

"Ah, a hard no on that. Very sorry."

I look up and stop reading the papers that she's thrust in front of me to sign.

"Sorry about that," she says. "I'm a dog lover myself. I mean, we all are. We're a dog family. We've got a bunch of them. We breed, sort of informally. That's why I asked if you wanted one. But here, in the hotel, we run a tight no-dogs ship."

I feel as if I might begin to cry. "Anywhere you can send me nearby that's pet-friendly?"

She looks at me for a moment. Then her eyes dart from one of the brothers to the next and the next. "You know, what is it they say . . . *Don't ask, don't tell?*"

"That's my motto," I say, nodding.

"Is he quiet?"

"Is who quiet?"

"The dog."

"Oh yes. It's a she! She is very quiet. The quietest dog you've ever seen. Or heard. Or not heard."

"Well-behaved?"

"Oh, extremely!" Lies and more lies.

"How long are you staying?"

"Probably just the one night. Maybe two."

"Okay, just don't let me see her. Also, don't let those fellows see," she says, nodding in the direction of the three white beards. "No one here can keep a secret."

"Got it! I'm so grateful, you have no idea." I don't ask who we are keeping the secret from.

"Just the one dog, right? You don't have any other creatures in that car of yours out there? No gerbils, or turtles, or pythons, or a cat stuffed in that bag or anything? Cats are a definite no. I'm allergic."

"No cats!" I assure her. "No pythons, gerbils, or turtles either!"

Possibly a moth, I do not say. For all I know, assuming it was ever really there, it has crawled inside one of my bags.

"You won't even know we're here," I add, pushing thoughts of Gumby, of Hoppity, of the chewed-through internet cord, to the back of my mind.

CHAPTER 16

About the Dog

I HAVE NEVER been without a dog, save for a few months in between getting a new one and mourning the one I had just lost. And each dog, while very different, has also been the same.

First there was Benjamin, a giant, gentle white retriever mix, who, like Luna, had different-colored eyes.

When I was small, Olivia and Harry told me I sometimes crawled around on my hands and knees, fetching objects with my mouth, drinking out of the water bowl on the floor. On more than one occasion, I tried to eat Benjamin's food, and probably got a few bites in before I was discovered.

So close was our bond that for a year or so, my family was concerned I might have developed some species confusion.

While I have loved every dog best, it is possible that I loved Benjamin especially best. Technically he was the family dog, but he chose me as his person, sleeping at the foot of my bed and often beside me, his big furry head on my pillow. He followed me everywhere; when I took a shower, he spread himself out on the bathroom floor, waiting to lick the drops of water off my legs when I emerged. When I returned from school in the afternoons, I found him waiting for me by the door.

I was sixteen when Benjamin died in his sleep. He was about three years younger than me, roughly thirteen, although we never knew for sure.

There had been no plans, at the outset, to get another dog. Harry and Olivia had treated Benjamin well, but they were not dog people. You can tell dog people from not dog people—their affections were stiff and forced, and they seemed nervous just walking him around the block, even though I know they loved him like the family member he was. They did not stop and have doggish conversations with strangers—did not ask, for example, the provenance of an unusual-looking dog, or inquire about how someone managed to find a breeder of an Australian shepherd who did not band the puppies' tails. They turned to me, a child, for advice when it came to medical decisions. I sometimes wondered why we had a dog, although I was grateful that we did.

After Benjamin passed, I struggled. I went about my life, forced myself to school and did well enough. I practiced cello, kicked the soccer ball, performed whatever duties were required of me at home, but I felt hollowed out. It was nothing overt. My loss was quiet, private, and not something we talked about, because when it came to emotions, we mostly kept them to ourselves in our family. And yet, a few weeks later, Olivia and Harry suggested we get another dog. I pushed back at first. There could be no dog like Benjamin, I protested. Benjamin was the only dog I ever wanted. But I overheard them talking sometimes and could grasp key words that involved my name and the words *lonely* and *depressed*. I eavesdropped on calls that had to do with puppies. And then one day another dog appeared. Another white retriever mix, this time a girl, whom we named Lucy. She was more petite than Benjamin, who had been squat and muscular, built like a small pickup truck. Lucy was lithe and slim, and she did not have those heterochromatic eyes. She, too, chose me. Or perhaps it was simply that she sensed my need. Whatever the reason, we quickly bonded, and once I graduated college, I took her with me to my first apartment.

By the time I met Richard, I was on to the next dog, Stella. Stella was the first dog in Vera's life, followed by Ruth—a not very doglike name, Richard insisted, as if the names that came before were somehow more appropriately canine. When Ruth died, Richard suggested that with Vera going off to college perhaps we had reached the end of our run with dogs. I pushed back, but he pleaded with me to give it a break, to at least see how it might feel not to be tethered to the needs of another creature. I tried, but with Vera out of the house and Richard in the basement, I felt as if there was no ground beneath my feet, that I was swimming through the days, or even drowning. It wasn't until Luna came into our lives that I could again fully breathe.

Richard could have lived without a dog. He could have lived without most everything except the weather, and, apparently, Elaine. But he tolerated, or seemed to tolerate, the things I loved. Not that this ought to matter much; it's not as though one falls in love with the expectation that every like and dislike will align. Couples compromise on all manner of things more important than pets: decisions on whether to instill a religious orientation in children, and if so, which one; where to live when careers force geographic shifts; what sorts of education will suit their family best; or even how often to have sex. And money, even in the wealthiest of homes, must still manage to stress.

For a while Richard accepted my canine needs. If somewhere along the way he developed a strongly held aversion, he failed to voice this until Luna came along, and suddenly it was a thing.

Richard was not much of a fighter, but about this, we fought. How was it possible that I had agreed to take a puppy in without consulting him?

It was not an unreasonable question. I was completely in the wrong, but Richard and I were barely speaking at that stage. Besides, there wasn't much choice. From the moment I saw Luna, I knew we belonged together. She was a tiny puppy at the time, shy and frightened. She had just come off a van of yelping homeless puppies, my neighbor, Magda, told me. Magda had agreed to foster her, to take her in until they were able to find an adoptive family.

I didn't know my neighbor well—although we lived side by side in a duplex, she was renting and had only recently moved in. Our street saw a lot of turnover, perhaps because the small-ish size and relatively modest price of the homes seemed to at-tract more transient people, or sometimes couples who left after a few years, once they began families and moved to the suburbs for larger homes and better public schools. Richard and I had lived there for the entirety of our marriage. The house—three bedrooms, a finished basement, and a small leafy yard—had plenty of room for our family.

Magda had knocked on our door a few days after she had taken in the puppy, saying she had to go out of town overnight for a family emergency. I agreed to watch her, and that was that. She was a white Lab, or something Lab-like, and she, too, had those fantastic different-colored eyes. As soon as she crawled into my lap, I knew I had to take her in and that her name was Luna.

Two weeks later, a moving truck appeared in Magda's half of the driveway, and before I had a chance to ask where she was going, she was gone.

Richard seemed a little shocked when he realized the puppy situation wasn't temporary, as had initially, and truthfully, been advertised. The moving truck came and went, but the puppy remained. We should have discussed it. Mea culpa. But then, maybe we should have discussed Elaine.

To my credit, I didn't say that. Besides, I truly don't think the puppy acquisition was tit for tat so much as a survival mechanism. What Richard did not understand is that I was depleted by his troubles. I had effectively lost my husband, on top of which I had, quite jarringly, an empty nest. I needed Luna as much as she needed me.

The three of us peacefully coexisted in our upstairs-downstairs arrangement for a few months as Luna chewed through various household items, including several pairs of Richard's socks.

We didn't get into a full-blown fight about Luna until the day she gnawed through the internet cable. She disconnected Richard from the weather for nearly thirty-six hours, until Verizon could come to make the repair.

CHAPTER 17

Stuff

I HAVE SO much stuff in the back of my car, one might think I had decided to run away from home before I decided to run away from home. It takes me three trips to transfer my belongings to my hotel suite, and each time I open the car door, I scan the surfaces for the moth.

First there is my small duffel, and my tote bag full of books. One of the sweatered men tries, again, to help me, but I insist that I've got it under control.

Next is the bag of kibble that I picked up at Giant while Luna scarfed my lunch. If I'm not supposed to have a dog, then it's hard to explain to the sweatered men what I'm doing with a forty-pound sack of dog food—the only size they had—that I can barely lift. I wrap it in my coat, then wrestle it through the lobby, stopping midway to adjust my grip.

"You got a body in there?" a different sweatered man inquires.

"Ha! Maybe I do! The Ghost of Christmas Past," I say stupidly, the first thing that comes to mind.

"Well, let me know if you need help," he says, forcing a polite laugh.

I drop the food in the room, then return to the car for another trip, this time with Luna wrapped inside the coat like a burrito. As we make our way through the lobby, something falls from her mouth, and one of the men rushes over to pick it up.

"Whoa, what happened to this poor fellow?" he says, handing me the mutilated Gumby. "Looks like he just returned from combat."

He does. Worse than he did this morning when I stuffed him into my bag. He's covered in bite marks, and one of his arms has been severed at the shoulder.

I'm out of witty, or rather, not so witty, retorts, so I take Gumby, stick him in my pocket, say thanks, and rush through to the elevator to better disguise the fact that in my arms is a wriggling puppy. It's only when the doors close that I realize Luna's long wiry tail is sticking out of one end of the parka.

I bring Luna directly to the bathroom, with its circa-1950s lime-green tile and tub, and close the door to contain her before returning to the car one last time. Ostensibly I'm checking to see if it's okay to leave it parked there, but really, I want to look once more for the moth. It must have burrowed somewhere—in the seat crease, or under the floor mats, although it's also possible that it flew out of the car. But now that I am seeing white-bearded men in duplicate and triplicate, I entertain again the disturbing possibility that maybe the moth was never really there.

Using the flashlight on my phone, I shine the light on the dashboard, in the cup holders, on the seatbelt straps, between the seats, and on the floor. There is no moth, but there is so much other extraneous stuff, especially in the back, that it reminds me of a book I once read about the women of the British raj, who hired fleets of camels to transport their many suitcases and sometimes even their pianos for their summer retreats. It's not intentional, this nest of stuff, but it might pass for an exhibit in the Museum of Everyday Life. Perhaps one called "Mom." In addition to Vera's cleats and the soccer ball, there are a bunch of empty water bottles, and I'd forgotten that I'm still carting around a pair of snow boots.

Sometimes snow boots are simply the things a person wears on her feet when it snows, and sometimes they are the portal for every possible snow-boot-adjacent memory imaginable. Snow boots were the footwear choice for my cousin Evan when he was a toddler, for example, and for an entire eighteen-month stretch, he refused to take them off, even in the heat of summer. I miss Evan. It's been more than two years since I last saw him. Maybe once I pull myself together again, I can fly to Tokyo to catch up.

Snow boots also make me think of all the times Richard warned me about the weather and I shrugged him off, like yesterday, when I wound up in the traffic hell of the Chesapeake Bay Bridge. Or last winter, when I was caught in a nor'easter while on a trip to New York with Vera to visit colleges. Richard had told us it was coming, and we both shrugged. Vera shares my laissez-faire approach to all things weather: If it rains, we will get wet. If it gets hot, we will remove a layer of clothing. *What's a little snow?*

I can still feel the bite in my toes from my frozen, weather-inappropriate shoes on the day we toured Barnard. I had ensured that Vera was properly dressed, but before the city shut down that day, we had to find our way to a shoe store where I bought one of the last pairs of snow boots they had left. Not just unfashionable, they were also the wrong size, which is at least part of the reason they now live in the back of the car.

I wish I could make these memories stop, but a gate has opened, or maybe just the back hatch of the car, and a nostalgia cyclone has begun: Over there is an old college boyfriend I haven't thought of in years, now an anesthesiologist in Texas; and here is a trip for ice cream with Harry in Bethesda one summer before going to the movies, a waffle cone with coffee chocolate chip; learning I was pregnant with Vera; her difficult, but not especially complicated, birth; her baby-naming at Olivia and Harry's house, followed by a bagel brunch; pushing the stroller through my favorite part of Rock Creek Park; the many birthday parties; the first days of school; the soccer games galore.

A thought occurs to me, standing in the dusk, staring into the back of my car on a frigid winter evening in Point Pleasant, West Virginia: These are family memories. They are not Richard memories, per se. Richard was there but also not there. Not really. He was there in body, but not in spirit. Once his weather phobia was brought under control, all he wanted to do was chase things. Chase a storm. Chase Elaine. Chase who knows what, or who, else.

I force myself to conjure a Richard memory, and this is what pops up: a vacation we took ages ago that I haven't thought of in years. Richard wanted to go skiing, so we flew to Vail. I don't ski, plus we had a toddler, but I figured I could hang out with Vera in the lodge, read books, drink hot chocolate. Not exactly a vacation for me, but I didn't push back.

We were eating dinner that first night in a cavernous, touristy hotel restaurant with a vaguely western theme—the chandelier overhead appeared to be made from antlers, and taxidermic animal heads hung from the walls—when his phone rang. A colleague's mother had died, another reporter on the weather desk was out with the flu, and the East Coast was experiencing record amounts of snow. Might Richard step in to help? They wanted him to get to Boston, pronto.

He went into a flurry of booking flights. I encouraged him to go, of course. I had worked hard to help him get to the point where he was even able to chase the weather, so I certainly wasn't going to hold him back. I tried so hard to be supportive and cheerful that I was in denial about my disappointment—not just about being left to make my own way back from Colorado with a three-year-old but also about being there in the first place, about pretending this week of babysitting Vera while Richard went skiing had anything to do with a vacation for me.

I don't know why I'm being pelted by these completely random memories right now. Perhaps being in West Virginia has loosened some nut in my head. Or maybe that was the work of the second bang of my head, even though I barely felt a thing.

"Time is just a construct to keep everything from happening all at once" is a line often attributed to Einstein, but the internet will tell you it's from a 1921 short story called "The Time Professor" by Ray Cummings. Staring into the back of my car, time is less a construct than a deconstruct, and it is continuing to dissolve into a montage of largely insignificant yet weirdly specific memories now of Vera, mostly but not entirely in reverse order:

- Helping hang her clothes in her dorm room this fall, using up all of the colorful plastic hangers we acquired at the Container Store. *"We should have bought one more pack,"* I remember saying.
- Sitting on the sidelines and cheering her on as she ran down the field in her orange jersey the day her school played Holton-Arms. I was camped out on a blanket with Ruth (a blanket not dissimilar to the one Officer Keel gave to me on the bridge, now that I think about it). A light rain had begun to fall during the game, and I thought to myself how fortunate that Richard was not there. That thought quickly morphed into its opposite—how *unfortunate* that Richard was not there, and how sad it was that my entire marriage, that Vera's entire childhood, really, revolved around the weather.
- Vera getting her braces off, quipping about how she couldn't wait to gnaw on chicken bones, a reference to our stern orthodontist who reminded her, at every visit, not to do so—as if she ever did.
- Vera selling Girl Scout Cookies in front of the grocery store on Newark Street, running out of Thin Mints.
- Vera in the beanbag race during field day in elementary school, taking second place, beaming in the photograph with the sack on her head, missing her two front teeth.
- Reading books to her in the rocking chair, trying to get her to fall asleep.
- Then, unexpectedly, I am back where our family narrative began: There is Richard on that rooftop in Delhi, pouring me wine, talking into the early hours of the morning.

All of these memories are rushing at me, slashing like horizontal rain, until suddenly they are interrupted by the sight of Richard and Elaine, lying in our bed. The image is so specific that I have to remind myself it's not something I saw with my own eyes.

I slam shut the back door of the car, and it's like I've turned off the spigot. The memories cease to flow. The moth fails to appear.

CHAPTER 18

I'm Fine

NOT A WHOLE lot open at this hour," says one of the brothers when I head back down to the lobby to inquire about restaurants.

"It's only just after six," says another.

"Yeah, but it's the day before Christmas Eve. Christmas Eve Eve, if you will. I think everyone is already gone," says . . . someone.

"Gone where?"

"Gone wherever they're going."

"I think the bar over in Gallipolis is open. They have burgers."

"The last thing she needs is a bar."

I consider objecting to this statement, even though it's true. I have no interest in drinking alcohol, or otherwise merrily cavorting. But on what basis, I wonder, are they making this assessment? I am refreshed, having showered, washed my hair, and put on fresh clothes. I've even scrubbed my puppy clean. I'm in tip-top shape, or at least as close as I'm able to get right now.

"I said they have burgers. Although a drink might do her good."

Now I'm wondering what this reverse assessment, that I *need* a drink, is meant to convey.

"No, look at her! Clearly she ought not drink and then drive back across the bridge by herself at night."

The bridge? *That bridge?* I certainly do not.

The three men look at me, assessing and assessing and assessing.

"No, I do not need a drink," I agree, "and I'd prefer not to drive. Is there any place within walking distance? Also, is there a store nearby? Did I see a grocery store when I drove into town? I need to pick up some rice for the dog." Luna's stomach still seems wonky, plus I'm about to switch her to a new food, so I figure I should pick up some rice to help calm her system.

"What dog?" asks a brother.

"No dog," I reply, remembering that I am not supposed to have a dog. I'm about to correct myself, to cobble together some implausible explanation about seeing a dog tomorrow but picking up the rice tonight, but mercifully we seem to glide right over this charade and move on to the next subject.

"How is she going to cook rice?"

"Isn't there a stove in the suite?"

"No, Alma put her in 403. The suite with the kitchenette is occupied."

"Oh, that's right."

"There's another guest?" I ask.

"Yeah, the crypto guy. He arrived this morning. We let him have an early check-in."

"The crypto guy?" I ask, puzzled. Why would someone in crypto be in this town? But then, what do I know about crypto? I remember that I saw a Bitcoin ATM between the bridge and this hotel, so maybe that has something to do with it.

"Yeah, nice guy. A little strange though. He's been coming to town for a while, always stays here."

"Why?" I ask. "I mean, not why does he always stay here, but why does he come so often? I guess I read something about how crypto is moving into the small towns. Energy is cheaper when you get away from the cities. Something like that."

Their blank looks are inscrutable.

"Well, you have a point," I say, still babbling. "I don't have a kitchen so I might want to get some precooked rice."

"Well, whatever you decide, you'll probably want to go to the Piggly Wiggly," says a brother. "And right across the street is the oriental joint. They ought to have rice."

I cringe at the word *oriental* and consider correcting him, but then I cringe at my cringing. I don't want to come off as some woke city girl.

"What's that?" I ask.

"There's some Japanese or Korean or what-have-you place a couple of blocks away. You walk out and go right, then left, then right."

Already I am lost. Left *where*? Right *where*? Who are these people with an ingrained sense of direction, and why don't I have one?

"Do you have a piece of paper so I can write that down? I have a knack for getting lost," I say.

One of the brothers goes behind the registration desk and

hands me a pen and a pad of paper. When I remove the pen cap, ink spills onto my hand, then onto my coat, and drips onto the rug. *Of course it does*, I think. It's been that kind of day.

"What the what? How did that happen? I'm so sorry," he says, handing me a tissue from the box on the counter.

Apologies are exchanged. They apologize. I apologize. They tell me not to apologize.

"It's not a big deal. It's just an old coat. Truly, don't worry about it."

"I'm sure Alma doesn't want this leading to some bad Yelp review," a brother says.

"Please don't worry. I'm not a Yelper."

"Ha! That's a good one," says brother number three. Or two. The room feels like a kaleidoscope. I need to get some food in my stomach, and some fresh air.

"You know, I think I remember that place! I think I saw it on my way in. The hibachi steakhouse?"

"Yup. That's the one."

"Perfect," I say.

"You really okay walking there on your own?"

"Really, I'm fine!" I repeat, a broken record.

CHAPTER 19

Crypto

THE HIBACHI JOINT looks like a Hollywood set, more like the Platonic ideal of a hibachi joint than an actual hibachi joint, with the moonlight illuminating it theatrically, accentuating the tangle of telephone and electrical wires overhead and causing the awning to glow.

Inside, Bing Crosby's rendition of "White Christmas" is so loud it practically assaults. A plastic pink cat with a clock embedded in its belly sits on a shelf, its tail wagging, keeping time. A Santa hat has been planted on its head. Wreaths, lights, a small tree in the corner—Christmas in every direction.

I think of a joke that Richard used to tell back in happier, joke-telling days, when he even cooked us dinner once in a while: When he made too much of something, far more than our family of three could eat, he would say, *They didn't have less.* I imagine him here, looking around, deploying that quip to describe what some might consider to be an overabundance of holiday cheer.

The thought makes me miss him a little in a way that's hard

to parse. Do I miss him because I miss *him*, or do I simply miss having someone beside me? Also, I don't miss him as much as I should. It's been years since I asked for a table for one, and there is something thrilling about this, being an independent person again, even if, admittedly, I find myself at—of all the places in the world—a commercial junction at the foot of the now reconstructed bridge that claimed my parents' lives.

Drained, celebratory, depleted, and weirdly elated, I am greeted by a young, perky, blond-haired, blue-eyed hostess who is, unsurprisingly, wearing a Santa hat. I try to suppress the admittedly sexist thought that she looks like a cheerleader, what with her short, pleated skirt and saddle shoes. She leads me to a large, red vinyl booth in the center of the empty restaurant. I believe she is simply trying to give me a comfortable spot, but the hugeness of the booth and my centrality in the space only amplify the fact that I am alone.

I thank her and ask for a menu, but she motions in the direction of a plastic picture holder on the table, next to the salt and pepper shakers, that houses a QR code. I try to open the link but accidentally snap a picture, and then when I try again, I realize I am nearly out of battery. I plead for an old-fashioned menu instead. When the waitress grudgingly drops one on the table, it's so thick it might pass for a novella. It's filled with so many combination platter possibilities that I wonder if I ought to take notes.

There is hibachi chicken. Hibachi steak. Hibachi shrimp. Hibachi vegetables. Hibachi chicken and steak. Hibachi steak and vegetables. Hibachi shrimp and steak and vegetables. Various types of lo mein, with some of those combinations all over again. Then there are pages of sushi options, including a long list of cleverly named rolls: the Crazy Girl Roll, the Under Control Roll, the Charcoal Roll, the Turn Over Roll. There is mercifully no Bridge Roll. Nor is there a Moth Roll. No Keep Your Eye on Your Head Roll. No If Bridges Could Talk Roll. Also conspicuously absent: the Where Am I and What Have I Just Done to My Life Roll.

The cheerleader is back before I finish perusing, but rather than beg for a few more minutes, I land on the vegetable combination.

"Are you sure?" she asks.

"I think I'm sure," I say. But I'm not sure at all. "Why do you ask?"

"We're known for the steak."

"Ooooh, that sounds good, but I've been leaning toward more of a vegetarian diet. It's not a hard-and-fast thing. Sometimes I eat meat. My daughter tells me I'm what they call a flexitarian." I don't know why I share this information. It's more of an aspirational thing anyway, to eat less meat. I could just lean in and, per her suggestion, order the steak.

"I'm not sure I caught all that. You've become a *who?*"

"A flexitarian."

"I haven't heard about that one. Is it a religious thing?"

"No, just trying to be more mindful of what I eat," I say, regretting each word. "And how about some sake. Warm. You know, with those tiny cups?" I'm not sure I really want alcohol, but now I feel the need to prove to her that I'm a regular person who sometimes indulges, and not some sort of leaf-eating nun. "And I need a couple orders of white rice."

"Just rice?" she asks. "Your meal comes with rice, you know."

"It's for my dog."

"Oh, so you want it to go?"

"Sorry, yes, to go. Just the rice. The rice for the dog. Not for my meal. Which is for here."

"Not a problem," she says. She then stares at me for a moment. "Are you okay?"

"Of course I'm okay! Do I not look okay?" I don't mean to sound hostile. I've just had it with this question.

"No, you totally look okay," she says, forcing a smile. She seems to pick up speed as she walks to the kitchen, like she's trying to get away.

I tell myself to get a grip, to calm down, to self-improve, although when I take my hat off and fluff out my wild, still-damp hair, I realize that might take some work. I probably look a sight. Perhaps she thinks I'm indigent, coming in from the cold, treating myself—on Christmas Eve Eve—to a warm meal.

A jingle at the door indicates the arrival of another customer. In walks a man, alone. The blond waitress greets him excitedly. I think they are going to embrace, or give each other a peck on the cheek, but they do not. Still, they stand at the front of the restaurant talking for what strikes me as an unusually long time.

She appears to tip her head in my direction, likely signaling to him that there is a customer—*a flexitarian!*—sitting alone in a booth. She then leads him, mortifyingly, to the table directly across the aisle from mine.

Does she think she is doing me a favor? Matchmaking? I stare at my wedding band, which I have not yet removed. I am not looking for anything. Correction: I'm looking for a lot of things, but not for a man. And even if I were, probably not *this* man, although there may be nothing wrong with this man.

Not that I know, of course, given that I know nothing other than that he is wearing a puffy orange parka, a broad-brimmed hat that might or might not be a Stetson, cowboy boots, and tortoiseshell glasses. He is of average male size and height and is not unattractive, I can't help but notice, yet something about him looks incongruous. It might be the beard, which doesn't seem to belong on the face. Or maybe the preppy glasses, which look mismatched with the otherwise rugged ensemble. He reminds me of a German shorthaired pointer, the way the brown head atop the spotted torso looks like it's been accidentally attached to the wrong dog.

Then again, it might be me. I think of the brothers in the hotel, and how everyone and everything appears to me slightly off.

Whoever he is, what is he doing in Point Pleasant, West Virginia, the night before Christmas Eve, in this hibachi restaurant, alone?

Also, given all the empty booths, why did the waitress have to seat him right here? I focus my gaze on the pink tail-wagging, vaguely dystopian timekeeping cat.

I try not to look to my left, yet if I keep staring at this stupid cat, I fear it is going to hypnotize me. Besides, it is awkward, and vaguely rude, to not at least acknowledge the man sitting across from me in an otherwise empty restaurant. I nod in his direction. He nods back. My work is done.

What I have absorbed in my further, quick assessment is that he has a sweet, nonthreatening face. He looks like a country-western singer. But also he looks like a college professor. Something about him makes no sense. I look away, then back at the cat, at my hands, at the table, then retrieve and stare at my phone. I shouldn't be using up battery, but I look at Instagram and see that Olivia has indeed posted the picture of me and Luna, preparing to head off, supposedly to Ohio, in the car. She has captioned it: "Bon voyage, my love!" I think of the promo for her radio program and wonder if this is a double entendre: goodbye, have a nice trip, as well as good riddance to my niece whom I'm about to humiliate on National Public Radio.

Mercifully my order arrives just then, so I am at least able to occupy myself by swirling food around with the chopsticks, taking inventory of this rather dull mixed platter of wilted vegetables, entrée D-11. I insert a piece of broccoli into my mouth and begin to chew.

"You're not half bad at that," he says.

"At eating?"

"At chopsticks."

"Thanks," I say, avoiding eye contact. Eating with chopsticks is second nature to me, but I don't say this because then he might ask why, and I would probably begin to blather, disclosing too much about my life—like that Harry and Olivia set out chopsticks whenever we ordered Asian food, or that I spent a fair amount of time reporting stories in Asia—because I am constitutionally incapable of not oversharing information about meaningless subjects but don't want to encourage him in any way, although I sort of do, if only out of curiosity because who is he and why is he here?

"You're new here," he says. His voice is deep and gravelly. Country-western singer might not have been the worst guess.

"I'm not here, really. I'm passing through."

"Ah, I see. A stranger comes to town."

"Well, as I said, I'm not really *here* as in 'coming to town.'

I'm 'passing through.'" I make air quotes, although it's not clear even to me which part of this sentence I am attempting to flag as ironic.

"Did you know there's only two kinds of stories in the world?" he asks, ignoring my clarification.

"Yes, I did. A person goes on a journey. And a stranger comes to town."

"John Gardner."

What are the odds, I wonder, that I should sit in a hibachi steakhouse in close proximity to the bridge where my parents died, in search of my story, and meet a stranger who is quoting one of the master craftsmen of story construction? They are slim. Very slim. *Of all the hibachi joints in all the towns*, I think, but I don't know where I'm going with that thought.

"Which one are you?" he asks.

"Which one am I what?"

"Are you the person on the journey or the stranger who comes to town?"

"Well, as I said, more than once, I'm not really 'in town.' I'm just passing through."

"You do like those air quotes, eh?"

"Cute," I say. "Bad habit, I guess. But technically speaking, I guess I'm both."

"I've lost you there."

"I'm both the person on the journey and the stranger who comes to town. Because if you think about it, isn't it all the same story?"

"Perceptive," he says, sipping at the beer the waitress has just set down in front of him. I don't remember him ordering a beer but gather, from their effusive greeting at the door, that he must be a regular. "I suppose you can look at it that way. It's all a matter of point of view. Of who is telling the story."

"Okay, this is kind of crazy. Are you messing with me?"

"Do I appear to be messing with you? I'm just sitting here, drinking my Sapporo."

"You're a writer, right?" I ask. Only a writer would know this adage about the stranger. Either that or a teacher of writing. Or a teacher of writing who is also a writer who happens to be actively not writing.

"Why would you say that? Do I look like a writer?"

"I don't know. What does a writer look like?"

"Frazzled. Bookish. Ink-stained. Bespectacled. Like you."

"Frazzled? Me? Okay. Bookish, maybe, and bespectacled, and I can explain the ink stain. That's not my usual look. Just a leaky pen."

"Sure, that's what they all say."

"So you're not a writer?" I ask.

"See any ink stains? My field involves crypto . . ."

"Seriously? Are you the crypto guy who's staying at the hotel?"

I hadn't meant to let that question, with its obvious implication that I, too, am staying at the hotel, slip out.

"I don't know. Depends how many other crypto people are staying at the hotel, I guess."

"I assume that's your idea of a joke."

"Must be me then. Yes. Just for a couple of days. I've got a bit of research to finish up."

"But why here?"

"Why here what?"

"I don't know. I guess I never thought of West Virginia as a place for crypto, but then I don't really know much about crypto. I confess I don't understand this whole NFT thing. Or is it NTF?"

"I think it's NFT. Nonfungible tokens. But that's not the kind of crypto I'm talking about."

"Oh, like Bitcoin?"

"So you're a writer *and* a humorist?"

The waitress reappears and sets a plate of sizzling steak in front of him. It looks much more appetizing than my vegetable platter.

"Wait, did you even place an order?" I ask.

"He always gets the steak," she explains. "Like I told you, it's the best thing here. It's called a steakhouse for a reason."

"I hear you're a *flexitarian*," he says, confirming my suspicion that they were talking about me. "Bummer. This would have been a good time to flex. You don't know what you're missing." He then turns to the hostess. "Got any hot sauce, Bea?"

"You know I do," she says. "For you, anyway. I'll be back in a sec."

"You're the best," he says.

"You know it."

I roll my eyes at this rom-com flirtation, benign as it seems to be, but I don't think either of them notices.

"Actually, I did buy some Bitcoin, but I'm not sure it was my finest moment," he says. "But my nephew, he's a crypto guy." It takes me a minute to realize he's back to talking to me.

"Yeah, I read about it dropping or something. But I don't follow the financial news that closely."

"Neither do I, although I do dabble. But you've got the wrong crypto. I'm talking cryptozoology."

"Let me guess. Bitcoin for zoo animals."

"Ha, definitely a humorist."

My phone vibrates, and I flip it over and see that Richard is calling. I have never, in all our years together, failed to answer his call, even when I perhaps should have. That statistic is misleading, however, in that for the past couple of years, we have only occasionally been farther apart than the distance between the basement and the master bedroom. What I need to tell him about my whereabouts, about Vera coming home, about my state of mind, involves a much longer conversation than I'm prepared to have here with the timekeeping cat staring at me and this crypto guy eavesdropping. I let the call go to voicemail and turn it back over so I no longer see the screen.

"I'm not trying to be funny," I say. "Rather, I have no idea what you're talking about. What's up with the zoo business? And what does that have to do with crypto? I'm truly not following."

"Cryptozoology is a science. Although technically some would tell you that it's pseudoscience."

"Like fake news? Fake science?"

"Sort of. Although I'm not sure that it's fake science. That's just the definition you'll find in dictionaries. I mean, if enough people believe in something, it's worth paying attention to, don't you think? But enough about me. What brings you here?"

"Wait, back up a minute. What do you mean about the things people believe in?"

"A whole bunch of things, but what I'm talking about here mostly has to do with the story about the moth. Not sure if you've heard about it, since you're just passing through, or whatever it is you say you are doing."

"What about the moth?"

Bea returns and sets down the hot sauce.

"Thanks," he says. "By the way, how's the team going?"

"Oh, great. We have a really talented group this year," she says. "I came straight from practice. Didn't even have time to change."

"They're lucky to have you."

"Thanks, Ingram," she says.

Aware, again, of my peripheralness, I consider asking him what in the world they are talking about. How nice it would feel to belong. Yet also how nice it is to feel, for a day or two anyway, like I do not.

The man who is apparently named Ingram does not need to be asked the question. "She coaches cheerleading at the local high school," he volunteers. "Which you can probably tell from her outfit."

"Ha, I was wondering," I say.

"If it looks like an elephant . . ."

"I thought it was 'if it quacks like a duck.'"

"I think both are true. Also a horse."

"I've never heard a horse before."

"Well, strictly speaking, I think it's a zebra."

"Then it has something to do with cheerleading."

"You've nailed it."

I glance at his plate as he douses the meat in hot sauce. It looks very good, this D-25. I have a bit of hibachi envy.

"It looks like you might want a bite?"

"Sorry, I don't mean to stare."

I watch him cut a piece of steak and put a forkful in his mouth. It smells so good, and I want a bite so badly, I feel like I might start to drool the way Luna does when I hold a dog biscuit in the air and try to get her to sit. I select a carrot from my vegetable medley and try to muster some enthusiasm.

"Truly, you don't know what you're missing. And wait for dessert. The deep-fried Oreos? Incomparable."

"Surely you are kidding me."

"You don't know about the moth. And you don't know about the deep-fried Oreos. I guess you really *are* just passing through. Does that mean you've never heard of the Mothman?"

Have I heard of the Mothman? LOL, I want to say. The Mothman has only been one of the chief preoccupations of my life. But I don't say this. I want to know what *he* has to say about the Mothman.

"I've heard something about it, but what do you mean?" I ask disingenuously. I hope it doesn't count against me if someone up there is keeping track of my recent spate of untruths.

"Pretty much everyone who comes here is here for the Mothman. It's become quite the tourist attraction. There's an annual festival, and there's even a museum. You haven't been?"

"Like I said, I just got here, and I'm just passing through."

"So you keep saying."

"Tell me more about it. And about the moth."

"Somehow I don't fully believe you don't know about the moth . . . Everyone around here does, but if you are seriously asking, there was a catastrophe. The bridge collapsed. The Silver Bridge, the one right out there. Well, not literally the one out there. It's been rebuilt," he says, gesturing vaguely toward the left. "The original bridge gave way during rush hour on December 15, 1967. Forty-six people died."

"Two were never found, right?"

"Yes. But you don't know anything about it," he says.

"Well . . . maybe I know about the bridge collapse, but that doesn't mean I know anything about the moth," I bluff.

"In the weeks prior to the bridge collapse, a lot of people around here thought they saw a creature that looked like a giant moth. But it also looked like a giant man. A moth man. It had big, sturdy, hairy legs. Some say it was ten feet tall. Others say it had a ten-foot wingspan."

"That seems rather exact. And terrifying."

"True on both counts. But if you think about it, once the words *ten feet* get into the story, it tends to be repeated whether it's accurate or not. But the one thing everyone is quite certain about are the eyes. They were bright red, like bicycle reflectors."

I think of the moth in the car, the eyes so red and bright they seemed to bore right through me. "You don't believe it's true?" I ask.

This conversation is so surreal that I wonder if I'm imagining this entire scene—the restaurant, the pink timekeeping cat, this crypto man, this story he is telling me. I've spent a lifetime being told not to talk about the moth—I derailed my career by simply raising the subject—and now we are talking about it in such casual fashion we might as well be talking about the weather—the sort of weather that is not hugely fraught.

"Which part? That it was ten feet tall? Or that it ever existed?"

"Either. Both."

"It's not my job to believe. I'm interested in what other people believe."

"In a cryptobiological sense?"

"Cryptozoological, if you will."

"Right."

"Right. So you haven't had a look around yet? It's your first time here, you say?"

"Correct. I just got into town, like, an hour ago. And it's cold and dark, so I haven't seen much of anything. Although I apparently have a view of the river from my hotel room. I can't wait to see it in the light of day."

"Ah, did Alma put you in suite 403?"

I pause to chew and digest his question. "She did. It's not creepy at all that you know this. But while we are on the subject, who are those guys in the lobby? Are they guests? Or do they work there? Or live there?"

"Ah, you are definitely new to this place, stranger. Those are the famous Evett brothers."

"That sounds like a band."

"You're confusing them with the Avett Brothers."

"Ha, maybe I am. What makes them famous?"

"They own the hotel. Well, they don't own it exactly. Alma does. But it's a family business. It's been around for a couple of generations. But also they are known for their dogs. They have a big farm about five miles or so out of town."

"If they are known for their dogs, why do they have a no-dogs policy at the hotel?"

"Who can blame them? I love dogs, but if I owned a hotel, I'm not sure I'd want to deal with the mess or possible destruction."

"I suppose that's true," I say, Luna's recent behavior being exhibit A.

"Well, if you aren't here for the moth, what brings you here?"

"As I've said, I'm just passing through. But if it makes you happy, we can amend that to say I'm a stranger who comes to town *and* who is just passing through."

"Whatever makes *you* happy, stranger."

"Enough about me. You still haven't told me what it is that you do. I mean, I get you are in crypto something, but what does that mean?"

"I study the supernatural. Not to change the subject, but you appear to be staring at my steak."

"I am not staring at your steak."

"I think you are."

He passes a forkful of meat across the aisle. I stare at it longingly, the utensil hovering above the linoleum floor.

"Seriously, I'm not eating your steak. I hardly know you. Not to mention . . . germs."

"Suit yourself," he says.

As he begins to withdraw his arm, some sort of animal instinct kicks in. I grab his fork and stick a piece of steak in my mouth.

"You're right," I say. "It's not bad."

He waves to Bea, and from across the restaurant she waves back and asks if he is ready.

"Two forks," he says.

My phone vibrates again. I look at the screen. It's Richard:

Olivia said you left for a job interview? WTF?

I put the phone in my pocket without replying. I can't believe that Olivia is still leaning into this absurd cover story.

I don't really know what I'm doing, but I'm not at all sorry to be here, in the best hibachi joint in town, talking to this cryptozoologist, waiting to eat deep-fried Oreos. Life is full of surprises, and whatever it is that is happening here in this strange restaurant in this strange town holds the promise of answering my many questions, not to mention advancing my narrative rut.

CHAPTER 20

Orion

BACK IN THE room, I prop myself up in bed, fire up my laptop, and, having forgotten to ask about the hotel wireless, mooch a few bars of internet from an open network named COFFEEMOTH. Absorbed in my private drama of these past two days, my rhythms thrown off by travel, I've lost track of what is going on in the world.

The first thing I see when I log onto the website of the *Washington Post* is the following headline: "Rare Moth Species Found at Airport."

Moths, moths everywhere.

I am aware that I am always on the lookout for coincidence, and that I sometimes behave irrationally in pursuit of making pieces of information conform to my theories and thereby make sense of my life. As a writing instructor, I operate on the possibly misguided assumption that every story must loop back neatly to its logical end. But not everything can be wrapped up in a bow, and it's unrealistic to expect closure, as much as we desire it, for every loose end.

And yet, what are the odds that this story has just popped up? I click, of course.

It's a picture of a moth, not entirely dissimilar to the one that haunts me and that I saw in the car. It has those same red eyes, those sleek dark wings, that mighty, fierce gaze. It appears to be staring at me from inside the internet.

I sit up straight and begin to read.

Apparently customs agents discovered the larvae and pupae of an unidentifiable species inside the seedpods a passenger was transporting from Ethiopia. Experts were summoned, and they discovered it was a moth not seen since 1912.

"The moths, whose black-and-gold-dotted wings resemble a cloudy predawn sky, were discovered in September and looked to be a member of the moth family Pyralidae," the reporter notes.

I read this again and can't help but break the sentence into stanzas.

> *The moths, whose black-gold*
> *Dotted wings resemble a*
> *Cloudy predawn sky.*

It's not just an admittedly minor moth coincidence; it's multiply coincidental: a weather and moth haiku. And the moths are from Ethiopia, a country I visited many years ago on assignment, although I'm certainly not suggesting this last part is meaningful.

Perhaps the cryptozoologist, this Ingram person, whom-ever and whatever he is really, might know something about this moth. Although why do I care? Am I simply looking for a reason to keep the conversation going? I suppose that I am. It was a fun evening, refreshing to be my own blank slate: not a wife or a mother or a former journalist, not an orphan or a moth-obsessed niece. Not a writer who can't write. This evening I was someone else: just a stranger passing through town, eating steak off a fellow stranger's fork, sharing an order of fried Oreos, which, with their creamy, viscous liquid oozing from their burnt fried shells, is unlikely to sit well in my stomach. It was just a lark, this being someone else for an hour, but it was strangely exhilarating. It felt possibly like a fresh start.

As I start to drift off, I remember the call from Richard that I did not pick up earlier, the text to which I did not respond. At times, especially when I am falling asleep at night, alone but for my dog, my feelings can muddle. The unadulterated anger about Elaine seems almost a healthy thing; at least that form of betrayal is concrete. But I sometimes feel responsible for the rest. Ought I have been better able to help him through his so-called shame? Should I have been able, somehow, to prevent it? Might we have found ways to survive it?

Words are not the only way to communicate. I think of how he would lie beside me at night, tracing the scars on my back. When we first began to date, it took months before I had the courage to let him see me in the light, to see the thick web of scar tissue stretching from shoulder to shoulder. He said he thought it was beautiful, that the pattern made him think of the constellation Orion. He traced, with his finger, the line he thought resembled Orion's hunter's bow. He never asked me how I got those scars. Not that the answer is especially compelling—falling into a patch of tomatoes, my skin ripped by the rusted-out wire cage—but still, why did he not ask me questions? And more to the point, why did I think his lack of curiosity was okay?

Nevertheless, I can't fight the compunction to be in touch, to at least be a responsible co-parent, so I message him to say that I'm okay. Then I put the phone on silent and fall into a deep, dreamless sleep.

CHAPTER 21

Vision

THE SOUNDS OF something thudding to the floor, of paper ripping, of items spilling, then rolling, cause me to bolt upright. I then hear a dog, munching. I don't have to see it to know it: Luna has helped herself to breakfast by chewing open the bag of kibble I've left on the credenza by the door. How she reached it is a mystery, but then, I frequently underestimate her dexterity—she is as stretchy as Gumby, at least before he sustained his injuries and lost an arm.

On the upside, perhaps this means she is feeling better, although appetite, of course, is not always a reliable barometer of a dog's state of health. I remember watching Benjamin eat, then vomit, then eat his vomit, then vomit again.

I jump out of bed and scold her.

"No, Luna, no!"

She looks at me politely, ears pricked, listening, then continues scarfing up the spilled food.

"I got you rice!" I tell her. "I need to mix it into your food.

Plus, we are switching food, so we need to transition—a little bit of both foods this morning, mixed with rice!"

Again, she looks at me, then turns her attention back to the kibble on the floor. I bend and begin to scoop it up. Although I believe I have retrieved most of it, some has rolled into the corners and under the furniture. Luna has her head underneath the credenza, her chest pressed downward, her tail sticking up. Downward dog. I squat to look around for any stray bits of food but realize I can't quite see what is going on without my glasses.

Although I wear glasses for both distance and reading, my vision is not completely awful. I can see well enough to get around—although I wouldn't dare drive without my glasses— and I can even read if the text is large enough and positioned correctly. Still, without them, things are a bit of a blur, especially from across the length of a room. I can't identify the chewed-up object lying next to the doorframe by the bedroom, for example. I'm assuming from the general shape and size of the object that it's Gumby, but as I move closer, I see that it's not. Another foot closer and I see that it's a pair of glasses. *My* glasses. My now-mangled glasses. I lean over and pick them up and see that they are not just a little bit mangled, if there even is, by definition, such a thing. Rather, they are beyond-repair mangled. In far worse shape than I might have imagined possible. So mangled that mutilated Gumby, in repose atop the desk beside my keys, looks hale in comparison, like he might get up and run a marathon.

"Luna!" I yell. "Bad puppy! Bad, bad puppy! Bad!"

I am aware that even in my most angry, threatening voice, I sound neither angry nor threatening. Nevertheless, Luna and I are in such sync that she knows she has done something wrong, far worse than the initial sin of spilling the dog food.

She hangs her head low, then tucks her long tail between her legs, which is kind of a sad sight.

"What have you done, Luna?"

She looks at me with those startling, heterochromatic puppy eyes, and I instantly soften.

I know it's my fault. She is a puppy. Puppies chew things. Puppies eat anything they can reach. Or, in this case, bat off the bedside table. In my defense, who would ever consider the possibility of a puppy eating a pair of spectacles? I bend to retrieve them, annoyed but not yet alarmed, because it will take me a moment to understand the gravity of the situation. It's not just that one of the temples has detached, or that the remaining temple has been heavily gnawed, but the lenses are full of tiny, toothy indentations. I put them on, and they sit crookedly on my face. Even when I straighten them, it is harder to see with them on than off, so badly mutilated are the lenses.

I go to the computer to look up nearby opticians and nearly forget that without my glasses it is hard to see the screen. I enlarge the type, reposition the computer, and determine that there is an optometrist across the river in Gallipolis, Ohio. It is currently seven thirty, and the office opens at ten.

One aspect of one new problem, potentially partially resolved.

CHAPTER 22

Chief

IT'S BITTER COLD outside, and an icy wind whips off the river. I fish through my pockets for my hat and gloves to no avail, then wrap my scarf around my head and tie it beneath my chin. It's what Vera calls my babushka look, which I doubt she means in a fashion-forward kind of way.

Luna pulls me hard toward the left, where I can see and almost smell the coffee from the café across the street, presumably the place from which I am stealing bars of internet. I get it; I, too, would rather be there inside a cozy coffee shop than here in the bitter cold, but she needs her morning constitutional, and I need some exercise after all the driving I've done over the last two days. I coax her to the right, and we head behind the hotel, where we connect to a walkway that leads alongside the river.

There's an entire other world back here, including an amphitheater. It's like stumbling onto an archaeological ruin, except the opposite in that everything looks new. I guide Luna along the walkway, where we see a couple of signs memorializing the Silver

Bridge collapse—at least, I'm pretty sure that's what they are. I can only see what I can see without my glasses.

We pause before a giant painted mural that lines the walkway, stretching the equivalent of a city block. All I can see is a blur of figures. It appears to be a gruesome, bloody montage. I'm guessing these are the British fighting the Native Americans, but they could also be the American settlers battling the British. Or the Americans battling the Native Americans. Carnage and more carnage, none of it is good. I see bodies strewn along the forest, lying in pools of blood. I turn away.

Farther along the path, I see a statue of a Native American chief. Cornstalk is his name, and it's written in such large letters that even a blurry-eyed woman with a sporadically bleeding head can see it. Cornstalk is holding a machete-like object. His headdress is resplendent, and his expression fierce. Whether he would approve of this depiction or find it racist and reductive, I can't say. Behind him is a mural of yet another hideous battle, quite possibly the same one, but who knows, because all I can make out are figures, trees, and a lot of blood.

A tug on the leash brings me back to the moment, and I turn toward the river. What appears to be a couple in the distance is moving toward us, bundled so tightly in parkas and scarves that it's hard to get a sense of who they are until they are smack in front of us.

A female voice emits through the fabric of a checkered scarf and squeals, then squats in front of Luna, rubbing her ears. Before I can do anything about it, Luna is in her lap, licking her face. Luna then pulls the wool hat off her head, as if she is as curious as I am to see who this person is. More squeals erupt, both human and canine, and a long mane of magenta hair spills to the young woman's waist. It's a beautiful, nature-defying color, somewhat alarming in its brilliance, at least compared to this grey winter morning.

"I'm so sorry," I say.

"Oh my gosh, no apologies! I love her! I want to take her home!" Magenta is young, not much older than Vera, I think.

"She's all yours," I joke.

"Oh wow," says her partner. "There he is. That's the chief."

"The one who put a curse on this place?" the young woman asks.

"Wait, what?" I ask. "A curse?"

"Oh yeah. He put a curse on this whole area on account of what they did to him."

"What did they do? I mean, I can imagine, sadly. But it's the first I've heard of him, I'm embarrassed to say. I'm just a stranger in town. I'm just passing through."

"This place is totally haunted," the woman says. "That's part of why we came here on our honeymoon. It's one of the most haunted places in the country. We're doing a ghost tour."

A honeymoon? They look too young to be married. I hesitate before speaking, fearful of saying something inappropriate about marriage given my current nihilistic mindset.

"That sounds romantic," I lie. What I want to say is: *Beware of stray nightguards on the bedside table. Of friends who are not friends. Of egos that inflate into memes.*

"Tell me about the curse," I say instead.

"I wrote a paper about Cornstalk for a history class in high school. I don't remember every detail, but he was a Shawnee leader," Magenta says. "His name in the Shawnee language was

Hokoleskwa. He led a raid against the colonialists back in the 1760s."

"He was, like, the main guy in the Battle of Point Pleasant—"

"There was a Battle of Point Pleasant?" I ask, then regret, the question. Obviously, there was a battle. That's what this mural in front of me is about. I've been so obsessed with my personal history that I have failed to consider there might be a whole other narrative, one with historical implications.

"Yup. In 1774. It was also called the Battle of Kanawha. It was brutal, between the Virginia militia and the Shawnee. Also the Mingo. They were trying to stop the militia from taking their land in the Ohio Valley, but the Shawnee were outnumbered. Cornstalk was forced to cede the land that is now West Virginia and Kentucky," Magenta explains.

"So that's why there's a curse?" I ask.

"No, that happened later. I mean, there are different versions of this, but during the Revolutionary War, he advocated for Shawnee neutrality. He was a diplomat of sorts. Or he tried to be. He went to Fort Randolph to try to talk to the colonists, but they just tossed him in prison. No surprise given the way we've treated Native Americans. They arrested his son, too, and wound up executing them both in retaliation for the death of one of their soldiers. But not before he put a curse on this place."

"Right," Mr. Magenta agrees. "He said something like, 'May the strength of the peoples be paralyzed by the stain of our blood—'"

"'I was the borderman's friend,'" Magenta cuts in, attempting a stern male voice. "'I never warred with you . . . For this may the curse of the great spirit rest upon this land.'"

Susan Coll

"It was much longer than that. You can find more on the internet," he adds.

"So what has happened? Since the curse, I mean."

"You know about the Mothman, right?"

"I've heard something about it," I bluff.

"And the bridge collapse."

"Yeah, again, I've heard."

"Well, before the bridge collapsed, there were sightings of a giant creature. Like a moth. But, like, with big hairy legs," he says.

"Were they hairy? Or just really muscular?" she asks.

"I don't know. Both maybe?"

"Some people think it was a bird. A really big bird. A sand-hill crane is one theory. Or maybe an owl."

"There are other components to the bird theory," he says. "Like some who believe that the moth, or the Mothman, whatever you want to call him, was an incarnation of the thunderbird."

Now *this* is something I've never heard. "Meaning what?" The only Thunderbird I can think of is a car.

"The thunderbird is a spirit. A giant bird. He carries lightning in his beak. His flapping wings cause thunder. I mean, that's the myth."

"You sure know a lot about this," I say.

"I'm doing a master's degree in Native American studies," he says, forcing me to reevaluate his age at the very least.

"So wait, what is the connection?"

"Between what and what?"

"The thunderbird and the Mothman."

"I mean, who knows. People see what they want to see, right?"

Luna has now rolled over and is enjoying a belly rub from Magenta.

"That's fascinating," I say. "I hadn't heard about the curse."

"Well, that's only part of the curse. There are so many things . . ."

"Like what?"

"Like lightning. Like floods?" Magenta says.

"Like also plane crashes. And there was a mining disaster. Also a train derailment. And a tornado that killed a bunch of people," her husband adds.

"The water supply was poisoned too. And there was an accident at the nuclear power plant."

This recitation makes me think of the ten plagues that God inflicted on the Egyptians, according to the story of Passover, when Pharaoh refused to let the Jewish slaves go: *blood, frogs, lice, flies, pestilence, boils, hail, locusts, darkness, death of the firstborn.*

"Yeah, also they built a monument in Cornstalk's honor and planned a dedication. The night before the ceremony, they were going to set the monument up. It was huge, like more than eighty feet tall, but there was a freak lightning storm. It hit the crane that was going to install the monument, so they had to delay the whole thing. Then when they finally rescheduled it, there was *another* lightning strike. It damaged the capstone and some of the granite."

"No way," I say.

"You can read about it."

"On the internet," Magenta adds.

"That's unbelievable."

"Oh, there's more. A lot more. Also floods, constant floods—that's why you have that floodwall," he says, pointing toward the concrete structure that flags the river, which I hadn't fully registered as anything other than part of the architecture.

"There was an explosion at the jail. A freight train derailed. There was a collapse on a construction site. Fires galore."

"So many fires," she adds.

At some point along the way, this story has become overstuffed enough to lose credibility. But then I stop and ask myself how the narrative of a giant moth appearing before the collapse of a bridge might have struck me as believable to begin with.

"We'd better go, babe," the man says. "We're meeting Lulu for breakfast, remember?"

"Yup!" She turns to me, as if she owes me an explanation. "Lulu is my cousin. She lives in Gallipolis, right across the bridge."

I nod, unsure what else to say. Part of me wants to know everything about this young woman, even though she is a stranger whom I will presumably never see again.

"I hate to say goodbye to this beauty," she says. "One last belly rub!" Luna happily complies. When Magenta rises, she is completely covered in Luna's white fur.

"It was nice to meet you. Have a nice honeymoon!" I wave, then add absurdly, "Good luck in graduate school!"

Have a nice life, a happy marriage. Run for your life, I do not say.

CHAPTER 23

The Eyes of Gallipolis

WHILE TALKING TO the honeymooners, I had continued to fish through my pockets, hoping to find my hat and gloves. Instead I found only plastic bags to clean up after Luna, and enough elastic hair ties to keep Bea-from-the-hibachi-joint's cheerleaders in ponytails for several years.

Hopefully they are back in the hotel room, although it's possible I left them at the restaurant last night. For the life of me, I can't remember if I had them as I walked home, exhausted and distracted, on a sugar high from the deep-fried Oreos, and a touch tipsy from tiny cups of sake that apparently add up.

It hadn't occurred to me that it could be quite this cold in West Virginia, although that said, it might be less bad if I were appropriately dressed. Still, the idea that it should be somehow warmer here than in DC is my bad sense of direction talking. In my mind the word *Virginia* means South, but in reality, I'm roughly on the same latitude as I am back home—possibly even a little bit north.

Thinking longingly of coffee, I turn back with Luna and

head in the direction of the hotel. Just as I'm about to open the door, the cryptozoologist appears on his way out. He is still wearing that Stetson-style hat, but now, instead of the orange parka, he has on a red and black buffalo check jacket. I laugh, without meaning to, at the coincidence, which is of course not a coincidence so much as a Christmas thing, or a style thing— or, for all I know, a West Virginia thing, or basically, when you think about it, just a thing. Plaid. It is one of the most ubiquitous fashion choices in the world, probably dating back hundreds of years. I think of Scots. Of tartans, even though I don't really know what a tartan is, apart from it possibly being the name of a sports team somewhere.

"What's so funny?" he asks.

"Am I laughing?"

"You are smiling. Penny for your thoughts?"

"Tartan."

"Carnegie Mellon," he says. "My alma mater."

"I'm sorry, what?"

"You said Tartan. I said Carnegie Mellon. That's where I went to college. All of our athletic teams were called the Tartans."

"Seriously? That's so weird."

"Yes, why? Did you go there too?"

"No, just, I was thinking about plaid. Because of your jacket. It's not a big deal. It's one weird thing after another is all."

"It's a strange place. Weird things happen here," he says.

"Either that or I need coffee."

Something about his getup still looks like a costume, but I can't say which part is out of place. I try on my country-western singer theory again and imagine him with a guitar strapped to his chest and a glass of whiskey, belting out a tune. "A Stranger Comes to Town," perhaps. A mournful ballad set in a hibachi restaurant in a town made famous by its tragic history.

He doesn't break into song. Instead, he bends down and caresses Luna. She jumps up and licks his face. She is having quite the social day already, and it's not even nine.

"Beautiful pup!" he says, laughing. "What's she called?"

"This is Luna. She's not shy."

"Well, since you mentioned coffee, best cup of coffee around is right across the street."

"Yeah, I noticed that earlier." I look back at the café, in front of which sits a sandwich board with a blue chalk drawing of what might be a giant cup of coffee, but for all I know it could be a bowl of soup, or even a chicken with a beak. All I can make out, given my optical situation, is a round object with something protruding from the side.

"That sounds great. I'll head over as soon as I get Luna upstairs." I take my coat off and wrap it around her as I scoop her wriggling body into my arms.

"What, may I ask, are you doing?"

"Like I mentioned last night, no dogs allowed in the hotel. I have to sneak her in. I mean, I'm not *totally* breaking the law or anything—Alma told me it was okay for her to stay as long as we all pretend this isn't really happening. And to not tell the brothers, even though I think they know."

"Ah, kind of a wink-wink thing."

"I guess that's what it is, yeah. Wink-wink."

"That coat doesn't suit her, so why don't you take it off? She looks like more of a leather jacket kind of gal. Or maybe denim. Let's bring her to coffee."

"Yeah, you're right about that. I think she's part Lab, part motorcycle, so maybe a bomber jacket would be good. And that's a nice thought, but she can't go inside a restaurant, and I don't want to leave her outside."

"What do you mean, she can't go in? She's your guide dog, right?"

This is clearly intended as a joke, and yet, as it happens, I am unable to see. Or at least to see well.

"She's the most poorly behaved dog in the universe, so I don't think I'll get very far with that for a cover story."

"I'll vouch for you," he says. He is squatting now, giving Luna a fierce ear scratch. She is easy, Luna. Won over, in love, she's ready to call a truck and move in with him. I remember his easy manner with the waitress last night. He seems to be one of those people everyone likes. There is definitely something about this Ingram that is strangely compelling, but being compelled by a man is the furthest thing from my mind given that I'm still detangling from the one I've got. Besides, I've come here for a reason—not to further complicate my life.

"I'd certainly prefer to bring her along," I say, "so I guess there's no harm in trying. But it's funny you should say that, about her being a guide dog. She chewed up my glasses this morning. Completely destroyed them."

"Well, there you go! She created a job for herself."

I contemplate Luna as a guide dog. She would pull me straight into a tree, or traffic, or the frigid waters of the Ohio River.

"Like I was saying," he continues, nonplussed, like a dog destroying eyeglasses is a completely normal thing. "It's not even a lie."

I follow the cryptozoologist across the street and into the café, and the waitress begins to fawn over him so aggressively that I don't think she'd notice if Luna jumped up on the counter and ate the muffins right out of the case, a maneuver she appears to be contemplating.

"Ingy, honey, where've you been?" she asks.

Honey? Do I feel a little . . . jealous? I bat the thought away.

"I told you I'd be back. And here I am. Can you get me one of those lattes? I like it extra frothy. And I'll take an order of those pancakes, but tell me first, where is the maple syrup from?"

"It's from the supermarket, hon."

"Ha ha, what I'm asking is, is it Canadian maple syrup? Or is it the fake-o-rama stuff?"

The waitress laughs as if this is the funniest thing she's ever heard. "It's whatever comes in the jug," she says. "You're hilarious."

I add *food snob* to the confusing list of details I have assembled about this man. Conflict averse, I ask for black coffee and a muffin. I point to a brown blurry object in the case, not sure whether it's dotted with chocolate chips or blueberries, and I do not ask. I'm just grateful that no one has voiced an objection to Luna's presence, and I figure the less attention I draw to myself, the better, although I know in reality that *Ingy* is simply sucking up all of the energy in the room, and that if he were not here, charming this woman behind the counter, I would have been escorted outside and deposited on the curb in a hot second.

We take our food to a high-top table, and Luna curls at my feet and pretends, for a few minutes, to be a well-behaved dog.

"So, *stranger*," he says, emphasizing the word. "Not to belabor it, but you haven't told me what you're doing here."

"Like I said, I'm just passing through. I'm on my way to a job interview. Although I've been thrown a curveball. I might now be a little bit stuck."

"I'm all ears," he says. He takes his hat off and sets it on his lap.

"Well, like I already told you. The dog ate my glasses. I need to find an optician."

"Did the dog eat your homework too?"

"Very funny. I'm sure that's next. But I'm serious. The thing is, I can't drive without my glasses. I can see well enough to get around, but not to get behind the wheel. I have an extra pair of glasses at home, but that doesn't do me much good here."

"Where's home? Maybe we can go get them."

I'm not sure how much I want to disclose to this stranger, this cryptozoologist, this man named Ingy, so I am deliberately vague. "The DMV," I say.

"You live in the Department of Motor Vehicles?" he asks. "That's a first!"

"Ha ha ha. I never thought of it like that, but yes. That's how we sometimes refer to the DC, Maryland, Virginia metropolitan area. It's colloquial, I guess."

"*Colloquial*," he repeats with a hint of sarcasm. "Fancy. Well, I guess that's a long ride, but I can at least drive you to the optician."

"I'm not looking for any favors, but that's kind of you. I'll call an Uber."

"Yeah, but you can't take your puppy in an Uber."

"Right, but I can put her back in the hotel room. That was my plan a few minutes ago, as you likely recall."

"But you need your guide dog."
"You have a point. I guess I do."

✕   ✕   ✕

It is unremarkable, the drive over the bridge. It's a letdown of sorts—no violins play, my heart does not race, I don't cry or scream or grip the sides of my seat. I don't even think deep thoughts. If anything, my blurred vision casts an artful tinge across the still water, distracting me with serene thoughts of museums, museum cafés, museum gift shops, a cute cubist robot I once bought at the Andy Warhol Museum in Pittsburgh, of a pair of earrings at MoMA in New York. I keep expanding the thought, thinking about museums on my bucket list, which expands to other cities and countries, creating a travelogue longer than my life span will likely allow, deliberately filling, even cluttering, my mind to keep it from drifting toward the subject of bridges, or at least a certain bridge, which happens to be the one we are on.

There is a scene in the Mothman movie where, after the bridge collapse, the Ohio River is filled with Christmas presents bobbing on the water. It's a haunting image that is hard to shake: all those carefully wrapped gifts that will never be delivered. Lost gifts, lost family members. It's presumably fiction, this image, this scene, conjured by the filmmaker, but who knows, and who cares? Sometimes such minor fictions speak more powerfully to reality than reality itself.

If only bridges could talk.

How crowded it must have been on the bridge during rush

hour, just before the holidays, as people rushed about, hyper-engaged in the hunting and gathering of holiday provisions. We could talk about that, the bridge and I, or we could talk about corroded bridge joints, or vehicles plunging into the water, or a giant lurking thunderbird, or a sandhill crane, or an owl, or the Mothman. Or Chief Cornstalk and the curse. The stain of blood.

Before my imaginary conversation concludes, we have reached the other side, and I am no wiser than when I began.

⋈   ⋈   ⋈

There are so many things I want to ask this man Ingram, chief among them is still the question of his improbably named profession. I want to know other things, too, like where is he from, does he have a dog, what kind of music does he like, what is his favorite food, what kinds of books does he read? How might it feel to touch the stubble on his cheek? Also, is he married? And what does it mean that I am even thinking about this? It's just a safety check, I tell myself. The more I ground this person in normalizing details, the less likely he is to be a psychopath.

As if. I have read enough newspaper stories and watched enough episodes of *Law & Order* to know this is not even remotely true. But if he is, hypothetically, a serial killer, wouldn't he identify in some more conventional way—as an insurance salesman, or a pediatric oncologist, or a middle school history teacher—rather than lay on the weirdness by identifying as a cryptozoologist? Were Vera to tell me that she had accepted a ride from a man about whom she knew next to nothing apart from his study of cryptids, I'd likely deliver a lecture about Stranger Danger, which was a unit from her kindergarten class that was supposed to teach safety—don't accept candy from the stranger, don't get in the car with the man because he has a cute puppy—but had the unintended effect of giving her nightmares for years.

I get that things don't always fit into a tidy box, and yet I like the box tidy even if I, myself, feel like my seams are showing, like my stuffing is coming out. But this is all moot because here we are, together in his truck, and he seems to be benign. Before I can begin my interrogation, he pulls into the parking lot of a strip mall and points to the storefront of an optical shop.

"That was fast," I say. We have been on the road for only ten minutes.

"Yup. Light traffic this time of day. You run on in. Luna and I will wait in the truck."

I feel a twinge of hesitation. I hardly know this man, but then, what's the worst possible outcome? Would he really kidnap my dog? Besides, if he did, he'd probably track me down to return her as soon as she chewed holes in his shoes.

I coax my mind toward more productive thoughts, such as the errand we are here to run. In front of me is the optical shop, Eyes of Gallipolis, in the window of which is the stencil of an oversized pair of thick black-rimmed spectacles that make me think of the fashion designer Iris Apfel. A wreath adorns the door, and sleigh bells announce my arrival when I swing it open.

The small shop is bustling with customers who seem to have popped in to pick up their new glasses, or to get an adjustment, the day before Christmas, which is not something that would have occurred to me but makes all kinds of sense. Many people have likely taken the day off from work to catch up on errands, crossing things off their to-do lists before hosting relatives or preparing to leave town. This means I have to wait some fifteen minutes until it is my turn to talk to an employee of Eyes of Gallipolis, who turns out to be a cheerful young woman sporting chunky red frames that dwarf her delicate face. She looks strangely familiar.

"I'm Autumn," she says. "What can I do for you, doll?"

Doll? She seems too young to be employing such an old-fashioned, possibly sexist term of endearment. I know I ought to bristle at this, but I don't mind when a taxi driver calls me *luv*, or a receptionist calls me *hon*. Perhaps this means only that I have a thick skin, or that it takes a lot more than that to ruffle my feathers. Or maybe it's a sign that I'm starved for affection.

"Do I know you from somewhere?" I ask.

"I don't think so, but I hear that a lot. I guess I have one of those faces. So how can I help you?"

I open the case that holds my glasses and show them to her. She lets out a belly laugh so loud that heads turn in our direction.

"Jorge, you have to come see this one!" she calls to her colleague. Jorge looks exasperated, but it's not clear whether the source of his annoyance is Autumn's interruption or the customer he has been assisting since I walked through the door—a dapper, mustachioed gentleman who looks to be in his seventies, and who has by now tried on what appear to be more than two dozen pairs of frames, all of which are piled into plastic trays, rejected and waiting to be sanitized. He walks over, looks at my mangled spectacles, and roars with laughter. Soon I have a small audience of both employees and customers gawking at what had once been my lovely, overpriced frames.

"You win," Jorge says to Autumn.

"I think I do. This is even worse than the lady last week who put her Ray-Bans down the garbage disposal."

"Oh, way worse," Jorge agrees. "What happened here? Let me guess: You ran them over with the car."

I think of Gumby and wonder where he might fit into the hierarchy of mangled things.

"That would have been better," I say. "At least I'd have myself to blame. But this was my puppy."

"Your puppy? Wow, good work!"

"Have you thought of giving it a rawhide to chew on?" asks an eavesdropping customer, an older woman in a light blue ski jacket with old-school lift tags dangling from the zipper, who might or might not be affiliated with the man auditioning frames. I don't know how to respond to this without saying something regrettable. I mean, she has a point, but I don't need this kind of advice right now, so I nod in her direction and force a thin smile.

"This is a tough one," says Autumn. "I wish I could help you, but these are beyond repair. The lenses are toast. And the plastic, no way to bend that back. If it was just the temple, that would be easy, but the bridge is nearly snapped in half. Best we can do is order you up a new pair, hon. Do you have your prescription?"

"Not on me. Can you get the prescription off the old pair?"

My question is met with another round of belly-laughing that goes on a bit too long before Autumn regains her professionalism and says, simply, "No."

"What do you suggest?"

"Best thing," she says, "would be to reorder from your

optician. I'm assuming you didn't buy them here, as we don't carry this brand."

"Right, the thing is, I'm traveling, I'm on the road, and I need my glasses to drive home."

"Got it," she says. "Let's call your optician and get the prescription so we can get them for you within a week."

"A week?"

"Well, you're right, probably a little longer, maybe ten days, given that tomorrow is Christmas. Then we're closed the next day, and with shipping delays . . . probably safer to assume ten days."

"Oh boy. That's not going to work. I can't stay here that long. Do you have an optician on staff? Maybe they can do a quick exam? Put in a rush order? Or is there someplace else around?"

"So sorry. No—there was a one-hour optical place about an hour away, but it closed a few years ago. And Varun, our optician, is in LA visiting his fiancé's family. They got special passes to Disneyland because his sister works there, and he's off until after the New Year, so let's get a copy of your current prescription," Autumn says. "Even if you don't want to put in an order, we'll at least have it as a backup solution. Assuming it's still good. If not, you might want to start over with a new exam. Another thought is that if it's a straightforward prescription, we might have contacts on hand."

"It's not straightforward," I say. Nothing is ever straightforward with me. "Plus, I can't really deal with contacts. I have trouble getting them in, and then, once I do, they irritate my eyes."

Autumn seems to regard me with pity, like I'm a person with a lot of problems.

"But sure, go ahead," I say. "Call my optician." The plan won't work, but it's not like I have a better plan, other than asking a family member to come pick me up, which is pretty much the last thing I want to do—explain my whereabouts, signal my inability to manage, advertise the bad behavior of my dog.

I begin to casually browse the frames. Perhaps it's time for a new look. But before I even select a pair to consider, Autumn has returned.

"They're closed," she says. "They will reopen on Monday. And by the way, I see the shop is in DC. Is that where you live? I spent a few years there too. Grad school and then after grad school."

"Oh wow, where did you live? What did you study?"

Before she can answer, we are interrupted by one of her colleagues who has a question about a missing order, and Autumn excuses herself to go into the back of the shop. I linger a few minutes, hoping she might return so we can continue the conversation, but more customers have entered and the phone is ringing, and now someone else is calling Autumn's name, and I get that it's time to leave. The Eyes of Gallipolis has tried to do right by me; it's not their fault they have failed.

"Have a happy holiday, everyone!" I cry on my way out. A merry jingle from the spray of bells on the door confirms my departure.

CHAPTER 24

Cryptids

AND THE STRANGER returns," he says in the theatrical tone of a sportscaster, like he's telling listeners that I've just tied the game with a grand slam. "Where to next?" he asks as I climb into the cab and strap on my seatbelt.

"Don't you want to know the outcome?"

"I don't want to pry."

"Well, fine then. I don't really want to talk about it anyway since I'm basically stuck."

He looks at me, a silent invitation to elaborate, which I ignore. I'm still processing the fact that I am effectively stranded here in West Virginia until I can either get a new pair of glasses after the holiday weekends, or find a ride home, retrieve my spare pair of glasses with a slightly weaker but still good enough prescription, and then come back to pick up my car. But in the latter scenario, I don't know what to do with Luna. The answer is, of course, dependent on how I transport myself back to DC. I could probably fly, although I have no idea where the closest airport is, and I know from past experience that certificates will be required to verify that Luna is up-to-date on vaccinations, plus an appropriate travel crate will need to be expensively procured.

(Why do I know this? I once made the poor decision to accompany Richard on a weather assignment in pursuit of an epic Nevada sandstorm. Olivia and Harry agreed to watch Vera, but since we were driving, I decided to bring the dog. I don't know what I was thinking. It was a harebrained thing to do, and it involved some forty hours in the car, but this was before I knew better, or perhaps more to the point, before I could see the ways in which the weather might come to completely dominate our lives. That, and there was a certain romance to the idea, a recapturing of youth, this somewhat reckless adventure. As it happened, the storm was something of a bust, plus our car broke down on our way out of town, failing to start again after we had detoured to a casino and managed to lose $538 at blackjack. It was an ancient Volvo with 140,000 miles—it had been Richard's car before we married—and the mechanic told us it would take a week, maybe even two, to ship the parts. The cost of one to two weeks in a hotel was more than the value of the car, not to mention that we had to get back to Vera, so we sold it for scrap and flew home—but not before having to find a vet who could sort out the paperwork with my vet in DC and issue the appropriate documentation.)

I suppose I could ask Richard to drive to West Virginia and bring my glasses, but that's low on my list of favorite options. Besides, it would require him to leave the basement, not to mention encounter the possibility of weather on the road. The easiest and most logical thing would be for him to overnight the glasses—surely he could figure that out, even if it meant arranging to have the package picked up at the house—although

Susan Coll

with holiday delays, that would still likely take a couple of days. That option would also require telling him where I am—not that he'd care.

"I guess let's head back to the hotel, if you don't mind," I say. "I need to figure out next steps."

"I think your next step is the museum, if I may be so bold. I'm meeting a source there at eleven thirty. Why don't you come with me?"

"A source? What, are you on assignment for the *Cryptozoology Times?*"

"Sure. Yes. Let's say that I am."

I shoot him a look that means, *What the hell?* He shrugs.

"I don't want to interfere with your meeting. But definitely I will stop in and check out the museum before I leave." I'm just assembling words here, then spitting them out. I have no immediate plan to leave, although it goes without saying that I need one, or at least I will once I answer whatever questions I have come here to ask, which are not entirely clear even to me.

"You won't be interfering. In fact, you might find it interesting."

"Who or what are you meeting? Or rather, who or what is your 'source'?" I say, framing the word in air quotes.

"You and your air quotes. Little Miss Sarcasm. I'm meeting with a survivor, if you really want to know."

"That would be *Ms.* Sarcasm, if you will. With a survivor?"

"Of the bridge collapse."

I don't know why I assumed he meant a Holocaust survivor. The legacy of years of Hebrew school, I suppose.

"What's your interest in the bridge collapse anyway?" I ask.

"I don't know what it is you think I do, but I study cryptids."

"And this is meant to be illuminating?"

"Sorry, I figured you might be interested in the moth. I think you indicated as much last night."

"Did I?"

"Maybe not. Maybe it was an assumption."

"And a cryptid is?"

"A cryptid is a mythical creature, or maybe disputed mythical creature is the better description."

"Disputed mythical is redundant."

"Touché. But I guess some are less disputed than others. Like Bigfoot. Or the Loch Ness Monster."

"Wait, so you are saying those are real?"

"I am not saying those are real, but I am saying those are at least more well-known. When you mention the Loch Ness Monster, no one says, 'Who, what?'"

I am about to split another hair, point out the many absurdities in this conversation having to do with one disputed mythical creature being less disputed than another. But I am both tangled in my thoughts and interrupted by the ringing of my phone. The ID tells me it's Vera.

"Just a sec," I tell him. "I need to take this. Hello!" I shout into the receiver. Again I hear only static. "Hello? Hello? Hello?"

There is no reply, and the line goes dead. I remember how this was always happening in the movie about the Mothman. Frequent connectivity problems. Lots of static on the line. I feel a little spooked.

"Spam call?" he says.

"My daughter. She's calling from overseas. Hang on, let me send a text."

Have you sorted out your travel?

"So you were saying?"

"I wasn't saying anything," he replies. "I believe you were about to pick a bone with me about cryptids. But what I was going to say is that the Mothman is likely just a cryptid, albeit less well-known than some of the other more commonly accepted cryptids."

"Okay, sorry to nitpick, but what do you mean by *likely just a cryptid*?"

"Well, there were a lot of . . . shall we say strange goings-on in the area around the time of the Mothman sightings."

"Again, define *strange*. I mean, was the Mothman itself not strange?"

"Yes, but you remember Indrid Cold?"

"Not really. Maybe?"

"From the movie. And the book."

"Which book?"

"The Keel book. *The Mothman Prophecies*."

"Keel? Seriously?"

"Seriously what?"

"I was just dealing with someone named Keel. Officer Keel. On the bridge. I'd forgotten that's the name of the author."

"On what bridge?"

"A different bridge. Never mind. It's too weird. Just a coincidence. So what about this Indrid Cold person?"

"Well, you want to talk about a stranger who comes to town . . . He is the original. Around here anyway. Around the time of the first sighting, there was a sewing machine salesman driving along I-77. His name was Woody Derenberger, and he was heading home after a business trip when he had to pull over to deal with one of the sewing machines rattling around in the back of his truck. He then saw a bunch of lights and thought it was the police, but it was an aircraft of some kind . . . like a you-know-what."

"Like a flying saucer? *Please*."

"Well, nothing that cliché, but whatever you want to call it, it was a UFO. And this man appeared and asked Woody to roll down the window so they could talk. The man said his name was Cold. Indrid Cold. He looked normal, but also . . . kind of not normal. He was wearing a blue suit, or something that looked like a blue suit. But it looked odd. It was made of shiny material. And something about his shoes was weird too. It was like he was trying to fit in and look normal but he didn't really know how to do that."

"And what did he want?"

"Not clear."

"Okay. Sure. And the point of this is?"

"Well, you're the one who asked. But the point is that after Woody reported this to the police, there were apparently a bunch of other very similar sightings."

"Okay, still, really not trying to be sarcastic—I'm asking sincerely . . . Oh shoot, my text didn't go through! Cell service is terrible around here."

"Strange. I'm not having any problems."

"Really? Mine seem to be endless. Maybe I need to run an update or something. Or maybe it's time for a new phone. I'm still not sure I understand why you are telling me this about the sewing machine salesman," I say.

"I'm saying that the story of the Mothman is so intertwined

with UFO sightings that it's not clear if the Mothman is some-how related to the aliens, or if he is a run-of-the-mill cryptid."

"A run-of-the-mill *minor* cryptid."

"Indeed."

"And back to this Indrid Cold character a minute. Did he . . . *say* anything else?"

"Great question. He did. He told Woody not to be fright-ened. He said, 'Do not be afraid.' In a sort of strange, sing songy voice. Again, like trying to be normal but not quite achieving that. And then—this is my favorite part—by way of farewell, he said, famously, 'I'll see you in time.'"

"'I'll see you in time'?"

"Yeah. Kind of brilliant, eh? Like it can mean so many things. For example, this might have been Cold just being awkward, trying to fit in but not entirely saying the right thing. Or he was saying the entirely *right* thing, because time is fluid. So maybe he is saying exactly what he means. They will meet again . . . not in a particular geographic place but rather somewhere in time."

"Backing up, do you believe in all this stuff?"

"I told you, I'm interested in cryptozoology."

"So does that mean, like, you are interested in cryptids, or are you studying the people who believe in cryptids?"

"Yes."

"Not a helpful answer."

"I'll tell you more about that, about what I do, but first you have to tell me something about yourself. Why are you here?"

"What is this, truth or dare?"

"No. It's a game called Human Interaction. I've told you a fair amount about myself, and you have told me close to zero, apart from that you have a sweetheart of a puppy who is also a destructive Tasmanian devil."

"That's a cryptid, too, right?"

"No, that's a real thing."

"No way. It's a cartoon animal. Like a *Looney Tunes* thing."

"It might be that, but it's also a carnivorous marsupial that hails from the island of Tasmania."

"How did I not know that?"

"It's presumably not an important thing for you to know in your day-to-day life, not that I have any sense of what that entails, other than a lot of people attempting to call you, to no avail."

"It's complicated."

"Evidently. Oh, wait . . . I love this program," he says, turning up the radio volume. The road is clogged, and we've been crawling back toward Point Pleasant, getting stuck at nearly every light, and now, when we are finally about to move through the last intersection before the bridge, a fire engine approaches from behind, requiring all traffic to merge to the right. The siren is loud, but not loud enough to drown out the unmistakable voice of my aunt.

"Do you ever listen to this program?" he asks. "*The Storyteller?*"

"I'm familiar."

"She's great. Olivia Oliver. Love that name. Seems like your kind of thing."

"What seems like my kind of thing?" I ask defensively. Then I cringe, remembering the promo yesterday. Why in the world is Olivia bringing this private matter to the radio-listening world? *What if someone you love refuses to let go of the past? To stop asking questions that make no sense? To acknowledge that these* *constant, nonsensical questions are creating problems in the present?* The only reason I can think of is not especially generous. She is protecting herself, throwing me under the bus, telling her version of the story, making it look like I'm somehow unhinged.

"You indicated last night that you are a storyteller, or at least a writer or reader or something storytelling adjacent."

"I did?"

"Do you remember anything about our conversation? A stranger comes to town? John Gardner? Et cetera? Or did the sake erase your memory?"

"Of course I remember."

Luna, who was napping in the back seat of the cab, wakes up and crawls into my lap. Perhaps she recognizes Olivia's voice.

He turns the volume up to compete with the siren. Olivia is midsentence. She has on her show, as a guest, a psychoanalyst, and they are on the subject of obsession.

"Aren't we all story-obsessed, in a variety of ways?" the psychoanalyst asks. "With our own stories, of course, but think of the addictive nature of television dramas, or even gossip."

"Sure," Olivia says, "but this is more extreme in that this person I'm talking about—and it's delicate, because it's someone I know—seems stuck on a single story that happened more than fifty years ago. She continues to ask questions and is never satisfied with the answers."

"Sometimes the questions asked tell us more about the person asking them than the answers do," the psychoanalyst says.

"That's true. It's like she's always searching. But for what? Sometimes it's not even clear what it is she wants to know. It's like nonsense. It's like asking: 'How blue is a mile?'"

"How blue is a mile!" Ingram says. "That's a good one!"

I'm trying to tamp down my anger. This is patently absurd. My questions about how my parents died are nonsense? Granted, I understand that my queries sometimes wind up focusing on the moth. But has Olivia ever considered this might be a way of avoiding the more painful subject of how I became orphaned?

As bad as this is, an even more alarming thought occurs to me. What if I wind up in her book? I can't bear to think about this, or to listen to another word. I lean over and turn the volume down.

"If you don't mind, I have a headache." I am using this as an excuse, but now that I say it, I realize it's true. Just a dull throb that has come on all of a sudden.

"Whatever you say. Although I'm curious. I mean, who isn't stuck on a story? Everyone in this town is still stuck on a story, for good reason, especially those who lost loved ones in the bridge collapse. What's wrong with that? It's a way to remember the past. As long as it's not ruining their lives, as she says."

"Exactly."

"If you feel up to it when we get back to the hotel, come with me to the museum. We can bring Luna."

"I'll see," I say. "But I'll probably pass. I need to figure out how to get home."

"We can worry about that later. I'm telling you, you need to go. Not going is kind of like going to the beach and not playing mini golf."

"I go to the beach all the time and I never play mini golf."

"Well, there's your problem right there," he says.

"I didn't know I had a problem."

The fire trucks move past us, but by now the light has again cycled to red. We wait a few minutes longer before crossing back over the bridge. I look out onto the still waters and try to blot out thoughts of Christmas presents bobbing in the wake of the collapse.

CHAPTER 25

A Brief Interlude about Hair

AS LITTLE KIDS, Samantha and I both sported pixie cuts. We pleaded with Olivia to let our hair grow out long, but she refused to budge on this position. She told us she was afraid of long hair, worried that it would wind up full of knots. About this she wasn't wrong. Once I was old enough to push back convincingly, I let mine grow out, and it wound up so badly tangled that the only solution was of the surgical sort. Olivia stood over me with scissors, trying to isolate the clot, which she then cut with a snipping sound that is triggering to remember—this little piece of me, now excised. She then deposited it in my fist, victorious, a little souvenir of me that looked like something a cat might cough up.

Even as an adult my hair hasn't become much easier to manage, but I still wear it long. It offers me protection in a way that is difficult to articulate but might have something to do with being able to cover my scars. Samantha continues to boldly wear her hair short, and I'm full of admiration for the way she looks—stylish and confident, without the need for a cloak.

Knots or no knots, this short-hair mandate seemed overly harsh, an infringement on my autonomy, not that I had the vocabulary, as a child, to describe it thus. Olivia is one of the most progressive women I know, but she has a hard edge—or maybe it's just that she lacks a soft touch—and is not the sort who would pause to consider the effect her edict might have on my behavior all these years later, today, as I find myself in some quiet rebellion, unable to adopt a style most would consider more befitting a woman my age.

A defiant mess is how it looks right now, and I feel Olivia's silent judgment.

I've agreed to meet Ingram in the lobby in five minutes, so I run a brush through my hair, pull it into a ponytail, then change my mind and let it back out. I'm not preening so much as simply freshening up. A little lipstick is not meant to be suggestive of caring what I look like, because all I am doing is walking across the street to go to a campy museum about a minor cryptid with a cryptozoologist and his "source." Nor is putting on a clean pair of jeans and changing into one of my favorite go-to sweaters—a beige striped Pendleton that I've had for nearly ten years. I take a quick look in the mirror, and even with my blurred vision I see a hint of my white t-shirt peeking through. Closer inspection reveals a rather large hole just below the right shoulder, and it looks, suspiciously, like the work of a moth.

CHAPTER 26

The Mothman Museum

HAVE YOU CONSIDERED wearing a hat?" Ingram asks.

I'm reminded of how bitter cold it is as I stand in front of the hotel, my hair blowing wild in a sharp wind that feels like it's moving in two different directions.

"Useful items. They keep the head warm in winter," he adds.

"Hilarious," I say. "Do you do stand-up?"

"Funny you should mention. I do an open mic every Thursday in Pittsburgh."

"Seriously? Are you from Pittsburgh? Oh, wait, Carnegie Mellon."

"No. And yes."

"Okay, well, whatever that means. Save your words for the open mic. And yes, hats are great. But I'm on a roll, losing things left and right. First my glasses—not that I lost them technically, but they are nevertheless lost—and now I can't find my hat or gloves."

"Those situations might be related."

"That's true. But it's also possible that I left them at the restaurant last night. I'll give them a call later, when they open. I asked the young man at the registration desk if maybe he'd seen them, but he said no."

Luna puts her paws on Ingram's chest as he drops to his knees, shifting her too-big puppy paws to his shoulders. Now they are nose to nose.

"You two seem to be hitting it off," I say, which is clearly quite an understatement. "And who is that kid anyway? He looks too young to be working at the hotel."

"That's Alma's nephew, Ian. He's filling in for the day while she does her last-minute Christmas shopping."

"Got it. He seems like a sweet boy. Christmas shopping—that's something I sort of forgot to do." I don't know why I say this. I have no reason to procure gifts. Olivia and Harry think gift-giving is too . . . something. Commercial, perhaps. Or bourgeois. I'm not sure what their objection is, but growing up I had Christmas envy, jealous of my friends who had Secret Santas and Secret Elves, stockings over the fireplace, stacks of presents beneath the tree. Even most of my Jewish friends had parents who bestowed gifts at Chanukah, sometimes one per night. My aunt and uncle were generous. I had everything I needed, and it seems petty to gripe about this particular idiosyncrasy: their refusal to give in to what they considered holiday hype.

"Well, perfect then. The museum has a gift shop. You can get anything you need. Including a hat."

⋈   ⋈   ⋈

He's not kidding. The museum, at least at first sight, appears to be one gigantic gift shop filled with moth-related tchotchkes. Coffee mugs, key chains, books, t-shirts, notebooks, posters, buttons, caps, and pretty much anything a person could think of, imprinted with the image of the Mothman.

Again I am reminded that this thing that has haunted me for decades is, for most people, nothing but a shopping opportunity. One with spectacular markdowns, to boot; over in the far corner is a rack where everything on it has been reduced by half. This poor moth, I think, and the many ways in which it has been appropriated. If it was on Twitter, it might have a few things to say.

Pushing more deeply into the moth bazaar, I see maps, flashlights, pennants, a dog bowl. Looking up, I see a bunch of framed movie stills hanging on the wall. There is Laura Linney, the actress who stars in the Mothman movie, dressed in her police uniform. She looks both fierce and fetching in this costume, with the most perfect hair I've ever seen.

Her first appearance in the movie occurs when Richard Gere, aka John Klein, finds himself in that trippy, bendy time-space vortex that leads him to knock on the door of the first house he sees after he winds up, inexplicably, on the bridge. The possibly deranged, possibly visionary man who owns the house corrals him into a pink-tiled shower and puts a gun to his head. Laura Linney appears to defuse the situation, to calm everyone the eff down. She has such a sweet disposition, commanding yet exuding warmth and wisdom. I want to be her best friend.

The man with the gun is explaining that John Klein has

shown up three times in a row in the middle of the night, to which Richard Gere says:

"Something's very wrong here. I don't know these people. I have never been here before. I'm from DC."

I have a moment of déjà vu, or double déjà vu, since I've seen this movie more than once, but then I trace the memory to Vera, propped up in bed, watching this movie, this line of dialogue audible through her door. The memory is the memory of an absence. The absence of us talking about this, ever. Sure, Vera knows my parents died in a bridge collapse in West Virginia, but she is unaware of my unspoken rift with Olivia over her refusal to talk about it. And Vera doesn't know anything about the moth, other than what she saw in that movie. What this says about me and my parenting, whether I am causing family history to repeat by not talking about the things we need to talk about, is something I've not thought about until this moment.

In another photo I see Richard Gere in the newsroom of the newspaper where his character works, which is the same newspaper that employs my husband, notwithstanding the fact that he now works remotely from the basement of our house. Although John Klein is not my husband, Richard Klein—the former being a fictional character—and I am already aware of this coincidence, each time I am reminded of this and see the resemblance, it fells me all over again.

I pick up a t-shirt with a campy decal of the moth and consider whether it would be a good gift for Vera, or if it would creep her out. Before I am able to decide, Ingram is at my side.

"I found a good hat for you," he says, handing me a pink Mothman beanie.

"Pink, eh?"

"Now that you mention it, you seem more of a military green."

"That's true, but it doesn't sound like a compliment."

"It's possible that it is, but I suggest we continue this discussion later. Right now, let's go to the museum."

"I thought this was the museum?"

"This is the gift shop. The museum is in the back," he says. He is holding Luna's leash, and he leads us both toward a register at the far end of the shop. Again, I marvel at how no one has objected to the presence of a dog.

Ingram covers the modest entrance fee for us both, and I pay separately for the hat, which I decide I'll give to Vera. Then we push through a turnstile into the museum. It's not at all what I expected, not that I had any particular vision of how it might appear. It's a large, bright room filled with photographs and newspaper clips, with life-size replicas of the Mothman, and more sundry movie paraphernalia. An unexpected Mothman archive tucked into the back of a moth-themed gift shop, all of it meticulously assembled. I didn't know it until now, but I've been waiting all my life to walk into this very room. This thing I have had locked up inside me that has been regarded as some dark, terrible secret, is not only real but has been turned into a shrine.

The entire history of the Mothman, of the bridge collapse, of the weird UFO stuff Ingram was just telling me about, is all here, in row after row of display cases filled with newspaper clippings. Unfortunately, without my glasses, I can only make out the parts that are in large print, which means mostly just the headlines.

I brace myself and begin to read.

"Quick Trip to Store Meant Gone Forever."

"They Didn't Make the Game."

"Bridge Cracked at 4:30."

"I'm Just Going onto the Bridge': Dad's Last Report from Taxi."

"Divers Begin Search for Untold Loss."

"Eight More Bodies Recovered on Sunday; One Yet Unidentified."

I want to read every word of every article preserved beneath the glass, hoping to find something about my parents. I'm staring hard, moving my face closer to, then farther from, the glass case, trying to find some sweet spot where things might come into focus. A hand on my shoulder startles me.

"Easy, stranger. I didn't mean to scare you. It's just me," Ingram says. He is with an elegant, older woman, who wears her long grey hair in a braid.

"I want you to meet my friend. This is Cynthia Rodriguez," he says.

"I'm Cassie," I say, extending my hand to shake, a gesture that feels weirdly formal in a setting where a giant inflatable moth dangles over our heads.

But Cynthia extends a hand, and when I take it in mine, it is warm and soft.

"Lovely to meet you," she says. "Ingy told me all about you." This is such an odd thing to say, that all I manage is a mumbled response. What he might have told her, I cannot begin to imagine.

"Turns out we had some miscommunication," he says. "My fault, I'm sure. Cynthia thought we were going to grab lunch—she hasn't eaten yet—and since it's just about that time, we're going to head over to the café. I figured you'd like to join, *Cassie*." He overemphasizes each syllable, clearly amused to have discovered that I have a name. "What's it short for?"

"Who says it's short for anything?"

He gives me a look.

"Constance," I say. "Maybe you two could go ahead to lunch and I'll join you in a bit? I just got started here."

"I think you should join us," he says. This seems presumptuous. I met this man only last night, and here he is, giving orders. But something in his voice tells me there's a reason he wants me to come.

"I want to read a few things here, although without my glasses . . ."

"We'll come back," he says. He sounds decisive, and decisive is what I need right now. That plus some lunch, so I follow them out the door, the faux guide dog leading the way.

CHAPTER 27

Condiments

IT IS EASY to underestimate the power of perspective, how the slightest shift in point of view casts a situation in a very different light. Two days ago, I was a woman stewing in my too-quiet house, tiptoeing around my mercurial husband, sometimes quite literally; I would take off my shoes when I walked through the kitchen so he wouldn't be disturbed by my footsteps overhead. He didn't have a temper—I might have welcomed an occasional flash of anger since that would at least have given me something, in the moment, to address. But in the catatonic state that was our marriage as of late, it was simpler to leave him be in the basement, to not disturb him at his bank of screens, hunched over his keyboard, tapping out the weather news:

A PASSING STORM WILL BRING ICY RAIN TO THE NORTH. THEN POSSIBLE SNOW.

This seemed to make him happy. Domestic interactions ranging from the subject of our marriage to banal inquiries about dinner? Not so much. Who even knew where Elaine fit into his happiness quotient. Or if she did at all. Meantime, I was sinking. It was as if the weather had finally won. I was becoming paralyzed by inertia, buried beneath the weight of his stupid weather haikus.

Now the world looks very different here in the Moth Café, accompanied by a scholar of minor cryptids and his so-called source, although that might have something to do with the fact that I cannot properly see.

Ingram leads us to a table in the corner and asks us each what we would like to eat. I'm too embarrassed to admit that I'm unable to read the menu on a chalkboard above the counter, so I say I'll have whatever he is having. Cynthia says that sounds perfect, and she'll have that too.

"Does that mean you are prepared to flex? Flex Friday, perhaps?"

I remember my steak envy last night and tell him yes, Flex Friday. How did he know?

At the counter he engages in some light banter with the woman from this morning. Everyone seems to know him. They talk first about college football, then about some man named Dennis who works at the local gas station and just slipped on the ice and broke his arm. Then they switch to the subject of weather, of all things, and I hear the words *cold front*, and I hear the word *snow*, but I can't hear anything that comes after that because Cynthia puts her hand on top of mine and begins to speak.

"Ingram tells me you are just passing through town. Are you here as a tourist?" she asks. "Or are you here for a reason?"

I decide to keep it simple. "I'm just passing through," I say.

"Ah, I thought maybe you had some personal interest in the bridge collapse, that maybe you'd lost someone."

"Interesting. Why would you think that?" I feel a little spooked, but then, it's a low-hanging fruit of a guess. There are surely countless family members of the departed, as well as of survivors, who come to this town to pay their respects. Besides, what is wrong with me? Why am I shutting down on—never mind interrogating—this lovely woman?

"I just assumed," she says. "Ingram called me first thing this morning. He said I should join you both for lunch, so I figured . . ."

"He did?" I glance back over at him. He is now staring up at the menu. "He told me you were a source, although I don't know what that means. Or what he does."

"Well, I am a source, but we've already spoken for hours. I'm not sure I have anything left to tell him. He seemed to want me to meet you."

"Do you know why?"

"He probably thought we'd like each other. That's Ingram for you. Such a friendly sort."

"I only met him last night. And I'm not really here. I'm not supposed to be here, is what I mean. I'm just passing through, and I have to get home. My daughter is on her way from Barcelona," I overshare. "And now I'm stuck due to my optical situation."

"He mentioned that. To be honest, I don't like to talk about this whole thing anymore. I've tried to put it behind me. I lost my husband and my daughter in the bridge collapse. But his work is important. And if he thought we should talk, then we should talk."

This man seems to know more about me and my intentions than I know myself.

"He thought we should talk? About what?"

"He didn't say. I mean, he didn't say explicitly that we should talk. I just assumed he wanted us to talk. But we don't have to talk. Or we can talk about something else, like the weather."

"Please, no. Anything but the weather."

"What are you two talking about?" Ingram is juggling three iced teas while holding Luna's leash, and he sets them on the table without spilling a drop.

"We're talking about talking," I volunteer.

"That sounds scintillating. Meanwhile, I was talking to Maggie over at the counter about the weather. She says there's a storm, something they are calling a bomb cyclone, moving in from the east. Also from the north. Basically, two storms are converging."

"A bomb?" Cynthia asks.

"Not an actual bomb. That's the name for when a storm gains strength quickly and grabs a bunch of moisture from the winds. Basically, it means it's going to snow. A lot."

"How do you know all this?" I ask, as if the weather is a proprietary thing that belongs to Richard alone.

"I heard it on the radio while you were dealing with your glasses, but also I was just getting an update from Maggie. She's got the Weather Channel on back in the kitchen," he says.

"Wait, so you are saying there's a huge snowstorm headed this way?"

"That's what I said. Yes."

"So I'm kind of double-stuck?"

"I guess you could say that. But not my fault. I didn't orchestrate the circumstances."

"Sorry," I say. "I didn't mean to sound accusatory. I'm . . .

surprised." I'm so used to Richard advising me about the weather that for a brief, misdirected second, I'm annoyed with him for not warning me, notwithstanding the fact that he doesn't know I'm here. "How much snow are they predicting?"

"Two feet, maybe more. Could be less."

I know I ought to panic at this news, but I think of my hotel suite with its beautiful view of the river, of the giant bag of kibble that ought to keep Luna fed for weeks, of this curious man who has attached himself to my dog, of my mangled glasses, and wonder if this approaching storm is a gift in disguise.

We have momentarily run out of words. The only sound is of liquid rushing through paper straws as we sip our iced teas, until Ingram speaks.

"Cynthia, do you mind if I tell Cassie your story?" he asks.

"Please," she says. "I think it's important to keep the story alive, but please stop me if it's too much."

Rather than begin to talk, she turns silent.

Ingram jumps in. "So, Cassie, the last time Cynthia and I met, she told me about her experience. She was on the bridge, driving home from visiting friends in Huntington—that's in Ohio, on the other side of the river—when it happened."

"When what happened?" I ask. I mean, I know about the various things that happened, but I don't know if he's talking about the bridge or the moth.

"We were all in the car," she says, taking over. "Me and George and our daughter. And suddenly it started sort of swaying. Then, sort of . . . shaking. Kind of like an earthquake. And then, I know this will sound weird, but a kind of sliding . . . like a piece of the roadway opened up and we glided right off into the water. I know some people said they fell, or dropped, but not us. It was like we drove into the water. And there was this noise. You've never heard anything so loud in your life, a gnashing sound. Metal grinding on metal. Like the noise a monster would make, like Godzilla. But do you know what the most surprising thing was?"

I can't even begin to imagine, given what she's described. I shake my head no.

"It was the quiet right after. First, all that noise, and then . . . silence for the longest time. What is the saying—the calm before the storm? Except in this case, the calm was right after, although only for a moment. After this terrible, terrible quiet, there was screaming, shouting, total commotion. But it was that brief jag of silence that still haunts me. I always have the radio going in my house, in the car, wherever. I can't bear the silence.

"And you know the other thing I remember?"

"What?" I ask, still processing what's she's said. I'm free-associating, or maybe disassociating, thinking of the cello music I'd been listening to while I drove across the other bridge, the way it sounded like cold grey steel.

"The cold water. It was unbearably cold. It started coming into the car. The window was partially open. I don't have any memory of opening it—I was a smoker back then, so maybe I had rolled it down? And maybe that enabled me to get out? I don't really remember that detail. But I do remember trying to get them both out. George seemed to have blacked out. I opened his door somehow—I don't even know how I did that, it's a total blur—but I remember that he didn't move. And my daughter . . ." She stops and takes a long slow sip of iced tea. "I got her out, but I couldn't save her."

I don't know how to respond, but after a moment I tell her how sorry I am and ask how she got to safety.

"I started to swim. Then I clung to something, a piece of the bridge maybe? And then a boat came by and picked me up. They told me how lucky I was, the temperature was something like forty-four degrees. There weren't a lot of survivors. I guess people lost consciousness pretty fast from the cold. I also remember I was starting to get kind of goofy. Like you know how people say they saw a white tunnel or saw God or whatever? It wasn't like that exactly. It was more like I was hallucinating, dreaming. I remember walking down the hallway at my daughter's elementary school. She was wearing her Blue Bird uniform. She so wanted to be a Camp Fire Girl."

She looks back down at the iced tea, which is now empty, and pointlessly swirls the straw. We are all silent for a few minutes.

"Can I get you more?" I ask as if more iced tea will numb the pain of what she is telling us, will make this beautiful, terrible image of a girl in a Blue Bird uniform somehow less tragic. But then, it shouldn't be less tragic—this is the point of telling the story. To keep her daughter's memory alive. In fact, now that I've heard this story, I'm pretty sure this Blue Bird will live with me for the rest of my days.

She shakes her head no. She's had enough iced tea.

"I'm sorry to stir all this up again," I add.

"No, it's okay. It's helpful to talk about it."

"Where were you going when you were on the bridge, if you don't mind my asking?"

"Like Ingram said, we were on the way back from Huntington—that's in Ohio, on the other side of the bridge," she repeats. "We'd been visiting friends, and then I stopped at a toy store in Gallipolis. I'd ordered some presents for my nieces—pogo sticks—and the shop had called earlier that day to tell me they were in. This was before you had your internet shopping with overnight delivery and your drones and whatnot," she interjects. "The toy shop is long gone, which is too bad."

"I'm sorry," I say, like this is my fault, or at least the fault of my generation, our online shopping habits having led to the collapse of this particular franchise, of brick-and-mortar shops generally.

"You know, back when you had to get in your car and go fetch things yourself."

"I got it," I say. "How old were your nieces?" I don't know why I ask this other than to steer the conversation toward something possibly more upbeat, which turns out to be an epic fail.

"They were little angels, those girls. They still are. Well, one of them is. One is gone."

"Gone?" I hope, for a brief moment, she means *gone* as in *moved out of town*.

"Drugs," she says. "Started in middle school and never got better. Lord knows we tried everything. But Lizzie is with us. Married with kids, probably closer to your age now—and all of them, they buy everything online. Always on their phones! I'm not good with remembering everyone's age—I've got sixteen nieces and nephews. Well, no, now that's thirteen. An unlucky number. The drugs got to some of them too. But those girls were young at the time of the accident. I'm going to guess around six and ten. They are George's sister's kids, the oldest of the entire clan, and he adored them."

"I'm so sorry," I say stupidly. I have no shortage of questions, possibly too insensitive to ask. *Do you remember the sensation of falling? What was it like to be trapped, even for a moment, in the car? What kind of car was it, model and year? Did they recover the car? Were you injured? Did you know anyone else involved in the crash? What was the weather that day? Did you happen to see my parents?*

I want to know those answers, but what I really want to know is whether, in the weeks and days preceding the crash, she had seen the giant red-eyed moth.

The waitress appears with three platters of turkey and mashed potatoes, drowning in pools of gravy, with cranberry sauce on the side, before I can get any questions out other than one to do with Ingram's meal selection.

"What is this, Thanksgiving?"

"No, it's Christmas Eve."

"Ah, so it is," I say. I should be grateful for this holiday meal, I realize, because it is likely all I'm going to get this year.

Christmas music pours through the speakers, accompanied by the sounds of our silverware clanking, of chewing and swallowing.

"You might be wondering what happened to those pogo sticks," Cynthia says.

"Weirdly, I am," I confess. My mind tends to seize on odd details like this. Perhaps it's the reporter in me.

"It was strange that amid everything that happened, I kept thinking about those pogo sticks. And you're not going to believe this, but they did survive. When they dredged the car, there they were, still in the trunk. My brother is pretty handy, and he managed to oil them, polish them . . . Whatever he did to them, they wound up working just fine. My niece still has them both. It's not like we keep them preserved as shrines . . .

They're still being used, now by the grandchildren. Somehow keeping them in use . . . well . . ." She trails off, and I worry that she's going to cry.

She recovers and continues. "It's kind of silly. I'd be happy to buy them new pogo sticks—they make much better ones these days, no doubt—but it makes me happy to see the old ones. I almost lost my temper once when Alicia, that's the niece who passed, couldn't find hers. It turns out she'd left it at her friend's house. No harm done, but I totally overreacted."

"Oh, I get it," I say. "People get attached to things, especially when they have to do with important events. Something similar just happened to me with an old toy, in fact. My aunt and uncle have this blue plastic . . . thing. It's a child's toy. You sit on it and hop, holding on to the head."

"Hoppity?" she says. "Yes, I remember it."

"You had one too?"

"No . . . Well, now that you mention it, I think my daughter had one. It was orange."

"Mine was blue."

"Ha, like that blue one that washed up onshore," she says.

"What do you mean?" That she might mean what I think she might mean is confounding. Then again, it could make total sense, now that I know what I know about the toy: that my parents might have bought it for me on this trip, that it might have been in their car before washing up onshore. Even so, this is quite the coincidence.

"I mean after the accident. I remember such details. Well, some of them anyway. Some of them I think I've blocked, and the doctors tell me that I likely passed out for a minute or two, but I do remember the horrible sound of the cracking. It was the loudest sound I've ever heard, earsplitting, painful, sort of atonal, hard to describe other than it hurt . . ."

I start to worry about her mental acuity, listening to her begin to repeat the story all over again, but maybe it's a thing she needs to do.

"And I remember how cold the water was, so cold that sometimes, when I'm cold, I think of that level of cold and know I can survive whatever I'm experiencing. And I remember that blue plastic toy sitting on the shore. I stared at it while they took care of me. I was in the back of the ambulance, and they wrapped me in blankets and were taking my vitals, but I could see it out the window, like it was a little bit of normalcy, a child's toy. I'll never forget it. It was like we locked eyes."

"You locked eyes? You aren't suggesting that it was somehow alive or supernatural or anything, are you?" I've heard so much weird stuff in the last few hours that I'll believe just about anything.

"Oh goodness, no. It had these eyes, plastic or inked in, I really don't remember that part. They were normal eyes. Not anything spooky, not like those eyes on that terrifying moth."

"Wait, what? You saw the moth?" I am trying not to shriek, but I am shrieking.

Instead of answering my question, Cynthia changes the subject. "This turkey, it's a little bit dry," she remarks.

"What you need is ketchup," Ingram says.

"Ketchup on turkey?" I ask.

"What are you, anti-ketchup?"

"Not at all. Since you asked, I'm a ketchup enthusiast. I just never thought to put it on turkey. Also, I mean, it's already waterlogged with gravy."

How we have so smoothly transitioned from death to condiments is beyond me, but it is also a relief. It's like going down a dark hole of internet sleuthing about the bridge accident, then clicking on an advertisement for boots.

"Oh, just you wait," he says. "Hey, Maggie, you got any ketchup?" he yells toward the kitchen.

"You got it, hon," comes a disembodied voice from behind the wall of the counter.

A moment later a bottle of ketchup is set in front of us. Cynthia turns it over and squeezes. Ingram locks eyes with me, as if daring me to try, so I follow suit.

"Okay, not bad," I say. "No offense to the chef, but this isn't the best ketchup."

"See? I figured you'd be a ketchup snob."

"Good grief, you're the one who was fussing about maple syrup this morning."

"Well, given that you're apparently a connoisseur, tell us: What's the best ketchup?"

"Have you ever had ketchup from India?" I ask.

"No, but have you ever had ketchup from Poland?"

"I have not, but I've had ketchup from Japan."

"They have ketchup in Japan?"

"Is this a serious question?"

"Um . . . It is, but why? Are you trying to ketchup-shame me?"

"No, I assumed, since you seem to be some sort of foodie, that you knew ketchup probably originated in Asia. Like it started out as a kind of fishy, briny situation. And now there's Tonkatsu sauce, which is sort of similar but also has Worcestershire sauce and maybe a little oyster sauce too. My brother lives there now, in Tokyo. My brother-*cousin*," I explain, although I don't know why. Ingram ignores this clarification and instead homes in on the ketchup.

"I like that you assumed that about me, that I'm a food snob."

"Yes, apologies. I agree that was a bit presumptuous. And yet it seems you are."

"I'm guessing you are not as condiment-savvy in DC though. Probably just your straight-up whatever it is you dip your hundred-dollar steaks into."

"Okay, there are so many things to say about that, but the first is how do you know I live in Washington? I mean, I told you I'm from the region, but I never mentioned DC. Are you stalking me?" I don't feel, in my bones, like this guy is up to anything nefarious, and yet it also creeps me out more than a little bit. Did he peek into my wallet? Inquire about me at the registration desk?

"Um, your license plates? On the car? I noticed it's an Audi, I might add."

"Oh, right," I say. "But that's still kind of presumptuous. How do you know that's even my car? And what about the Audi?"

He looks at me like this is the most moronic question ever asked. Which I guess it is, given that mine is the only other vehicle parked in front of the hotel, and we seem to be the only guests.

"Fancy car. I didn't notice it until we got back from the optician. But also, no big deal, it's just that in the movie about the Mothman, the main character—his name was John Klein—he also drove an Audi."

"Did he? I mean, I don't really remember the movie. I saw it once a million years ago," I lie.

"The scene when he first gets to West Virginia. When his car breaks down on the bridge and he has no idea where he is. He's in an Audi."

"Hmm. Weird. But meaningless," I say as if I ever think anything meaningless. In fact, I think this is extremely weird and possibly quite meaning*ful*. I don't know how I missed that detail, or what it means. "Still, that's really presumptuous. Hundred-dollar steaks. *Please*."

"You've got your Capital Grille or what have you. Right? You are driving a fancy car, you live in Washington, you have this designer puppy—"

"My dog is a rescue, and my car is a hand-me-down," I protest. "Also, I'm pretty sure Capital Grille is a Boston chain. And I know this is not the point, but DC is a great city for food. Lots of new restaurants opening all the time, test kitchens, ghost kitchens— Have you been to Union Market?"

"I have, as it happens. A friend who teaches at Georgetown took me to lunch there once."

Cynthia interrupts. "Since they're predicting bad weather this afternoon, I'd like to get home before it starts snowing. So, if you still want to, let's go out to the TNT area. I'll show you where I saw the moth."

"The *what* area?" is all I can think to say.

CHAPTER 28

TNT

THE CAB OF Ingram's truck is too high for Cynthia to reach without assistance, even with her foot on the running board. When Ingram gives her a boost, hoisting her from beneath the shoulders, then settling her into the front seat, I worry that he is going to snap her in two. But she's sturdier than she appears, and he seems to know what he is doing.

Luna and I pile into the back, and we set off along a road that hugs the river. We pass through residential neighborhoods, everything alight, twinkling with holiday cheer, even in daylight. Or so I think. The details are mostly a myopic blur set against the backdrop of an ominously dark sky.

"Here!" Cynthia says after a couple of miles. "Turn!"

Ingram is driving fast. He hits the brake hard and makes a sudden, sharp pivot to the right. Our ride turns bumpy as we turn onto a gravel road lined by trees on either side. Another mile or so, and the sky seems to grow even darker, or maybe it's just that the forest thickens, blocking what little sunlight there was to begin with.

Luna crawls into my lap, and I wonder if she is getting spooked.

"Where are we going, you guys?" I ask, trying to hide the worry in my voice.

"To the TNT area," he says cheerfully, like we're headed to an amusement park. "It's about a mile up the road."

"You still haven't told me what that is."

"I forget this is your first time here. It's an old munitions storage facility."

"Why?"

"Why which part? Why is it an old munitions storage facility, or why are we going?"

"Why to both."

"Ever heard of World War II?"

"Very funny."

"Well, it's not funny, really. This was where they used to store the TNT. Then it became a Superfund site. Deservedly so. They are still decontaminating. Or not."

"Oh, that's comforting."

"And we're going because that's where Cynthia saw the moth."

"Here, off to the right! Stop!" Cynthia instructs before I have the chance to process what he's said, which is perhaps a good thing because my instinct is either to insist on turning the truck around or to let out a primordial scream.

Ingram makes another sharp turn, like we are in a chase scene in a thriller. He then puts the truck in Park, perpendicular to a chain strung between two concrete poles, blocking our entrance to the road.

"This is it," she says. "Not right here, but a few feet in. Lots of other people saw it here too. Not all of them were in this exact spot, but in this part of the woods."

"It's right out of central casting, right?" Ingram says to me. "Like, you couldn't make this place up. Deep dark woods, munitions . . ."

"It does look haunted," I agree. I suspect *haunted* is not the right word, but since no one corrects me, I continue.

"What were you even doing here, Cynthia?"

"Oh, it was a big hangout spot. You know, where people came to fool around. But once it got a reputation for being the place to see the Mothman, it kind of became a thing. Honestly, I didn't believe any of that nonsense until I saw it myself."

"So you came out here looking for it?" I don't know why I ask this, but I'm doing some quick mental math, and she would have been in her midtwenties or so, a little old to be necking in the car—or maybe I've lost my sense of fun.

"Well . . . I don't talk about this much, but I'm an old woman, and George is long gone, and I'm starting to feel that bottling up secrets only makes it all worse."

Amen to that, I want to say.

"Me and George, we married too young. We'd been high school sweethearts, got hitched right away, and next thing I knew I had a baby. I loved George, but he was the only man I'd ever known, and then I met someone. It was a terrible time for me—and I lost my mind for this other man. It was hard to imagine anyone being attracted to me after I'd had a baby— George had certainly lost interest—and me and Rodrigo, we were sneaking around like kids.

"So I was in a bad spot in terms of talking about the moth,

because I wasn't supposed to be there in the first place. Sometimes I thought it was my penance—to have to live with the consequences of what I did. I'm a God-fearing woman, and I thought I'd brought on the bridge collapse by having an affair. I know that's extreme punishment, but truly, for years, that's what I thought."

Oof, this is so freighted I don't know where to begin, but I can't not respond.

"I don't think that's what happened, Cynthia. I hope you're not still beating yourself up. These things happen."

"I know that now. That's why I'm able to tell you this."

"What do you remember about it? About the moth, I mean?"

"Oh my lord, it was huge. Like, seven feet tall. It was grey . . . well, really sort of a grey black, with bright red eyes. Like they were almost on fire, those eyes. When we first saw him, he was wobbling, or it looked like he was wobbling. I wondered if it was a man who was drunk. But then, the muscles on the legs, those were not human, I'm telling you. And it started running surprisingly fast, and then all of a sudden, it took flight . . .

"One of the weirdest things, though, was that it just sort of lifted off. It didn't flap . . . It kind of went . . . *whoosh*." She extends her arm, then raises it, keeping her palm parallel to the ground to demonstrate. "It was remarkably graceful for a creature that heavy. That was the thing that made the least sense."

"*That* was the thing that made the least sense?"

"I mean aerodynamically. From a technical point of view. That was weird, for sure, but the main thing I can't get out of my head even all these years later was the eyes. They were . . . otherworldly. I don't know what other word to use."

"And this is where you were when you saw it?"

"Not exactly. We were about five hundred feet down the trail," she says, pointing into the woods. "Back then you could drive a little farther along, but now they've closed the road to cars. So we were in the car, and I had my eyes closed for a bit. That's how I kiss." She pauses, like she's summoning the kiss. "Well, it *was* how I kissed. It's been a while.

"Then, when I opened my eyes, I saw it . . . him . . . wobbling, running, then lifting up. Even once it was in the air, I could still see those eyes. They were so bright they lit up the sky like headlights, or spotlights, or even like a UFO, not that I believe in UFOs. I don't, for the record. And I'm saying that with no disrespect for people who do believe in UFOs, even though I don't believe in UFOs, because I just want you to know that I'm not a nutcase. Not that I think people who believe in UFOs are nutcases."

"I get what you're saying," says Ingram.

"Right. And a lot of people, some of my friends, they are pretty sure they saw weird stuff around that same time. And they think one thing begat another. First the Mothman and then the next thing you know there's this Indrid Cold character showing up and saying weird stuff like 'I'm a searcher' and 'I'll see you in time.'"

"A searcher?"

"Yes," Ingram says. "That was another thing Indrid supposedly said about himself."

"Then the creature turned around and came right back at

us . . . not in a menacing way, just like it was switching directions. That's when I heard the sound. Kind of like a roar, but
not a roar. I know that's not helpful, but it's hard to describe."

"Was it like the sound of the bridge when it started to fail?"
I ask. It's probably a stupid question, but I'm aiming to crack
this cold case by stringing together such previously overlooked
connections.

"No, not at all. This was different," she says with certainty.
"The bridge sound was awful, but it was at least of this earth,
comprehensible. But this . . . I've never heard a sound like
this. Not before, not after. It was deafening. Then it just
went . . . *whoosh*. And it was gone."

"Did it do anything . . . bad?"

"No."

"Did it say anything?"

"No."

"Did it try to attack?"

"No. Except I wound up with an infection right after."

"What kind of infection?" I assume she is referring an STD
she got from whatever else she might have been doing in that
car, but I'm wrong.

"Conjunctivitis."

"An eye infection?"

"Yes, there was a lot of conjunctivitis going around town
at that time," Ingram explains. "Except it seemed to be more
from people who had been around the UFOs than around the
moth, so that's part of what makes Cynthia's story especially
compelling."

"Why?" I ask, not sure what exactly I'm asking.

"Well, it depends on what you believe," Ingram says, "but one theory is the eye infections were caused by radiation from the spacecraft."

This is wackadoodle stuff. Or is it? It all seems perfectly normal: We are having a serious conversation involving the finer points of paranormal science.

"Spacecrafts are radioactive?"

"Well, sure," he says. "That's why they are so frequently seen hanging around nuclear power plants. They're recharging. Also, *spacecraft* is the plural of *spacecraft*."

"Seriously? You're correcting my grammar? Fine. How do *spacecraft* recharge? Wirelessly?" I think I'm asking a funny question, but Ingram says yes.

We are still in the truck, idling. He now moves the car a few feet forward, right up to the chain that blocks the rest of the road that leads to the trail. He cuts the ignition.

"There's another hypothesis," he says, opening his door.

"Wait, where are you going?"

"Now we walk."

"Are you serious?"

"Just a few feet. I thought you wanted to see the spot."

"This is close enough."

"Not really. It's just a little bit farther ahead."

"But there's a storm coming," I say, invoking the weather as an excuse, possibly for the first time in my life. I don't know what I believe and what I don't believe anymore. The cumulative effect of this conversation about the moth, about wirelessly charging UFOs, about the bridge collapse and the forthcoming bomb cyclone, about the fact that I am effectively stuck until I figure out how to get a new pair of glasses, and now apparently

Vera is coming home—it's all finally causing me to unglue.

"It's only two thirty. The snow is supposed to begin around four. We'll be back at the car well before three."

"I'd like to see it, if you don't mind," says Cynthia. "And I can't get out here on my own anymore. That's part of why Ingram and I met up today. He promised to bring me."

"Oh," I say. "I hadn't realized. Sorry, I don't mean to interfere."

"Not at all," she says. "Happy you came along."

Ingram helps her down from the truck, and Luna leaps out of the back, her leash still attached. I grab it as she tugs, clearly thrilled to be in the woods.

We walk a few yards in silence, the only sound the crunch of the leaves for a few minutes until Cynthia speaks.

"I guess I'm turned around now. I don't know for sure, but I think we want to go a little bit in that direction," she says. "There was a cement building. Like a bunker. It might be over there," she says, waving vaguely toward the right. "People came out here to do things they weren't really supposed to do, if you get my drift, but I swear, we weren't drinking or doing drugs. I mean, Rodrigo might have been sipping a beer. But we were both sober. Wait! There it is, just ahead," she says.

I see a low-slung cement building nearly buried under leaves. Or I think I do. Without my glasses I can't be sure. We continue moving toward it, Luna leading the way. "I hope we don't get lost," I say.

"We're not very far from the car," Ingram says. "It would be hard to get lost."

"Ha! You don't know me very well, do you?"

"Indeed, I do not."

We draw close enough to see that the small building looks like an igloo. Ingram approaches, walking through some bramble to reach the door, which he then swings open.

"Oh, no way am I going in there," I say.

"Suit yourself!"

He walks inside and Cynthia and I wait in silence. A moment later he emerges stealthily, then yells, "Boo!" which nearly gives us both heart attacks even though we are staring right at him, in daylight, when he pulls this prank.

"Very funny," I say, my hand on my chest. "What's in there?"

"It's empty."

"I thought it was full of TNT or whatever."

"It was. It's been cleaned out," Cynthia explains.

"I thought it was a Superfund site."

"Yes, but that was a while ago. They finished. Or so they say. They pretend to be done, and we pretend to believe them," she says.

I shift my focus from UFOs and cryptids to forever chemicals.

"There's more to it. More than most people know, or at least understood at the time," Ingram adds. "Not far from here, just a few miles up the road, was another government facility called the DLA."

"Let me guess: Department of Lunacy Assessment."

"Isn't that's a little redundant? Or maybe contradictory? Lunacy is elusive, and every time we try to assess it, we miss it. Fun fact about lunacy: Did you know the Russians thought lunacy was a mark of being closer to God? Like an open channel to him. The word is *blazhennyy*."

"And you know this why?"

"I know a lot of strange things, stranger."

"Because of being a cryptozoologist, presumably," I say. Very little about this man makes sense. He's talking like an academic. Or maybe a Russian operative.

"Precisely. Well, one more guess? Or should I fill you in?"

"Delicatessen Licensing Agency," I say, lamely.

"Good! You're getting very warm. Think Defense Logistics Authority."

"And that is . . . ?"

"That is where they store materials in case of war," Cynthia says.

"And that's relevant because . . . ?"

"Well, one theory—and not one I subscribe to, for the record—is that the government actually created some of the hype about the Mothman, about UFOs, to distract the public from what was really going on," Ingram says.

"Which was what?"

"No one knows for sure, but it's possible they were storing nuclear fuel, like enriched uranium, nearby, and they wanted to keep people focused on something other than what was happening right beneath their noses," he explains.

"So they what . . . created a Mothman?"

"Well, again, I don't believe this is the case, but nonbelievers, Mothman-deniers, whatever you want to call them, will tell you that maybe they just seized on the one thing—like the first sighting—as an opportunity. Then from there they did weird stuff, like maybe sending government agents out dressed a little oddly, giving them scripts, or just telling them to start flipping people out," he says.

"But what about all those supposed other Mothman sightings?"

"I'm going to take a quick look around the other side of the bunker," Cynthia says. "See if it brings back any memories."

"Be careful," I say, although I'm not sure what exactly I'm worried about, other than perhaps her tripping over a rock.

"Who knows exactly, but the government could have done some crafty things with helicopters, lights, giant balloons," Ingram says.

"I don't know . . . That's pretty far-fetched. I'm going back to the lunatic asylum theory."

"Well, sure, but then you've got more than one hundred documented lunatics in your asylum in a town that is, frankly, pretty staid and not prone to flights of imagination. I'm not claiming to know what was going on, but something was going on."

"And onto the scene comes the cryptozoologist, some fifty years late."

"Thanks for the vote of confidence, but there's more to what I do."

"You'll have to fill me in."

"I'd be happy to. Maybe over another hibachi dinner."

My first thought is banal. "I can see if they have my hat and gloves!"

My second thought is gastronomical. "I think I'd better skip the deep-fried Oreos this time."

It's only on the third thought that I realize he might be suggesting something along the lines of a date. Before I can respond, there's a rustle in the bushes, and then a small *chirp* or *cheep* that may or may not be a chipmunk. Luna jerks so hard on the leash that it slips through my grasp, and she is suddenly off and racing through the woods.

Without thinking, I run after her. She accelerates, hopping, leaping, flying through the air like some combination of rabbit and fawn. In fact, she looks so much like some rabbit-fawn hybrid that I hope it's not hunting season. Had I known we were coming here, I would have put something bright, like the bandana I have in my duffel bag, around her neck. But then had I known I'd be chasing after my dog all over again, I would not be wearing my stupid clog boots, and I would have doubled down on the search for my hat and gloves, or put on the beanie I bought for Vera, which is back in the truck.

Still, I give good chase, and as I pick up speed, I think of myself running along the bridge, and how if I could run a little bit faster, I might propel myself aloft.

I hear Ingram calling to Luna. Suddenly she stops, like she's considering his request, thinking about turning around since she knows she should, but then she decides against.

I continue running, then hear Ingram calling to me. "Come back here and stay with Cynthia! I'll get Luna!"

"I've got it!" I shout. I can't help myself. It's instinct. I'm a dog-mom, and I do what I must. But this time I've made a bad call. Luna is so fast that all I can do is follow the sound of her whooshing through the woods. Occasionally, from the distance, I see something leap in the air, a white gazelle, and I recalibrate, pivot in that new direction for what feels like half a mile. I have no idea if I'm moving deeper into the woods or going in circles, but I keep sprinting, even sometimes springing, and even though I'm frightened, I am also weirdly energized, until I feel my boot catch on something. It's a slow-motion fall—or maybe it's not—but I'm fully cognizant of the fact that I am once again slipping, or in this case tripping, and the next thing I know I'm face down on the ground. Again I think about how once a person begins to slip, it is easy to slip a little more, and then, apparently, to just keep slipping and slipping and slipping until slipping is all that's left. I now see the culprit is a rock, part of a circle of rocks that surrounds a firepit strewn with beer bottles.

Perhaps the moth hasn't been seen in years, but judging from this scene, the search party, or perhaps just the party, continues.

I get back on my feet and continue down a trail covered with forest debris—twigs, leaves, trunks of trees that have keeled over and are now disintegrating in place, covered in thick moss, until it occurs to me that I am no longer on a trail. I'm plain lost, and all I see is an impressionist blur that might be called *Winter Forest Scene*.

"Luna!" I yell into the forest. She does not reply, and the only sound I hear at first is my own voice bouncing off the trees, although a moment later I hear Ingram shouting, alternating my name with Luna's. He calls, "Cassie!" then pauses a minute. He then calls out, "Hey, stranger!" He then calls, "Luna!" Then just a general, "Yo!"

I answer, but he doesn't hear me, and as he continues to cry out our names, his voice is moving in the wrong direction. Or maybe it's me moving in the wrong direction, even though I am trying to move toward him, my unreliable sense of direction colliding with my lack of vision plus the sound of his voice ricocheting off the trees.

Now his words sound more like a song, or a chant, or an incantation, or even another language: Español! "Cassie! Stranger! Luna! Yo! Cassie! Stranger! Luna! Yo! Cassie-strangerlunayo!" The sound of his voice is moving farther and farther away.

The full gravity of the situation is slowly sinking in. I'm out here in the woods, alone, lost. In another hour or so, the sun will begin to set. It's cold and getting colder.

I then hear the chime of my phone, a sound so incongruous with the horror movie unfolding in my head that it takes a moment for my mind to adjust.

It's Vera, and it is so good to hear her voice, to remember normalcy, or at least what has passed for it in my life these last few years, that tears well in my eyes.

"Where are you, sweetheart?"

"Just landed at the airport. I'm in an Uber, on my way home. Where are you?"

"I'm on a little trip," I say. "I just . . . had a job interview." I hate myself for saying this, but it seems better than telling her where I really am right now.

"Oh, cool. I'm glad that's for real. I thought maybe it was some cover story Olivia made up. It's great that you are doing something for yourself, Mom," she says. "I was kind of worried about you. I mean, I haven't heard it yet, but Piper texted me about Olivia's show this morning. I don't know what she talked about exactly, I'll check it out when I'm home, but Piper seems to think she was talking about you."

Piper is my niece, Vera's first cousin. I can't bear the thought that people are talking about me, and I can't handle this conversation right now, so I invoke my wonky phone.

"I can't hear you, Vera. You're breaking up."

"Can you hear me now?"

I feel terrible, but I do not reply.

"Can you hear me now?"

I lock into the sound of my daughter's lovely, comforting voice until she gives up and the line goes dead.

CHAPTER 29

Bomb Cyclone

A SINGLE SNOWFLAKE falls. I catch it in my palm and stare at the delicate pattern, a tiny crystal, a lattice star. Can it really be the case that no two snowflakes are the same? Or is that just another old wives' tale, like the warning against letting the possibly concussed go to sleep?

I consider the etymology of the not-especially-feminist-forward phrase *old wives' tale*. I think of old wives' tales more as superstitions, like how if you have an itchy nose, you are about to get a visitor and, depending on which nostril is itching, a male or a female visitor. Then again, it might mean something entirely different: Someone is gossiping about you, about to put a curse on you, or about to kiss you.

The thought of kissing makes me think of bodies pressing together. It's been too long since I have kissed someone. I think of Ingram, of his incongruity, which has a certain charm. I think of taking off his tortoiseshell glasses and pressing my lips to his. I wonder what he might taste like. If his beard would scratch. If the kiss might lead to other things, although the part of this that is most compelling right now is less about intimacy or the erotic than about creating heat.

Fortunately, I have enough unfrozen circuitry in my brain to understand that I ought to move rather than stand here and contemplate snowflakes and kissing and kissing-adjacent things.

I begin to walk, or really hobble, in what I hope is the direction from which I came. I am beginning to wonder if I twisted my ankle when I tripped. But I no longer hear voices. I pull out my phone in the hope that I can reach Ingram, but then realize I don't have his number and don't even know his last name. It doesn't matter anyway since my screen is blank and the phone appears to be frozen. I put it down my shirt and secure it in my bra, hoping my body heat, at least what is left of it, might help warm it up so it will turn back on.

Another snowflake falls and another and another and I am back to thinking about snowflakes. I remember that Olivia once had on her radio show a snowflake expert with scientific bona fides, and she said it is true! Each one *is* different—that even if the snowflakes begin their journeys identically, by the time they make their way through the atmosphere, through humidity and vapor, each will change in individual ways. Naturally Olivia wove this into the subject of storytelling. She talked about how, for example, you can take the stories of hidden children during World War II, and even though the same set of circumstances sent them into hiding, no two narratives will be the same. She took that to the next level—it's not just that the details of their stories will differ but the methods by which the stories are told: oral history handed down from one generation to the next, memoir, photographs, diaries.

I walk a little farther, still calling Luna's name, but hear only my echo. It is now so quiet in the woods that it frightens me. I no longer hear Ingram calling, or Luna moving through the bramble. Even the chipmunks have stopped scurrying. I think about Cynthia's inability to abide silence. Quiet was something I used to crave back when my house was pure chaos with a young child, a dog, a husband who was pandemonium incarnate and somehow managed to create commotion for me even when he was on the road. He was never not there: I could hear him on the radio, see him on TV, read him in the paper. And he'd call from wherever he was and talk about the weather, about himself, his ratings, the listener feedback he'd just received, and only once in a while inquire about Vera or me.

Quiet is sometimes cathartic, but right now, what I wouldn't give for a little noise.

The pain in my ankle intensifies, and I decide to sit down for a moment under a tree, which at least provides partial shelter from the snow that is now falling more aggressively.

I think of home. Of piped-in heat. Of food in the cupboard. Of my spare pair of glasses. What was so wrong with any of that? And then I remember Richard in the basement. Elaine and her nightguard. This gives me a jolt, a second wind that propels me upright. I might not want Richard back. Elaine can have him. But I'm not going to make it convenient for either of them by freezing to death out here in the woods.

I trudge forward with a limp. I trudge and trudge and trudge. I don't know to where I am trudging, but my feet are growing numb and the pain is becoming severe and I'm starting to feel a little sleepy, so I sing.

I try to remember the lyrics to that song about the dog that has stopped its barking, the one I was listening to back when I was on the Chesapeake Bay Bridge. Didn't that song have something to do with West Virginia? Is that a crazy coincidence, or am I coincidence-obsessed? A sentence fragment having to do with being haunted by the past pops into my head. Weird. I sing this song for a long while, even though I know I'm mixing up all the lyrics, possibly even inventing some.

This keeps me going a bit longer. Then I think about how it's Christmas Eve. How much I love our version of Christmas. What I wouldn't give for some crispy, spicy tofu. For a dose of Will Ferrell dressed as an elf. How I wish I was home with my family, or at least with Vera. And I wish I had my puppy in my arms.

I'm free-associating as I freeze to death, my thoughts randomly pinging to the memory of the writer I once heard speak, who said that instead of outlining a story, instead of devising a plot, she thinks about music, about how a symphony tells a story and has its own narrative arc, and even a dialogue between instruments. At times the story speeds up, then slows down, then takes an unexpected turn, comes back around, somehow, to where it began.

I think of Richard Gere saying, "Something's very wrong here. I don't know these people. I have never been here before. I'm from DC."

I wonder why Vera was watching that movie. I know exactly why Vera was watching that movie.

I think of what Cynthia said about the blue plastic blob she saw, sitting on the riverbank.

I think of Ingram's name, and how it sounds like the man they keep talking about, Indrid. Indrid Cold.

I think of Uncle Harry. He would say something like, "Cassie! Be empirical!" And I would say, "Empiricism is over-rated!" Or something like that. I'm not entirely sure what I'd say because my head is so cold that I think my brain has begun to freeze like my phone.

I trudge and trudge and trudge, trying to keep these thoughts going, hopeful that if they all fuse together, some spark of logic will emerge.

I call Luna's name again, but it is swallowed by the wind.

Now I absolutely cannot feel my toes. The sun is low in the sky, at the intersection of *right about to set* and *completely set*, what I've heard called the hour between dog and wolf, which means it can be hard to tell light from dusk, good from bad, and I no longer know in which direction I am walking. I then begin to laugh because my sense of direction is so bad that if you let the setting sun scream its coordinates out to me or carved the four cardinal directions on the palm of my hand, it wouldn't help me.

I think of the story of the Marrano on the torture rack during the Spanish Inquisition, of the philanthropist who gives every-thing away, of the family smuggled by coyotes, of the soccer player with lymphoma, of the nanny facing eviction. I don't know how those stories end. I don't know *if* they ended or were simply abandoned when their authors gave up.

I don't know why I have spent my lifetime working so hard to make sense of stories. So many stories, not quite done. The world still spins, even without the tidy endings I desire. Yet here I am, possibly about to freeze to death in the woods, in an effort to tie up my own narrative. Perhaps this is the universe speaking to me, telling me that I should have given up.

Susan Coll

I sit down for a minute, fall backward against another tree, and then hear a deafening *whoosh*. I look up, and there it is: the creature I saw in my car, now a thousand times larger. I've been wondering where it went, and now I see it is here, in the sky, hovering over me. How did it get so big so fast? It has probably been munching on whatever it munches on, or rather what it munched on as a larva—sweaters, leaves, owl pillows from home economics class, Persian rugs—and has expanded, and is now so massive that while it is suspended overhead, it blocks the snow. The eyes are red, so bright they are blinding. It looks like a man. But also like a giant moth. Like something from a horror movie. But also, like something from a cartoon.

Where is that can of MOTHSLAY? I wonder. *And would one can be enough?*

Then, amazingly, the moth flattens, stretches, spins, turns itself inside out, becomes translucent.

"Do not be scared!" it says.

I wonder if it is evolving backward. Maybe it's about to become a larva, one that some entrepreneur will stick inside a plastic case and sell for people's amusement. Jumping beans! But wait, no, it's the wrong plastic case. The moth has become a dental appliance. It's a giant flying nightguard. It's a spacecraft, singular and plural. (But is that correct? Might Ingram . . . or Indrid . . . be wrong about that? Why am I always so quick to agree?) Everything is everywhere! Everything is everything! Time is just a construct to keep everything from happening all at once, because now it is a bluebird, both the brilliant, winged creature and the pre–Camp Fire Girl. And then it is the young woman from the Eyes of Gallipolis, and she looks so familiar, and I squeeze my eyes tighter and then see her behind a register, and then it clicks—she used to work in my neighborhood bookstore! But wait . . . Autumn is gone and replaced by . . . my mother? A woman with long dark hair riding in a powder-blue car, holding a lipstick-stained Silva Thin between her fingers. I call to her, but she doesn't answer, and I begin to cry. I want her to take me in her arms and protect me. I want to sit and talk with her for days. But now she is gone and has turned back into a moth, and this is causing my puppy to bark and bark and bark.

CHAPTER 30

The Frequency Illusion

OLIVIA IS THE self-proclaimed expert on storytelling, but I have theories of my own. One of them has to do with stories being preordained: A story knows where it wants to go and what it wants to be, and it is up to the storyteller to figure this out. I tell this to my students and frequently think about this myself. Were a writer to set a certain story in the summer, for example, it's possible that the whole thing wouldn't compute. Some stories are meant to be winter tales, in need of sleet and snow. Ditto for structure and point of view.

I might gently suggest to a student that his narrative wants to be in third person, not first, and he will grimace, push back, tell me that I'm wrong. But watch him come back into class in a month with a new opening. Dollars to donuts, he will tell me that I'm right.

The story is archaeological. It already exists. It wants to tell itself—or it doesn't. Either way, the job of the writer is to dig in the right spot.

I am explaining this to Ingram, or is this Indrid, who is

pressing something—a sweatshirt, maybe—to my head while Luna licks my face. As things come into blurry focus, I realize that I am lying in the back seat of his truck. Cynthia is up front, the engine is running, and the heat is pouring in. I wiggle my feet and they move, thank goodness. Ditto for my hands. I will still be able to type, should I come up with something to say.

"You are a hero dog!" he says to Luna.

"What do you mean?"

"She speaks!" he says. "You had us worried there!"

"What do you mean?"

"Luna found you and wouldn't stop barking. That's how I found you."

I am so grateful to be cocooned inside this warm vehicle that I try to give a pass to the fact that I have leaned into the most saccharine cliché of them all: I've been rescued by a dog. But at least it's a cliché I can live with quite happily.

"I was getting pretty worried about you, my friend. I helped Cynthia back to the truck and then came looking for you, but the snow is crazy. I've never seen it come down this fast. Plus it was starting to get dark. Good thing I had an extra flashlight in the glove compartment."

"How did Luna even find me?"

"I'm not sure she ever really lost you."

"Yeah, maybe she was playing kiss chase."

He looks at me, puzzled.

"It's a game Vera used to play on the playground."

Silence, still.

"Vera is my daughter."

"Ah, gotcha . . . Okay, I think we'd better get this looked at," he says.

"Get what looked at where?"

"Your head. At the ER."

"I don't know why everyone keeps going on about my head. Harry told me to keep an eye on it, and I've been doing what he says."

"Okay, well, I don't know who Harry is either, but your head is bleeding."

"It's fine, I'm telling you. Head wounds bleed. That's not an old wives' tale. Everyone knows it's a fact."

Outside, the blur of white is so wildly swirling that it looks like we are inside a snow globe. Or a snow tornado. I wonder if that's a thing. I'm tempted to ask Richard about this. There's a change—me wanting to talk to him about the weather! I imagine him down there in the basement, tracking this storm on his multiple screens. Then I see him wading through the snow in his knee-high rubber boots, microphone in hand. He's hanging on to a tree, pretending he's about to be blown away. Or maybe he's jumping into a snowbank, dropping to his knees, pretending to be swallowed.

Ingram pulls a scraper from the back of the truck and clears the windshield, or at least he tries to. He then gets back in the truck and puts the wipers on the highest speed before backing up. For a moment we seem to be stuck, but then he shifts gears and we move.

Then I remember—the giant thing in the sky, my mother, the bluebird, the nightguard, whatever it was—and a question pops into my mind.

"Are you sure it's a collective noun?" I ask.

"What are you talking about?" Ingram says.

"You know, are you sure the singular is the same as the plural?"

"Still confused."

"Can you look it up?"

"Sure. What am I looking up?"

"Spacecraft. Spacecrafts."

"*That's* what you're thinking about right now? I believe it's singular *and* plural. That's my understanding. But I'll look it up later. I'm driving."

⋈   ⋈   ⋈

Uncle Harry, pushing back on my frequent observations about coincidence, has told me about something called the Baader-Meinhof phenomenon, also known as the frequency illusion. Once you learn a new word, suddenly you notice it everywhere—in books, tossed about in dialogue, as answers to crossword puzzle clues. It strikes you as some great coincidence, but all that's really happening is that now your antenna is more finely tuned, picking up on usage when the word was already there.

I consider calling Harry from the hospital to tell him he's wrong. Suddenly the word *hypothermia* is on everyone's lips, and I'm quite certain it was not previously in such high rotation.

"Rest," someone—I don't know who—tells me.

I'm lying on a bed, and unlike the forest, it is very, very warm. Although when I close my eyes, I am lying under the tree again, but then, moments later, I'm in Vera's room, and it is full of tiny fluttering moths, small precious things, each one different, like snowflakes. Then they *are* snowflakes, and I am lying in a pile of snowflakes, but also they are moths, and then Uncle Harry comes into the room with a giant can of MOTHSLAY and I try to tell him these are good moths, not bad moths, and to watch out for the bluebird, but he doesn't hear me, and I scream.

Now, a man is standing over me, telling me to relax. "Take a deep breath," he says. "And another."

I close my eyes, open them again, and now there are three different people standing over me, every one of them saying, "hypothermia, hypothermia, hypothermia," like there is no other word in the world, until someone changes the subject.

"We ordered a CT," she says. "Looks clear. Possibly a mild concussion, though, so let's bandage her up and tell her to keep an eye on that head."

⋈   ⋈   ⋈

"Stranger! What a lousy way to spend Christmas Eve! But they are telling me you can probably go home soon. Well, not *home* necessarily, but we can get you back to the hotel for starters. Is there someone you want me to call? A . . . husband? The daughter you mentioned?"

I look up and there is Ingram, in all his incongruousness. Scruffy, awkward beard, orange parka, Stetson hat that could not possibly be for real, faux-intellectual tortoiseshell glasses unlike what any card-carrying cryptozoologist would wear. His eyes are a lovely hazel shade I had not previously noticed, and I can't help but stare. I want to take this man apart, turn him inside out, put him back together, figure out what makes him tick. This distracting and somewhat disturbing train of thought is interrupted by another.

"Where's Luna?"

"She's fine. The brothers have her."

"The brothers? Has she been sent off to some religious order?"

"No, the Evett brothers. She's at the hotel. She's fine."

"But what about *no dogs*?"

"These are special circumstances, obviously. She's in good hands. You don't need to worry about her."

We are interrupted by a man with a clipboard who looks too old to be practicing medicine.

"Good news," he says with some sort of lovely, lilting, hard-to-place accent. "I believe my colleague told you already, but the CT looks clear. We're going to release you. I just want to do another quick check of your vitals."

"But there was so much blood," Ingram protests.

"Head injuries can be messy. I'm not sure what happened, but it looks like she might have had a preexisting head wound. It must have opened back up. Maybe she fell in the woods, passed out, and hit her head again. Who knows for sure? The rest is your classic hypothermia. But she's stabilized."

He then turns to me and says, "You're lucky they found you when they did. And you're also lucky anyone was on call. Between the storm and the Christmas holiday, I'm the only doctor who was able to make it in since I live just a few blocks away. Can you sit up for a minute?" he asks.

I pull myself upright, then realize I'm wearing only a paper-thin hospital gown. It falls open in the back. Ingram politely looks the other way as the doctor puts his stethoscope to my chest, and then my spine, and then says, "Whoa! Those are some mighty scars! What happened there?"

"Oh, that's from when I was a kid. I was too young to remember, but something to do with me falling backward into a tomato patch, a scrape with one of those wire cages. It was torn up, and it tore up my back." I'm a little embarrassed to have him see this, to have Ingram right here too.

"That must have been one angry contraption. Looks like it got up and attacked you. Are you sure that's what happened? I mean, I can see how that might create some scarring, but nothing like this."

"I don't know. It's never really bothered me, and I never thought to ask."

"It's none of my business, but I think someone isn't telling you something. Although it's also true—and I'm telling you this as a man who is paid to live and die by data—not everything in this world has a rational explanation. We scratch our beards. We pretend."

"My uncle is a pathologist. He would beg to differ."

"Well, your uncle doesn't live in Point Pleasant, I presume. Things happen here that defy logic. But those scars . . . They are bringing me back."

The wail of an ambulance pierces the room, and there is a sudden clamor in the hallway.

"I'd better get going. Like I said, we're short-staffed tonight and there are a lot of accidents out there. The roads are slick. I'm going to discharge you—we're going to need this bed— but you probably ought to wait out this weather for a while. You can hang out in the lobby. There's a vending machine."

The implications of what this kind man has just told me are sinking into my possibly mildly concussed head, and I want to keep him talking.

"Wait, Doctor, can I ask you one thing? If you had to guess, what would you say about the scars? How I might have gotten them, I mean."

"I wouldn't dare offer up an official medical explanation, so this is extremely unprofessional, and obviously off the record—but it's making me remember another case. There was an accident here many years ago. I'm not sure if you know anything about the history of this place, since I see in your records that you're from DC—my cousin lives there, by the way— but we had a catastrophic bridge collapse, probably before you were born, or"—he glances back at his chart—"I guess you would have been a toddler. Anyway, the survivors—not that there were many survivors—wound up here. Some of them were torn up from the debris. It was bad. All that metal from the bridge, the cars, the glass. We did a lot of stitching that day. And there was this little kid, her back was a jagged mess. Who knows what exactly happened . . . Maybe she got tangled up with, or dragged across, a piece of the bridge cable? At first, we figured it was glass from the car window, but there weren't any shards, so it had to have been the bridge material. We didn't do a very neat job of it, but we got her closed. She's lucky she didn't bleed out.

"And speaking of lucky, you take care, miss. Stay out of the woods next time there's a monster snowstorm."

Turning to Ingram, he adds, "Please buy your wife a hat."

Ingram and I exchange a little side-eye, amused by this

assumption. I see him looking at my ring finger, which still sports the band. Removing it is such a radical act that, as certain as I am it's over, I've been hesitant to finally take it off.

"But you'll be fine. Just keep that gauze wrapped around the head for a couple of days—sorry we don't have anything to make it look less awful, but the mummy look suits you well. Give that ankle a rest too. And don't forget to keep an eye on your head."

CHAPTER 31

The Extras

INGRAM AND I consume approximately seven bags of barbecue-flavored potato chips, four bags of Peanut M&M's, and two tiny packages of oversalted cashews as we while away the hours, waiting for the storm to subside and the roads to clear enough to drive.

Partially sated and sodium-drenched, we stare, zombielike, at the television in the ER waiting room. Tuned to a local news station, the gizmo is loud, demanding undivided attention, impossible to ignore.

From these breathless reports, one might surmise that this bomb cyclone, right now, is the only thing taking place in the world. We learn it is an extratropical cyclone of historic, possibly even biblical, proportions. There is a wind chill alert, massive amounts of snow, zero-visibility conditions, all just passing through, en route to the Atlantic—so endure, folks! Courage!

More than twenty people have been killed, and hundreds of thousands are without power. There are pileups on roadways, vehicles engulfed by snowdrifts. Fleets of snowplows rendered motionless on highways. And this just in: a train derailment in eastern Ohio.

Again I think about how odd it is to be hearing about this from someone other than Richard. I feel as if I'm being disloyal. Then I remember that I have left him, that I have finally slipped the ring off my finger and stuffed it in my pocket. I just need to close the deal more officially. Whatever the reasons for my discomfit, it's a relief to let someone else opine, to be reminded that the weather is not a fiefdom ruled by Richard alone.

In the brightly lit television studio, a nattily dressed, mustachioed older gentleman who looks a bit like Captain Kangaroo is mansplaining the weather to a chirpy young woman in a red sweater. Her name is Janis, and she has reindeer antlers sprouting from her head.

"What a bomb cyclone means is that there was an extremely fast drop in a low-pressure air mass . . . and as the low-pressure air mass confronts the high-pressure air mass, it makes the winds increase. So, you see, it's all about the pressure. Hence *bomb*. The technical term is *bombogenesis*."

"I thought you said it's an extratropical cyclone," she says, looking perplexed. But I don't think she's really perplexed. I have faith in Janis. I think she knows of what she speaks, like she probably studied meteorology at Cornell and knows more about the weather than Captain Kangaroo, but she is dumbing herself down, as well as wearing the stupid antlers, for the sake of ratings.

"Same thing, Janis. It's also known as a nontropical storm. It has to do with the pressure dropping rapidly. What you need is a decrease of twenty-four millibars over twenty-four hours . . ."

"Okay, let's pause with the science for a moment and get out there in the field. Jason is onsite for us in Charleston. Jason, where are you, exactly?"

"Hi there, Janis. It's hard to tell, right? I'm standing smack in front of the Capitol Building, but it's impossible to see anything behind me with all the wind and snow swirling." Young Jason is bundled in a blue parka, wearing one of those fuzzy trapper hats with earflaps that make him look like a sheepherder. He is hanging on to a pole and looks like he's about to be blown away, except, unlike Richard, presumably for real.

A woman with a large Dalmatian pulling on a crimson leash passes behind him.

Jason tells us about a bad traffic accident as sirens scream in the background, which is confusing because there is also a siren screaming right here, outside the window, ferrying more people to the ER.

No sooner do I think this than the woman with the Dalmatian passes behind him again, coming from the same direction. Am I seeing double? Am I seeing this at all? It is, after all, something of a blur.

"Did you just see that woman walk by twice?" I ask Ingram.

"I'm not really paying attention," he says. "But those things happen."

"What do you mean?"

"People walk by, then walk by again."

"Well, obviously, but it looked like she walked by, coming from the same direction, within the span of a few seconds."

"That happens too. Goofs."

"Goofs?"

"Yeah, it happens in movies if you watch closely. There were some in *The Mothman Prophecies*. That same thing, now that you mention it. An extra walked by twice."

"Well, this isn't a movie. It's a live broadcast."

"Maybe you are seeing things. Or not seeing things, given that you don't have your glasses."

"Probably you're right."

I stare back at the screen and try to stop overthinking things, especially things I can't properly see. This Jason person reminds me a bit of Richard when he was young. Not his looks as much as his wired energy, his attitude, his cockiness. Perhaps Jason, too, is fighting demons, hoping that if he plunges headfirst into the weather, he can numb his own pain for a while before he self-destructs. Granted, I might be projecting on young Jason.

Eventually this breathless coverage lulls me into a fitful and very uncomfortable sleep that is interrupted each time another ambulance arrives and the hospital springs back to life. I think about what the doctor said, about the girl with the scars, about my scars not making sense, about how not everything in this world computes. How blue is a mile, I wonder, and is it possible that I've been asking the wrong questions all along?

Ingram dozes on and off too. We see the same storm footage of accidents minor and major, of downed trees, of a massive pileup on Route 95 in Parkersburg, what seems like a hundred times, but I don't see the woman and her Dalmatian again.

Finally, the sun comes up, the winds stop howling, and we climb back in the truck.

CHAPTER 32

If It Quacks

INGRAM'S TRUCK IS a weather-impervious tank, coursing through town as if this epic bomb cyclone has left behind a light dusting rather than three feet of snow. That said, someone somewhere was on the ball, and the snowplows have already cleared the main roads. We arrive at the hotel without incident and pull into the space next to a giant mound of snow, beneath which we are likely to find my car.

We both laugh at Luna, her face pressed up to the lobby window, looking like she owns the place. Her body begins to vibrate as we approach, completing the movement that begins at the tip of the rapidly wagging tail.

One of the brothers opens the door for us. I climb the stairs carefully, hanging on to the rail so I don't slip on the ice, but when I step inside, Luna practically knocks me over with her effusive greeting.

"Welcome back," the man says. "She is having the time of her life. Hope you are on the mend."

Luna now demonstrates her excitement by running in circles

around the lobby, jumping onto chairs, leaping, flying through the air. It's what Vera calls doing "zoomies."

"She loves the weather," he says. "You should see her rolling around in the snow. She sticks her head into a snowdrift and then pops it out again like a baby rabbit."

"Ha. I guess she's never seen snow before. Not like this anyway. We've only had a few dustings so far this year in DC. But the problem is she blends right in. That's part of how I lost her in the woods."

"Ingram filled me in," he says. "Glad you got through that okay. I mean, I hope you're okay. That head looks pretty rough."

"Oh, it's fine," I say, remembering that my head—this appendage that others keep commenting on, even though it has not bothered me in the least apart from how it apparently keeps spewing blood—is now encased in gauze. "Really, it's nothing."

"You should have told me about the dog," he says.

"But I did!" I protest. Or at least I think I did. He was there when I asked Alma. Or I thought he was there. Really, I don't know who was there since all the bearded men look alike, and for all I know, there could be even more of them.

"No, I mean I know Alma said you could sneak her in, but I never saw her, other than her tail. You had her all bundled up in your coat."

"Sorry!" I am not sure for what I am apologizing, but whatever it takes to keep him happy and on the pro-dog side. "Is there something wrong with . . . how she looks?"

"Of course not. It's just that she looks like one of ours."

"I'm not following."

"The white Lab, the heterochromatic eyes. Looks like she's got a bit of husky. That's what we breed. I mean, not deliberately—we're not breeders per se. We're not trying to do any fancy thing. It's just that our mom was a big husky person, and our dad loved Labs, so we've had these Luskies around since we were kids. There's possibly a bit of something else in the bloodline, too, but who knows, and we don't really care. Where did you get her?"

"I got her from my neighbor. In DC. But before that, she had come off a van. From a kill shelter in Mercedes, Texas. I don't know anything more about her, but when I saw her, I just about died . . . She looks like every dog I've ever had since I was a kid." I don't know why I'm telling him all this, but once I start talking about dogs, it's hard to stop me.

"I mean, not all of them have had the eyes," I continue, "but they're otherwise the same. I just keep getting the same dog over and over. Even when I'm not looking for it. Like this time, Luna sort of found me."

"Well, she would fit right in with our pack. I mean, it's not rocket science, the way dogs get made, but still, these are somewhat unusual. If you want to stop by the farm before you leave, we'd be happy to show you around."

"I'd love that! Speaking of which . . . given everything going on—the storm, my glasses, and I guess my head even though it's fine—I'll be here at least another night or two, assuming I can extend the stay on my room."

"No problem. We're quiet this week. However long you need," he says.

"I don't know how I'm going to get home, but I'll go up to my room and make a few calls and start trying to figure it out."

I glance at Ingram without meaning to, as if this man I barely know is going to help solve this problem.

"I'm going to head up too," Ingram says. "Thanks again for taking care of Luna."

Luna hesitates, torn between going back to the room with me and hanging out in the lobby. I coax her along, and we file into the elevator. But when the lift stops on Ingram's floor, she seems to know exactly where she's going and follows him out. He puts his hand over the door to keep it from closing as I call her name to summon her back, but she seems determined to stick with him, which is both amusing and depressing, her easy allegiance.

"So, stranger," he says. "Merry Christmas to those who celebrate. And I hope you don't mind, but I might be borrowing your dog."

"Appears so," I say. "And yes, same to you. I can't believe it's Christmas! What a crazy couple of days."

"Are we still on for tonight?"

"Tonight?"

"Hibachi?"

"Oh, of course. It's my annual Christmas ritual. How did you know?"

"Meet in the lobby at six?"

"Sure, if you promise to give me back my dog someday."

"I'll take that into consideration. Meantime, get some rest."

⋊   ⋊   ⋊

I crawl straight into bed, exhausted from my ordeal, but my mind won't settle. I keep turning over some of the odd scraps of information I've collected in the last couple of days. The way Cynthia casually mentioned seeing Hoppity after the accident, the doctor remarking on my scars. A possible scenario is starting to emerge, but it's so far-fetched that it must be dismissed outright.

A part of me is tempted to pick up the phone and call Olivia right now. Chances are she is expecting the call, having provoked it deliberately with that broadcast, but I'm not in the best frame of mind to confront her, and now that I have so many questions, I'm not even sure where to begin. I always tell Vera to take a deep breath, get a good night's sleep, count to ten, do whatever it takes to calm down before acting in anger. Now I try to follow my own advice, gratifying though it might be to call Olivia and explode.

⋈　⋈　⋈

I stare out the window for a while at the river. I remember the old black-and-white photos from the book I once snagged from the library and kept stashed under my pillow for months. It had pictures of children ice-skating on the lake, others walking across, creating their own passage during a particularly fierce winter storm. I can't see clearly enough to determine if ice is beginning to form, but I do know the sky is still grey, and the sun is still trying to glisten through the clouds in the morning light.

Perhaps if I stare long enough, I'll see a powder-blue Pontiac Bonneville crossing the bridge, a man and woman talking in the front seat, the woman waving a lit cigarette to punctuate her sentence, red lipstick staining the filter. Olivia once told me that my mother was not much of a smoker, that she liked to light them and leave them burning in the ashtray. For her, smoking was not a habit so much as a fashion accessory. I see the young man—handsome, curly-haired, dusky-skinned.

I imagine them in love. I imagine them fighting. I imagine them kissing, listening to loud rock music. The Beatles, perhaps. Maybe they are listening to the news. Or maybe they are driving in silence, until there is a sound so loud it is deafening. It's the sound of corrosion. Of metal splitting, cables snapping, asphalt crumbling. It's the sound of cars sliding, horns blaring, humans screaming.

Then silence. And most shockingly, absence. A bridge that was there is no longer there.

I try to imagine a child somehow emerging from the car, somehow getting to shore without drowning, freezing, or bleeding out, her back ripped open from detritus of the bridge. It is coming together and yet it makes no sense, still. Why the secret? This version of events simply can't be true.

If it looks like an elephant, I can hear Ingram say.

⋈　　⋈　　⋈

I don't want to talk to Olivia or Harry, and certainly not Richard, but my heart aches for Vera, and I want to hear her voice. I call, but she doesn't pick up. A moment later, a text arrives:

Jet-lagged. Napping.
Will call later!

Three heart emojis.

Then, a moment later:

Happy Xmas

I fall into a deep, dreamless sleep that lasts until the phone rings some six hours later. It takes me a moment to figure out where the ringing is coming from, since I don't recognize the sound. I look around and spy an old black still-shiny rotary phone on the bedside table. I pick up the heavy receiver, thinking it's been many years since I've pressed such a thing to my ear.

"Good news bad news," I hear Ingram say. I am again reminded that even after all we have been through in the last twenty-four hours, we still haven't exchanged phone numbers. "Which do you want first?"

"Let's get the bad news out of the way," I say. As my mind comes into sharper focus, I remember my puppy. "Is Luna okay?"

"Luna is right here deconstructing my shoelace."

"Oh, sorry about that. I should have warned you!"

"Puppies chew. No warning needed."

"Well then, out with the bad news already."

"Brace yourself. The hibachi restaurant is closed. Christmas plus storm, et cetera. Not sure which reason came first, but there you have it."

"Oh, that is indeed very disappointing. I was prepared to go full carnivore, even lean into the Oreo thing, it being a holiday and all." The thought of steak makes me realize that I'm quite hungry. Our junk food banquet at the hospital was full of empty calories, as unsatisfying as it was unhealthy. I haven't had a proper meal since lunch with Cynthia, which was more than twenty-four hours ago.

Susan Coll

"We'd better transition quickly to the good news before I start to weep."

"The good news is that we have been invited across the river to the Evett farm."

"What do you mean?"

"I asked Mitch if there was any place open for dinner, and he said just to come out to his sister's. He said it's an easy drive, right across the river, a bunch of family is coming, and they have plenty of food. Although . . . I forgot to mention the flexitarian situation, so I'm glad to hear you are amenable."

"Wait, who is Mitch?"

"Are you okay, stranger?"

"I'm perfectly fine. Just not sure who you are talking about."

"Mitch is Alma's brother. The guy from the lobby."

"Okay. Got it. And yes, I'll eat whatever they serve. That's very kind of them. But do me a favor: Please stop mocking me for trying to eat responsibly."

"I'm not mocking you, stranger. I admire you. Anyway, Mitch tells me they got out there with a snowblower, plus the county trucks came through. The roads are not great but they're manageable.

"Also, he said we should bring Luna. She can meet the other dogs. Everyone will love her. Their kids will all be there. You'll love them."

"It sounds like you've been there before."

"I told you, I've been coming here for a few years now."

"I still don't understand what you do. Or why you are even here since as far as I know there haven't been any Mothman sightings for some fifty years. In fact, I read somewhere that there was evidently a sighting in Chicago not that long ago. Why are you here and not there?"

"Oh, that Chicago thing . . . I don't know how much credence to give that one. I was out there for a while, in fact. That hoopla went on for a few years, starting right after 9/11. It's not clear if that was a subspecies of our Mothman, or hysteria, or something new, or a hoax."

"Did something bad happen?"

"What do you mean?"

"I mean, I thought the Mothman was a harbinger of something bad. I heard that sometimes people even have a sense of dread or despair after seeing it, and then something catastrophic happens, like the bridge collapse or Chernobyl or . . ."

"You know, I'm not convinced about Chernobyl either. There's some dispute—"

"Wait, something bad did happen in Chicago!"

"What do you mean?"

"The shooting in Highland Park, all those people killed while watching a parade." I realize as soon as I say this how ridiculous this sounds, a thought Ingram quickly confirms.

"This is called confirmation bias."

"Yeah yeah yeah, I know all about this stuff from my uncle."

"Then you know you are just corralling information to fit into the box to support your thesis. It's a normal instinct. But you could put a million different things in that box. Every bad thing that has happened in Chicago since 2011, when he was evidently first seen in the area, you could attribute to the Mothman . . . Well, not *to* him—he isn't causing anything to happen; he's just warning people."

"Do you believe this?" I ask. I mean, of course he must believe it. He's a cryptozoologist.

"It's a complicated answer, stranger. Better explained over dinner sometime. For now, let's just say I believe that people believe."

"You really do sound like my uncle. The experience of experience, he'd say."

"I thought your uncle was a pathologist."

"And an amateur phenomenologist."

"That's funny." And then he starts to laugh loudly, and he can't seem to stop.

"Why? I know it's weird, but what am I missing?"

"It's amusing, is all. A phenomenologist pathologist. My mother would love that. She wanted me to be a doctor. I did become one, just the wrong kind. Anyway, I'll see you in the lobby in an hour."

I don't know what he's talking about. He's a doctor? Of cryptozoology? But before I can ask, he jumps in with a request.

"Can you bring Luna some food? We should probably feed her before we leave."

CHAPTER 33

The Farm

IT's A FAILURE of imagination, I know, that until this trip, I had not paused to consider the physical beauty of West Virginia, notwithstanding the fact that, like any American of my generation, I can recite all the lyrics of John Denver's "Take Me Home, Country Roads."

Almost heaven is about right, at least here on the Evett property, where a picturesque clapboard farmhouse sits on some ten acres of snow-covered pasture, a large red barn in the middle distance. It's all so majestic I'm tempted to start writing my own lyrics for a song.

Luna leaps out of the car, already aware through the power of the finely tuned instrument that is her nose, that ahead are dogs galore. They, too, must sense the arrival of a canine visitor and come bounding out the front door. The other dogs, roughly eight of them—it's hard to distinguish the individual animals in this moving white blur—are some version of Luna except taller, shorter, fatter, thinner, a marginally different shape of floppy ear. A split second of tension occurs as they all stop and stare at Luna, possibly deciding whether she is friend or foe. Luna is either too oblivious or too full of puppy energy to wait for an invitation and inserts herself into the pack. Within seconds they are chasing one another and rolling in the snow.

The brother who is evidently named Mitch welcomes us and invites us inside, taking the package that Ingram presses into his hand. "Merry Christmas. Just a little something from me and Cassie," he says, presenting him with a gift bag that clearly contains a bottle of spirits.

I'm tempted to lean in and whisper to Ingram that I'll Venmo him my share, but that seems tacky, so instead I nod and smile in his direction, a gesture I hope he knows is intended as a thank-you.

"Come on in," Mitch says. "Throw your stuff right over there." He points to a mudroom filled with dozens of pairs of boots and a wide variety of coats, hats, mittens, and scarves strewn on benches and hanging on pegs. "How are you feeling, Cassie?"

"Oof, much better. What a night!"

"That head okay?" he asks.

"I'm absolutely fine!" I insist. "I just have to wear this very attractive bandage for a few more days. I'm so grateful to all of you for watching Luna."

"Of course. She's a sweetheart. Come on in."

Inside a fire is roaring, in front of which two big old huskies lie in repose, soaking in the heat from the comfort of fuzzy, round dog beds. It's warm and cozy and beautiful in here, right out of some *Dwell* spread about farmhouse chic. The only problem is that it's a little too doggy inside. I love dogs, but this is too doggy even for me. Still, I can tell effort's been made to clean the place up for this evening. It's almost certainly just been vacuumed, although I know from my experience with only one shedding animal that it's a Sisyphean struggle to keep clean any house in which a dog lives. Still, the smell of a wood-burning fire eclipses the odor of dog, and the way I feel right now, I could stay here the rest of my life.

Strewn along the mantel is a cone-and-berry garland with blinking lights, and Christmas cards hang from a ribbon. Eggnog is produced by a young woman who identifies herself as Charlotte, someone's niece. Orchestral Christmas music plays softly in the background, and I'm so happy to be here right now, so strangely comfortable with these people I hardly know, that I fantasize about curling up in this giant old leather armchair and falling asleep. In fact, I'm about to nod off when Alma appears with an oven mitt on one hand and a giant plastic baster in the other. She is accompanied by yet another large white dog and a chaotic bunch of puppies, one of which runs to me and jumps in my lap.

"Ha! Bernie seems to like you!"

Bernie! Funny name for a dog. "Maybe he likes me because I am already so covered in Luna's hair that he thinks I'm his mother," I say. I cleaned myself up, ran a lint brush over my clothes before leaving the hotel to try to look presentable, but I needn't have bothered. The puppy curls up in my lap, claiming me. Luna comes over and nuzzles him adorably.

Another man appears. He's tall and clean-shaven, with thinning red hair.

"I've heard a lot about you," he says, extending a hand. "I'm Gabe, Alma's husband. Alma tells me you snuck a dog into our hotel."

"I'm so sorry! I thought it was okay. I mean, I know I wasn't supposed to, but we had a tacit agreement . . ." I'm not sure if I should keep talking or if I'm digging myself a hole. I also wonder if this is something other than the lovely invitation Ingram advertised. Maybe I've been summoned to pay a price for my transgression.

"He's got a bad sense of humor," Alma says. "Just ignore him. We're all so glad that you're okay." She looks different than she did when I first saw her two days ago in the hotel. Tall and striking in her knee-high leather boots, she is wearing a stunning hand-knit sweater that looks like one you might buy in the overpriced gift shop of a ski resort.

"First, let me apologize. I hope this isn't an overwhelming dog situation for you. We usually keep them in the kennel—it's heated, don't worry. It's pretty nice in there, like a five-star hotel. But we have a Christmas tradition of letting them all come inside. If it's too much, let me know."

"No, no, it's fine. I love it," I say.

"I heard you had quite an adventure yesterday. Tell us everything," she says. "But give me a minute first. I need to go deal with the roast."

We pass the next hour regaling the Evetts with the tale of our debacle in the woods and our trip to the ER. I don't mention the part where I saw a variety of objects hovering in the sky, or where I finally had a moment with my mother, nor do I mention what the doctor said about the scars. Even without these juicy details, Alma appears to be listening, like she's hanging on my every word.

⋈   ⋈   ⋈

More people arrive, all family, so far as I can tell. There are two more couples, both with young children, and another family that I believe are cousins, along with their teenaged kids. Dogs run in and out, children play, logs crackle in the fire, and I count my blessings to have been invited, quite randomly, to this warm family event.

The dinner seating stretches from the dining room into the living room, with what appear to be three tables pushed together to create enough space for this large group. "I have a story," Gabe says after we have all gorged on the delicious pot roast.

There is a collective groan from the children.

"Please, no," one of the nieces says, but she seems to be laughing as she protests.

"It's a farm story," he adds.

"Oh, the one about the talking dog? That one's okay," a red-haired, green-sweatered boy who looks to be about eleven says.

"Thank you for the stamp of approval. Well then. We begin:

"A man is driving down the road when he spots a farm. He's not from around here. He's a stranger, just passing through town . . ."

I glance over at Ingram to see his reaction, but he is listening intently, a hint of a smile on his face.

"By the way," Gabe says, apparently speaking to me, "this story takes place in West Virginia, a few miles from here, in case you are wondering." He then resumes:

"And he sees a sign on the front porch of a house. And it says: 'Talking dog. Five dollars.' So he pulls over, of course. I mean, how could he not?"

"Wait, Uncle Gabe," one of the younger kids says. "Does

that mean you can buy the talking dog for five dollars? Or you can listen to him talk for five dollars?"

"That's a very perceptive question, William. The dog is for sale. But you are right to ask. That's too low a price for a dog. It's an old joke that needs to be adjusted for inflation.

"So anyway, he pulls over and knocks on the door and says to the owner, 'Can I check out the dog? See if it really talks?'

"And the owner says, 'Help yourself, dog's out back.' So he goes out back and sure enough, there's the dog and he starts talking and talking . . ."

"What kind of dog is he?" William asks.

"Another good question! He's like one of ours. Big retriever, of course. Part husky. So this big white Lusky starts to tell the man about his life. It's really something. The dog is retired now, he says, but he'd been CIA. He'd traveled everywhere and pretty much seen it all: the fall of Saigon, the Soviet withdrawal from Afghanistan . . . He'd even had dinner with Chairman Mao. His most harrowing adventure, he said, was sneaking into North Korea undercover as an arms dealer, then having dinner with Kim Jong-Un."

"I think you must mean Kim Il-Sung?" Alma asks. "You might have a timeline problem."

"It's a dog story, just go with the flow," Gabe says. "So the dog, he goes on and on talking. And this man, this stranger, is amazed. They talk for nearly an hour. The man then goes back to the farmhouse and knocks on the door and says to the owner, 'Your dog is amazing! Not only can he talk, but the stories he told! Are you really selling him?'

"And the owner says, 'Yes, you can have him. That dog's a damn liar; he hasn't been off this farm a day in his life!'"

There are a few laughs, a few groans. I can't help but laugh—I didn't see that punch line coming. The puppy, Bernie, who has apparently been under the table, jumps into my lap again and licks my face.

"That's my favorite story," says one of the younger kids. "I love it when you tell that!"

"It is a good story," I agree.

"Well, speaking of strangers," Alma says, "you still haven't told us what brings you to town, Cassie. I mean, when I saw your dog and told Gabe about it, we figured you were here to pick up a puppy."

"Really?" Nothing is further from my mind than acquiring another puppy.

"Oh sure. We have people come in from all over the country. These aren't pedigreed dogs obviously. They are mutts, but they're very popular. For whatever reason, people especially like the ones with the two different-colored eyes."

"Luna's enough puppy for me right now, but I'll know where to come next time." Then, for no reason, I begin to reminisce aloud about every dog I've owned, in reverse order. When I get to Benjamin, Alma looks at me like she's seen a ghost.

"I know Benjamin is not the most unusual name in the world for a dog," she says, "but—I'm going out on a crazy limb here, forgive me in advance—you aren't the daughter of . . . Well, now that I think of it, I can't even remember the family's name, so never mind."

I instinctively put a hand to my head and start worrying the gauze.

"What do you mean?" I ask.

"I don't know. Just a crazy thought. Never mind."

"I'm curious now."

"Well, a long, long time ago, we had this couple come in from DC. My dad was still alive, it was his farm then, but I was there that day too. This couple, they were friends of friends of friends . . . I don't even remember how they heard about our mutts, but we were trying to rehouse a dog, about a year and a half old. He was a fantastic dog, but the family that bought him originally, they were hunters and had hoped Benjamin—that was his name, which is why I'm telling you this story—would be a good hunting dog. We told them these aren't hunting dogs, but he wasn't having it. Then of course, we were right. He wouldn't retrieve. I mean, maybe he *could* retrieve if he wanted to, but the problem was he wouldn't leave the owner's side to go get the dead duck or whatever. He was what we call a Velcro dog. Overly attached."

"Or maybe the dog was a vegetarian," one of the kids offers.

"Good point. So anyway, these people returned Benjamin. They didn't want a pet, they said. They wanted a working dog. It's a little harder to place an adult dog, so we weren't trying to sell him; we just wanted him to have a good home. So, like I was saying, this couple came all the way from DC. They had a little girl with them, and they all stopped by the farm and stayed for lunch. We always vet the people who are taking our dogs, and they seemed like good folks. It's a terrible story though. It was kind of late in the day, and we talked about how maybe they should stay over and drive home in the morning, but they had a kid, and now a dog, and they were talking about all they had to do before the holidays, and they wanted to get home. So off they went. It was about four thirty. They drove onto the bridge at the exact wrong time . . ."

My body is processing this information more effectively than my brain. I stiffen. I sit upright. If I were a dog, my ears would be pointing high in the air to better absorb each word. This is the closest to an out-of-body experience I've ever had. Stranger, even, than my hypothermic hallucinations—if that's what they were—in the woods. This time the coincidence is so coincidental it can't possibly be true. I want to call Uncle Harry, to beseech him to apply some clinical epistemological concoction, to dismiss it as such-and-such bias, to make it disappear. But then I think of what the doctor told me yesterday, about the scars. I don't know how anyone, even Uncle Harry, can explain this away.

"The only saving grace of the story was that dog. He might have been a lousy retriever, but he was one hell of a swimmer. He saved that little girl's life."

"How?" is all I can ask.

"Someone said they saw her hanging on to his collar," Mitch says.

"I heard someone mention a plastic toy too," says one of the other brothers. "It was buoyant. No one knows for sure, but maybe the girl hung on to the toy for a while, then the dog. Who knows what really happened, but all three of them made it to shore."

"Do you know what happened to the girl?" Ingram asks.

"Nope. Strangest thing. I know they located her family. Her relatives, that is. Her parents died in the accident. Her aunt and uncle came to get her, but they were very private people. They didn't want to talk to reporters, and I heard later that when they tried to interview the family for historical records and such, they declined."

I ought to cry. Or scream. Or collapse. Let my head fall onto the table and dramatically convulse. Instead, I freeze; I'm in such shock that I let the moment pass without reacting, and before I know it, we have shifted seamlessly to the subject of dessert. This story, the most important story I've ever heard, is at the end of the day just another story told around the dinner table, not much different from the one about the talking dog.

⋈   ⋈   ⋈

After dessert, we move back into the living room. Although I am a new person now, with a new backstory, nothing here in the present has changed. More logs are thrown on the fire, the children discuss their favorite presents, the dogs romp through the house, and every time I set the puppy down, it crawls back into my lap.

Finally, everyone says their goodbyes. As we get ready to leave, Alma pulls me aside. "Just leave your keys with me," she says. "I'll take care of the car while you're gone."

"What do you mean?"

"I mean, while you go to DC to get your glasses, I'll bring the car over here. I can put it in the garage until you get back to pick it up. It's not a problem."

"Oh my. I didn't realize you'd heard my whole embarrassing saga."

"Embarrassing? You're talking to a woman who has lived through hundreds of puppies destroying more items than I care to recount. Why do you think we have a no-dogs policy at the hotel! I just didn't want you to worry about the car while you're gone."

"I appreciate that, thank you! I don't even have a plan to be gone yet. I have to call home and sort it out. Maybe I can get my daughter to FedEx my glasses or something. I'm sure there's a way."

"Oh, that's a good plan too. I didn't know . . . Ingram told me . . . Oh, never mind."

CHAPTER 34

Boxing Day

SOMETIMES YOU SET out to acquire a puppy, and sometimes a puppy sets out to acquire you. Clearly the latter occurred last night, when Bernie followed us out the front door of the farmhouse, hopped into the cab of Ingram's truck, then nestled into my lap.

"I guess we're taking him with us," I'd joked.

Something about it seemed strangely fitting given the paradigm shift that had quietly taken place at dinner. All those momentous details tucked so matter-of-factly into one more anecdote. The evening had left me a changed woman with a new story. So why not get a new dog?

Admittedly, that's not the most rational way to think about the situation, though nothing about my canine relationships has ever quite made sense. And yet, in this case, maybe it does. A dog saved my life. So why not surround myself with all the puppies I can?

Left unspoken, however, is the reality check. I am going to take Bernie the puppy *where*? And who is *us*?

⋈　　⋈　　⋈

Now it is the next morning, and we are back in the truck, heading east, two sweet white puppies with beautiful, crazy mismatched eyes curled up in the back seat. I look over my shoulder and see the big one is spooning the little one, as cute as anything you might find on one of those Instagram reels Vera sometimes sends to me; one adorable dog video after another, so addictive it's possible to lose an hour each time I pick up my phone.

An hour ago, before handing my keys to Alma, I did one last quick scan of the car. My keen scientific thought for the day was that if the moth was still in there, by now it would have surely keeled from the cold, then dropped to the floor. But it was nowhere to be seen. Again, I checked in every crevice, looked in the glove compartment and under the floor mats, to no avail.

"Are you sure this is cool?" I ask Ingram as he drives slowly down the main street. All but the coffee shop is shuttered this early in the morning.

"What do you mean?"

"Driving me all the way back to Washington . . . driving at all in these conditions."

"Don't worry," he says. "I took a good look at the weather. The storm's tracking north of where we're headed. We'll be fine."

"You still haven't told me what brings you east." Now we are on the same road we traveled with Cynthia on Christmas Eve, two days ago. As we pass the turnoff for the TNT area, I briefly fantasize about finding that spot again, seeing if I can recreate the circumstances, seeing if I can decipher any meaning in my delusions—the convergence of the moth, my mother, the nightguard, the poor sweet bluebird. But I know that wasn't much different from a dream, except for the part about almost dying from hypothermia. I'd simply been hallucinating, my brain playing loose with all the flotsam and jetsam it has accumulated these last few days.

A few miles beyond the turnoff, plumes of smoke bellow from a tall stack.

"What brings me east?" he asks after a moment, as if this is a trick question. "Oh, you mean why am I driving you to DC? I need to get back to New York to teach next week. I was going to head out in a couple of days, but it's good for me to get home early. I've got a couple of thesis students I'm working with and a bunch of meetings later in the week."

"Thesis students? Wait, you're a *teacher*? I thought you were a cryptozoologist. Although I suppose the two aren't mutually exclusive. Do you teach cryptozoology? Did you need a master's degree for that? Or teaching credentials?"

"I never said that I'm a cryptozoologist. You made an assumption."

"What do you mean? That's exactly what you said."

"No. I may have said that it's my field, but I never said I'm a cryptozoologist. That's not how I identify."

"Okay, mince some words, why don't you?"

Now we are on the ramp, entering the highway. The sun is poking through the clouds, and I reach for the visor that clips onto my glasses, then remember that I have no glasses to which to attach it. With my blurred vision and the sun in my eyes, the landscape looks so different this morning from when I first drove it that I don't recognize a single thing. Then again, since we are traveling in the opposite direction, I'm seeing all of this from a different perspective, so perhaps that shouldn't be surprising.

"Okay, enlighten me. Who are you really? Where do you live, and what do you do?"

"I'm Ingram. I live in New York. State, not the city of. And I teach at Bard."

"Teach what?"

"I'm in the philosophy department, going on some twenty years. Phenomenology has long been my field, one of them."

"No. No way. I don't understand." I so don't understand what is happening that I want to put my head in my hands and weep. I'm not even sure what it is that I don't understand anymore, so I seize on the most obvious part. "Your West Virginia license plate . . ."

"Oh, that. Funny coincidence. I borrowed my friend's truck. He used to teach at WVU. Small world, right?"

"Why?"

"Why what? Why did I borrow his truck? My car is in the shop. Someone rammed into me last week in the parking lot at the post office—surprising amount of damage. It's not drivable, and they can't even start working on it until next week. I have a rental in the meantime, but it's not a car I'd want to take on a trip in winter, so Morris said I could take his truck. Does that answer your question?"

"One of my many questions, I guess. Phenomenology? Is that why you were cracking up about my uncle? And why did you tell me you're a cryptozoologist or whatever it is that you said that made me think you are? And while we're on the subject, is that even really a thing?"

"Of course it's a thing, but you're making a whole bunch of assumptions here. I'm not lying to you. I study cryptids, that part is true, but that's in service of my book."

"Oh dear God. Et tu, Brute? You're writing a *book*?"

"*Now* what did I do?"

"You hadn't mentioned a book, that's all."

"Well, you never asked. I wasn't being fully transparent, yes, but I wasn't lying, strictly speaking. I let everyone I interview know about the project. I find it's better not to walk around telling people that I'm an academic. They might think I have an attitude, or that I'm setting them up to mock them somehow, and I don't, and I won't. I'm genuinely interested in the experiences of the people who experience these things.

"I'm not looking to pass judgment; I don't have answers as to why these sightings happen—but I'm fascinated by them, and by the people who see them. Like Cynthia, they tend to be honest, grounded folks, just going about their business—they are a snapshot of the general population, with some outliers here and there, sure. But I'm sorry if you think I misled you."

"You don't need to apologize to me," I say. He surely has no idea that it's the mention of his stupid book that has triggered me. Why is everyone in my life writing a book? Why am I, as he might put it, an outlier? Why am *I* not writing a book? Why do I think I need to write a book? Just because Olivia is writing a book, and Samantha is writing a book, and now Ingram, for the love of God, is writing a book, doesn't mean I need to write a book too! I try to normalize the conversation, such as it is, given that we are talking about cryptids.

"Okay, since we are putting it all out there, I have a kind of random, crazy question," I say.

"No question is too crazy."

"Evidently. So is there any connection between your name and the sewing machine salesman?"

"Say what?"

"That Indrid Cold character? Your name, Ingram. It's not the same, but it's not that different either. There are similarities."

"That they both begin with the letter *I*?"

"Sure. Same number of letters and syllables too. And both somewhat unusual."

"No connection. I'm named for my awful uncle Ingram, if you really want to know. He's quite the namesake. A hell of a guy. Had a couple of illegitimate kids, lost his house to gambling debts, did some time for writing bad checks. But anyway, you are thinking of the wrong guy. The alien, or whatever you want to call him—the guy who got out of the spacecraft and said, 'I'll see you in time'—that was Indrid Cold. The sewing machine salesman was named Woody Derenberger."

"My bad. Speaking of which, I looked it up. You are not, strictly speaking, correct about spacecraft."

"Remind me of the issue?"

"*Spacecraft* versus *spacecrafts*. Plural. There is a listing for *spacecrafts*."

"Seriously? I believe that is incorrect."

"You are arguing with the dictionary?"

"No. I guess I'd say it's not standard usage."

"That is exactly what it said. *Nonstandard usage*."

"That's my point. But as I was saying before you hijacked the conversation, as a phenomenologist, I'm interested in people's experiences. I want to know what they saw, or what they think they saw, and how it changed their perception."

"I don't know how this is possible."

"Which is *this*?"

"That you're a phenomenologist. That you're a writer. I mean, now I remember you were hinting, like pretentiously name-dropping John Gardner, sure, but then you seemed to want to throw me off with your ridiculous cover."

"Seriously, there's no cover. Everyone I talk to knows who I am. If they choose to identify me as the crypto guy or whatever, that's on them, not me. That's how they experience me. Just like they experience you as the woman with the puppy who is bleeding from the head."

"Do they? That's sad and embarrassing."

"Just a first impression."

"Jeez. Thanks."

"They get beyond that eventually. Maybe?"

"I guess that's who I am right now, so no mistake there."

"Well, since we're playing true confessions, who were you before, and who will you be tomorrow?"

"Oof. Profound." I'm silent for a long time, staring out at the snowy mountains. A rest stop clicks by. I see a sign for Dunkin' that makes my stomach rumble. Then, without fully meaning to, I begin to talk and I can't seem to stop. I hear myself over-share, expounding on the circumstances of my derailed journalism career. I tell him about my moth obsession. I tell him what I've just pieced together. And it feels so good to talk, to finally stop treating my life like it's one big terrible secret that even I'm not allowed to know. It pours out unchecked, all of it, core secrets opened, exposed to light, declassified, chapters flying into the ether.

I tell him about my dogs. Each and every one and in too much detail: Benjamin, Lucy, Stella, Ruth, and what I loved best about each one. I tell him about Vera, although I am not so lost in my own narrative that I bore him with the sorts of things that only her parents would care about—first steps, funny linguistic goofs, soccer trophies, ribbons at science fairs. I tell him about Samantha and Evan, about Olivia and Harry. Then I tell him about Richard, and about his weather obsession, and proceed to his so-called shame.

"Don't tell me he's that guy who predicted the Noah's ark situation. That's your husband? Good grief!"

"It's called an ARkStorm, technically."

"And then he faked some windstorm . . . *that* guy?"

"Yup. That's Richard. And . . . it's crazy that I'm telling you this, but maybe you of all people would understand . . . I've never told this to anyone before, but one of the craziest things in our marriage is . . . you're going to think I'm a nutcase . . . that my husband looks kind of like Richard Gere in the movie *The Mothman Prophecies*."

"John Klein, you mean?"

"Yeah, and it gets weirder. He works at the *Washington Post*."

"That is very weird."

"Seriously. I'm not even done. His last name is Klein."

"Your husband is named Richard Klein and he works at the *Washington Post* and he looks like Richard Gere. Let me process this for a minute. Is that a crazy coincidence, or is it possible that the director, or the screenwriter or whoever, saw your husband and his movie star good looks and noticed the resemblance to Richard Gere, and *that* helped inform the character?"

"You are such a rationalist. Never thought I'd say this to a cryptozoologist. But yes, that thought has crossed my mind. But even so, it's weird, right?"

"Oh, no question. And yet it makes perfect sense. I don't want to interrupt, but it's lunchtime. Want to stop and get a bite, let the dogs out for a few?"

⋈   ⋈   ⋈

I hadn't realized how long we'd been driving. We're in Maryland, and I recognize the exit where Luna and I stopped for lunch on Thursday. I'm a creature of habit. I take comfort in the familiar, even at the risk of it being dull, so I direct him to the parking lot, and we make our way to the *Sims* café.

This might be Bernie's first proper walk on a leash, and he yanks it around, a yo-yo on a string. People stop and stare. Someone even takes a video.

Not much has changed in the last three days: Santa still stands guard at the door, but he looks like he's lost his oomph, like his mojo is gone. There is such a thing as Too Much Christmas. You can see it. It's time to rest up for next year. The place is quiet. And the only buffalo plaid is on the professor of phenomenology, who is trying to blend into a landscape where he doesn't appear to belong.

The hostess with the peroxided hair greets me warmly like we're old friends. Her candy cane earrings have been replaced by tiny silver hoops.

"You again, with the puppy! Oh wait, now . . . two? Or am I seeing double?"

Ingram is standing over by the giant rock. The little puppy is trying to scale it, but he keeps slipping back down.

"Same?" she asks.

"Same . . . dog?"

"Same order?"

"Oh, sure. Good memory. Just make it two."

"It was two."

"Touché."

A few minutes later she delivers a couple of grilled cheese sandwiches and onion rings straight to the rock.

"Pretty good, right?" I ask Ingram as he unwraps the paper and takes a bite.

"Nearly as good as the Moth Café, but not quite."

⋈   ⋈   ⋈

"So this husband of yours, the Noah's ark guy, looks like a movie star, eh?" Ingram says once we are back on the road. Bernie keeps trying to crawl into Ingram's lap while he drives; then Luna gets the same idea. I look around for something to distract them both and find Gumby. I toss him into the back to be devoured by lions. Bernie works on his head while Luna gnaws on his remaining arm.

"He does, but good looks only get a person so far. I mean . . . it got him pretty far professionally. In his defense, he was good at what he did. Until he wasn't. But as for us, it's over," I say boldly. It's been over for a long time, but I can be a little slow to act. Which is really the story of my life—which I mean in a literal sense. It's like I know things, but it takes me a very long time to process them. A decade. Two. Three, even.

"I've spent my entire life aware that the story about my parents and the bridge collapse didn't add up, but what did I do about it? I think I may have deflected, spent all of my energy focusing on the moth."

"And yet look at what you just did. You got in the car on your own, and you figured things out."

"Yeah, sort of. I still don't understand why it's been a big secret. It's not like anyone did anything wrong, so far as I know. Am I missing something? Is there some reveal yet to come? Were my parents criminals? Spies? Living under some aliases? I don't think so. It sounds like my parents drove to West Virginia to get a freaking puppy! They were in the wrong place at the wrong time. Big deal. I mean, it's a huge deal, obviously, but why the secret about the whole thing? And why didn't anyone tell me that I was in the car?"

"I can't answer that."

"I'm aware. I'm just venting."

"Vent away."

Instead of venting, I scream. Something is fluttering in the back seat. Or else it's the universe, messing with my head yet again.

Ingram looks in the rearview mirror and glimpses the fluttering thing. "Some kind of insect," he says all matter-of-fact, like having an insect that is possibly a moth trapped in the car is no big deal, which I guess for some people is a shocking possibility. "Could be a stink bug. Or who knows what."

Both puppies are scampering back and forth. Bernie even climbs on top of Luna, trying to capture the thing, which has settled on the ceiling of the car. Luna stares it for a moment, then lunges, and this time succeeds.

"Well, it *was* a bug," Ingram says. "Now it's dog food. It's as simple as that. So you were saying?"

"I wish I'd seen it."

"Why? A bug is a bug. Well, most of the time."

"Can I tell you something weird?"

"Sure, that would be a nice change of pace. Nothing we have talked about so far is weird."

"It's possible this is the weirdest thing of all."

"Let's hear."

"So this moth that was in my car . . . Did I tell you about that already?"

"You did not."

"As Luna and I were driving here . . . well, really, before we were headed to West Virginia, we were on the way to my aunt and uncle's house in Delaware, crossing the Chesapeake Bay Bridge . . ."

"Oh, that's an awesome bridge! One of my favorites. A construction marvel. It's on my longlist of projects to study the people who experience gephyrophobia, on that bridge specifically."

"Yes, well, I guess design- and construction-wise it's awesome. Less awesome when you are stuck on it like I was. I had, shall we say, an episode. I don't have gephyrophobia, but there was an accident. Traffic was backed up for miles, I was stuck on the bridge, and it was starting to rain, a freezing rain, and Luna was going nuts, lunging back and forth like she did just now."

"So what happened?"

"There was a moth trapped in the car. I wasn't thinking too much of it at first, but then it landed on my seat, and it had these crazy red eyes. It looked . . . okay, you are going to think I'm nuts, but it looked like the Mothman. Or at least like the way they always draw the Mothman. These big eyes, bulging red."

"Oh, I just read something about that. They found some rare moth at the airport. From Ethiopia, I think."

"Exactly! I just read that too."

"Had you been traveling to Africa?"

"Not recently. I was there, yes, but a zillion years ago."

"So maybe it got into your luggage. Maybe it was, like, a pod, a cocoon."

"Are you serious? That was more than twenty years ago."

"I don't think I'm serious, but what do I know? I'm a cryptozoologist—or at least you seem to think I am. I only know stuff about cryptids. Not so much about real moths. But like the doctor said, there isn't always a rational explanation."

Maybe this thing *has* been trapped in my suitcase for twenty-five years, though it's highly unlikely. I don't remember the provenance of the duffel into which I shoved all my things, but the odds are stacked against it being the same bag I took to Ethiopia. Maybe the moth flitted into my car from another vehicle at a gas station, where I might have left the door open.

"Did you see that other strange bug story last week?"

"No," I say hesitantly. "Do I even want to know?"

"They found some insect in a Walmart in Arkansas. They say it hasn't been seen in North America in more than fifty years. They thought it was extinct."

"So?"

"They're saying it's an insect from the Jurassic era. The theory is that the bug may have largely disappeared for environmental reasons. But now they think it's possible that small pockets of the insects have quietly existed for years. And one of them had the misfortune of winding up on a truck en route to Walmart."

"Strange. It's like it broke through time. Or survived time. Or kind of existed outside time."

"Right? It's not the same, but it makes me think about the dogs of Chernobyl," he says.

"What about the dogs of Chernobyl?"

"Like I said, it's not the same, but they have studied some of the stray dogs that survived the disaster. When people evacuated, many had to leave their dogs behind. Officials tried to kill them, worried they might be contaminated, or be a menace— wild dogs roaming on their own. But . . . kind of like this Jurassic bug situation, some of them survived and bred and lived in their own enclave. Some of them right inside the power plant.

"Years later, when they did a study, they found that these dogs were genetically different. Their DNA was not the same as other dogs."

"That's scary. What does it mean though? Different in what way?"

"Inconclusive last I read about it. Just a curiosity. More evidence that there are strange things out there. Some of it can be explained scientifically. Some of it cannot."

"Don't you wish fewer things were inconclusive? It seems like everything is inconclusive. It might be nice to have an answer or two in black-and-white."

"I can tell you conclusively that we are approaching DC, and you need to direct me from here."

"Next exit, sorry. You'd better get over quickly. I wasn't paying attention." The next exit, an eighth of a mile from where we are, involves merging right across some four lanes of Beltway traffic, which is, luckily, mercifully light.

We exit the Beltway and merge onto River Road. I tell him to stay on this route until it ends and then turn right on Wisconsin. Every time I go this way, I say a little prayer of gratitude that Vera survived her high school years, recounting the names of two of her classmates who died in accidents on this stretch, new drivers, out late on dark roads.

I direct him another few miles and tell him to pull into an empty spot across the street from my house.

"So you were saying?" he asks, cutting the ignition and turning to face me.

"What was I saying about what, when?"

"You were talking about the man you call your husband. Dick, I believe is his name."

"Dick! Right. He is such a dick. I tried to help him through this. I've tried from day one. I never fully understood what the problem was, whether something terrible happened to him as a child, or he saw some scarring scary movie, like the way I'm still haunted by a too-early viewing of The Birds—but for whatever reason, he has always been weather-obsessed. We never talked about it in anything but a superficial way. But then, we never talked about my situation either. He was curiously not curious."

"Another word for that is *self-absorbed*. Not that I want to pile onto a man I've never met. Even if he sounds like a jerk. His wife, by contrast, is interesting."

"She is?"

"Well, I've just ferried her and her puppies of mass destruction on a six-hour journey, and we haven't stopped talking for a minute. So yeah, there seems to be something mildly intriguing here."

I don't know what it says about me that I have trouble accepting this at face value. I should just lean in for a kiss. Instead, I've got more stupid witty banter on the tip of my tongue, and I consider asking if he means there's something of interest in the sense that he wants to study me phenomenologically, or something less scholarly.

Before I can land on a response, he leans over and presses his lips to mine, and I lean into every romance novel cliché, kissing him hungrily, melting into his arms. He smells of sandalwood and laundry detergent that I believe might be Tide. I want to crawl across the gearshift and into his lap, but we are parked in front of my house and it is still light outside. Plus, we are a little old, and possibly too creaky, for sex in the car.

I think of Cynthia, in the car with her paramour, necking as the Mothman, red-eyed, circled above. On my busy street, it's more likely that the red eyes that might show up to disturb us would be from the headlights of a police car.

From my vantage point, my head on Ingram's shoulder, where I want it to stay all night, I see Vera's Corolla parked up the street. She has moved it from the driveway, and in its place is a sporty, red, electric Volvo with Delaware plates—Olivia's new car. I wonder what my aunt and uncle are doing here. Then, like this is the final scene in a slasher novel, I see what can only be the Elainemobile—Elaine's red Prius—parked just up the block.

"This can't be good," I say.

His expression changes to disappointment. "It seems pretty good to me," he says.

"Oh no, not that. That part is good," I say. "It's pretty great, really. I could do with a lot more of this. Maybe we can . . . make a date?" I see a group of people walking up the sidewalk and realize that anyone nearby can see us—not that I hugely care, but still. My family is inside my house, and I need to formally end things with Richard, or rather Dick, first. I pull away but take Ingram's hand. It's warm and soft and lovely, and I hold it tight. "But I think something is going on at home. Everyone is here. I'd better go deal with my life."

"I understand. So I guess this is goodbye for now?"

"Unless . . . Do you want to come in? You might need water, or a bathroom?" I can't imagine the drama of having him walk into my house right now—it's a very bad idea—but also I don't want to be rude.

"No, I'm going to power on through to my nephew's house in Baltimore."

I grab my bag from the back and affix the leash to Luna's collar.

"You're forgetting something," he says.

I look around, check for my wallet and cell phone. I have my keys. My head still sits atop my neck. "No, I've got it all."

"What about the puppy?"

"Oh, right!" I look at Bernie, who stares at me with his big mismatched eyes. If I thought walking through the door with Ingram might raise eyebrows, I try to imagine the looks on everyone's faces when I walk through the door with two dogs and they already think I'm nuts with one. I'm tempted to walk in with the whole entourage—this new, lovely man and these two adorable puppies—but I think of Vera and would never do anything, at least consciously, to upset her.

"What if I hang on to him for a bit?" Ingram says. "I'll take him for now. Next time we meet we can discuss future custody arrangements."

"That would be amazing. Thank you. And that's what I'm forgetting. I don't have your phone number."

"You don't really think I'd let you go without getting your number, do you? I'm going to AirDrop my contact to you right now."

"Well, aren't you fancy with the AirDrop." My phone dings, and there it is, his contact information. An email at bard.edu. A New York area code.

"I have a thought," he says. "I've got to go back to Point Pleasant in about two weeks. I've set up a couple more meetings. Want a lift to go back and get your car?"

"Really? You're going back? I mean, yes, but DC isn't exactly on the way."

"I can make it be on the way. Besides, we need to go back for hibachi, and to get your hat and gloves."

"Right. That's quite a loss. I've been losing sleep over it. But yes, I'll take you up on the ride. And hibachi. This time steak."

"It's a date. I'll be in touch. And I'll see you soon."

"I'll see you in time."

"Sooner than that, I hope."

I lean back in for another long kiss. The dogs have apparently had enough of this, or at least Luna has, and she begins to bark. Bernie leaps across the seat and pushes his way between us. He then licks Ingram's face and puts his tongue in his ear.

"You two, get a room," I say.

"That's a great idea," he says. "Except you need to join us."

"Soon," I say and lead Luna out of the car.

Part 3

CHAPTER 35

Reckoning, 1

I SET MY bags down on the front steps of our semidetached brick house on Ordway Street, then take Luna for a quick walk. We've been in the car for hours, and I need to clear my head before walking into whatever strange scenario is unfolding in the house.

It's a cold, crisp afternoon, and the sun, in its descent, filters bright through the trees. Our neighborhood always does Christmas big, and this year is no exception. The house on the northwest corner of our block has an inflatable Santa pulling a sleigh of reindeer that must be twelve feet tall, and judging from years past, we will be looking at this for a few weeks more, until it is replaced by an equally flashy Valentine's Day display.

Closing the loop on our block, I'm back at our house. But something stops me from walking up the steps, and it's not just the presence of Olivia's car, or the Elainemobile parked up the street. My mind is still swirling from everything I've learned on this trip, and I wish I had a few days to pull my thoughts together. Instead, I am going to have to plunge right into the maelstrom. I don't understand why on earth everyone is assembled here. Are they throwing me a surprise party, or staging an intervention?

I still can't bring myself to go inside, so I decide to walk a bit more, pay another visit to the giant Santa. I then circle around to the back of the house, walking through the alley and then entering our yard through the garage, inside of which sits Richard's car, which as far as I know he hasn't driven in a couple of years. I stare at the rows of dead azaleas and decimated perennials that need clearing out. Richard used to help me in the yard, but like everything else in our marriage, that's a thing of the past, and the detritus of our garden is now my problem, alone.

I'm some five hundred feet from the house and can see through the French doors a family sitting around the dinner table. Without my glasses I can't make out any details, but I don't need twenty-twenty vision for this: I would know each member of this family even if I were blindfolded.

Vera and Richard are seated at opposite ends of our oak dining table. Olivia and Harry are across from each other on the horizontal side. Next to Harry sits Elaine. There are take-out bags on the kitchen counter. I'm guessing Chinese, but that's pure conjecture. It could be Peruvian chicken, or something from the Indian restaurant a couple of blocks away, all of which are part of our regular rotation.

I'm observing these people like they are other, or maybe I am other, like the customers in the *Sims* café. And yet here they are, all of them, sitting around my dining room table, in my house. This enrages me sufficiently to propel me to the back door, which is, for better or worse, unlocked.

Vera startles. Then, five pairs of eyes stare at me, like I've just come back from the dead.

"Mom! What happened?"

"Oh my," says Harry. "Didn't I tell you to keep an eye on that head?"

I put my hand to my head and am reminded of the gauze. "It's nothing," I say. "I am perfectly okay. Long story, but I'm on the mend."

I let go of Luna's leash, and she bolts in the direction of the living room and begins to bark. Vera turns her attention to the front window, where a squirrel is hanging from a branch. This reminds me that I've left my bags out front. I walk through the dining room and then through the living room to retrieve them, and on my way back into the house I notice, on the credenza, five champagne flutes and an empty bottle. I feel hurt about having been left out of whatever celebration is occurring, but then remember that I'm the one who has fled.

"What are we celebrating?" I ask, setting my bags down.

"Richard's news!" Elaine says excitedly. I wonder if Elaine knows that I know about them. That I stuck her nightguard in my mouth—an act that still nauseates me to remember, and that will likely haunt me in my dreams for some time to come. Presumably Richard has told her that they are busted, but given his communication skills, who knows. This is not the time for that conversation, however, and I do not want to create a scene—at least not right now, not here with Vera in the room.

"What news?"

"He got an offer. Came in the day before Christmas."

"An offer?" Somehow, through this ordeal, he has hung on

to his job, so I'm not sure what she is referring to. A new job,
I guess.

"Yeah, it was really unexpected," he says. "I didn't mention
it, but a few weeks ago a literary agent reached out. She thought
I might have a good story to tell."

"About what?" I try not to sound mortified, but possibly fail.

"Well, that's what I asked too, but she had it all figured out. A
memoir. About rising to the top of my profession, then crashing
and burning, and then my comeback. Not that I've come back
yet, but the book will be part of the redemption strategy. It will
also double as a sort of how-to business book. About how to
come back from being canceled."

"I don't understand. Do you even know how to write a book
proposal?"

"She's one of those big agents who has people who do that
for you. They can write the book for you too, if you want them
to. And yeah, she sent the proposal out last week and said she'd
be taking offers after the holidays, but then we heard from
someone at Random House, and I guess they are doing what
you call a pre-empt."

"Again, I don't understand."

"Which part?" asks Olivia. "I used to be a book editor, as
you might remember. Plus, I just went through this when I was
shopping my book, so I can help shed light on the process."

I can't bear to be in this room a minute longer. "I'm exhausted
from the drive, and it's been a long couple of days. I'm going
upstairs to take a shower," I say. But then I see Vera staring at
my stuff. Her eyes seem to have landed on the shopping bag
from the Mothman Museum, which is on the floor next to my
suitcase.

I then see Harry and Olivia staring at the shopping bag too. "Where have you been?" Vera asks.

"Long story there too. I'll fill you in. I got you a silly little gift," I say, trying to be nonchalant. I hand her the bag and plant a kiss on top of her head. "I can't wait to catch up with you later, when everyone is gone." Then I walk upstairs and take a very long shower. By the time I emerge, Olivia's car is gone, and I can see through the window that Elaine has just turned on her ignition.

CHAPTER 36

Reckoning, 2

I SPEND MUCH of the night flopping around, trying to find a spot that will induce sleep. Luna is restless too. She curls into the backs of my calves, then, moments later, relocates to lie beside me vertically, puts her head on the pillow, and begins to snore. I know I ought to throw her off the bed, but it's a comfort to have her pressed beside me, an antidote to the dread of what I know needs to happen in the morning—to talk, or attempt to talk, to Richard. To bring this moldering marriage to an end.

I must fall asleep at some point, because the ding of my phone startles me, and it takes a moment to realize where I am.

There's a text from Ingram. I enlarge the image and see he has sent a picture of Bernie, sprawled out on a leather sofa, mouth open, tongue hanging out, tiny paws in the air, his white-and-pink belly face up.

Someone misses you.

You or Bernie? I type and then cringe. I'm too groggy to be texting. I sound like a lovesick adolescent.

I search my phone for a picture of Luna to text back and find the cute one of her in the car with her head on my shoulder, my road trip copilot. It's the photo Olivia took just before we set out from their house on Thursday, which she sent to me in addition to posting on Instagram.

Someone misses you too, I type, hoping to recalibrate, to dial it back to a cute exchange about pets.

I wait and I wait, but there's no reply. Maybe I've scared him off. Why on earth did I say that?

A few more minutes tick by, then a few more. I set the phone screen face down in frustration, then take a shower and dress. Finally, there is another ding.

Sorry, Bernie needed to go out. Are you trying to tell me something? he asks.

Now I am even more embarrassed. Yes, I want to say: I've fallen head over heels.

While I'm thinking about a more sensible reply, another text appears.

One Crazy Girl Roll, one . . . no, make that two orders of the Under Control Roll . . . and, depending on what time of day it is, I'll have either a beer or a green tea.

What on earth are you talking about?

You sent me the QR code for the hibachi restaurant. I figured you wanted me to place my order now, just to speed things up when we get there.

> OMG sorry! I thought I was sending you a picture of
> Luna, but I obviously did something wrong. I don't have
> my glasses on because . . . okay, never mind, you know
> that story! That reminds me that I need to find my old
> glasses . . . they're here somewhere.

I reach into the drawer of my bedside table to see if my spare pair of glasses is there, but my hand lands first on the nightguard. It's mine, not Elaine's, but it helps fortify me for what needs to happen next. And while I'm at it, I fish my ring from my luggage and drop it unceremoniously in the drawer.

I give myself a pep talk. I remind myself that it's been nearly a year since Richard and I have so much as shared a meal, sat together at the table, and exchanged snippets of our days. Had we been able to maintain even the illusion of coupledom, might that have been enough to yoke us together in perpetuity for the sake of our marital vows? Possibly so. My instinct, as a general operating principle of life, is not to blow things up. After all, we have twenty-plus years of shared history, a teenaged daughter, and extended family, not to mention a joint bank account and a house.

That said, there's nothing here. He has been living in the basement for nearly two years—except, apparently, when I am out of town and Elaine shows up. Is he a husband or a hemorrhoid, wrapped in neurosis inside a cloak of narcissism?

A friend in whom I confided my marital woes back when I discovered the affair told me that I wasn't ready yet to leave Richard, but that I'd know when it was time.

"How will I know?" I'd asked.

"When you learn he's been hit by a bus but you don't care."

I bristled at this cold advice. I do not wish Richard harm, and it's impossible for me to imagine, even now, not caring. But I have, with certainty, hit my wall.

Whatever is happening down there in the basement, whatever weather event is unfolding, whatever ear he is crafting—I truly no longer care.

⋈   ⋈   ⋈

I walk Luna around the block, then return and make two cups of strong coffee. I carry them to the basement, where I find Richard tapping at his keyboard, staring at his screens. It's a mess down here. The pullout bed on the sofa is unmade, there are wet towels on the floor, and a pileup of dishes corresponding roughly to the number of days I've been away has amassed on the coffee table.

I pull up a chair beside him. He looks at the cup, then at me, and grunts, which I know from twenty years of marriage is as close as he will get to a thank-you.

He rolls his head, but I don't know what that means. Is he acknowledging me, or is he relaxing tension in his neck?

"It's been a clarifying few days," I say.

Again with the head roll.

"I went to Point Pleasant. That's in West Virginia. The place where my parents died."

He remains unresponsive.

Luna bounds down the steps, looks around for a diversion, then squeezes under his desk. I see her moving toward the cord that connects the internet to the modem. For a brief mischievous second I consider letting her clamp her jaws around the cable, do to it whatever she likes, but instead I grab her and pull her into my lap. It might disconnect Richard from the weather for a while, but it would fall to me to get it fixed, and I have better things to do than haggle with home repairs.

I glance over at his screens and see on one of them a weather map with much of the New England states in pink. The states below New England, including DC, are blue. On his other screen I see lines of text.

"I nearly froze to death," I try. "I got stuck in a snowstorm."

When even this fails to get his attention, I realize something is wrong. I tap him on the shoulder, and he turns to me, startled, and removes his earbuds.

"What's up?" he says, sounding annoyed.

"We need to talk, Richard."

"Not a good time, Cass. I'm on deadline." But he concedes a little something, in that he puts back only one earbud.

"You're always on deadline. Every day there is weather and more weather. The weather never ends."

"This happens to be true."

"Give me a few minutes," I say. "In fact, take your other earbud out and let's take a walk."

"That's a hard no. Can't. There's a chance of snow, 33 percent. See the band?" he says, pointing to his screen. "The blue band there, that's snow."

I check my weather app. "Weather.com says it's 29 percent. And . . . just checking CNN—same."

"They're both wrong. They don't know what they're talking about."

It seems useless and beside the point to debate the comparative accuracy of forecasts, especially when talking to a meteorologist.

"It's a beautiful morning, Richard. I just walked Luna and the sun is out. There's no sign of snow, at least not yet, so we could almost certainly walk around the block without getting caught in a flash blizzard."

"Seriously, Cassie. I need to write tomorrow's ear."

"I'll write it for you." I look at him, my very handsome husband, my *Dick*, clad in a blue oxford cloth shirt and khaki pants, dressed for the office he hasn't seen the inside of in years.

"And I have a call with my agent in an hour."

I want to throw something at him, but alas, I'm not the throwing type. "Something that was there is now not there. Maybe it was never there," I say, spewing out the first few only barely sensible words that come to mind.

"What in the name of God are you talking about?"

"That's your ear."

"That's terrible. It has nothing to do with the weather. And it's missing a syllable."

"That's not really the point."

"It's not the point of what?"

"The point is that I can't live like this anymore." I consider elaborating, spelling out the many things I can no longer bear, but it seems unnecessary, and his response indicates that it clearly is.

"I'm going to have to call you back in a minute, Howard," he says. "My wife is having a moment."

"You've been on the phone this whole time? Your editor's been listening to this?"

"I don't think he heard. And besides, what's the big deal?"

"It's over, Richard."

"If that's what you want."

"It is."

"All right then. We can talk about logistics later. If you don't mind, right now I need to get back to work."

This is distressingly simple. I figured he'd put up a fight. That tempers would flare, tears would be shed, there would be pleas for a fresh start.

I'm glad, in a way, that he has pushed us to this point. Better this than spend the rest of my life rationalizing a dead marriage. And yet the nonchalance with which we have brought this very long, painful situation to an end is depressing. I thought we'd have some sort of closure. But then, perhaps there's no such thing.

CHAPTER 37

Reckoning, 3

I COULD STAND here forever in the doorway of Vera's room, drinking in the sight of my daughter. She sits at her desk, looking at the book beside her, tapping out notes. Her long hair spills down her back, and on her head is the pink hat. I keep still, staring, but she must sense my presence, and she looks up and smiles.

Her room has that half-lived-in feel—she's taken most of the things that once defined it, that made it uniquely her space, to her dorm. What remains is a high school time capsule: soccer trophies and ribbons, old uniforms, posters of boy bands she no longer listens to, and a closetful of clothes she will likely never wear again, including a beloved old pair of Frye boots, one of which has a hole worn through the toe.

On the wall above the desk is a bulletin board. Colorful pushpins hold in place small Polaroid photos of her and her friends in a wide variety of poses: at the beach, on the soccer field, at parties. A normal happy childhood—or so it has always seemed from my vantage point. At least Richard and I have successfully raised this lovely child, given her some footing, rendering our marriage not entirely in vain.

"That hat!" I say. "I'm glad you like it."

Instinctively her hand goes to her head, but she doesn't reply.

"What are you working on, sweetheart?"

"I have a big paper for my psych class due next week."

"Aren't you on break?"

"Technically, yes, but the professor said we can take until the end of the month."

"What's it on?"

"Intergenerational trauma."

"That sounds intense. Tell me more. I mean, I've read about this, about how children inherit trauma from war, from genocide, even if they didn't live through it themselves. Is that what you mean?"

"Yes. But it has implications in all sorts of contexts, with any sort of historical trauma. Or even personal trauma. And it doesn't have to be about an entire generation of people. It can occur within individual families."

"Interesting. Like what's an example?"

She turns to face me, and I am reminded of the degree to which we look alike, so much so that one might suppose I somehow spawned her without the help of a mate.

"Oh, I don't know, Mom. How about an example being a girl who grew up in a family where no one ever talked about anything meaningful. How this girl knew, from a very young age, that something very bad must have happened a generation ago."

She pauses and locks eyes with me. This is a challenge, I now see.

"And how all the silence haunts her and has in many ways defined her life," she continues.

It takes me a minute to absorb what she is saying: *What haunts me, haunts her.* How have I not seen this? I told her my parents died in a bridge accident but was admittedly stingy with the details, even the few that I knew.

"Go on," I say cautiously.

"This hat is a big step, Mom."

"Seriously? It's just a . . . silly souvenir."

"It's an admission."

"An admission of what?"

"That we have a connection to the Silver Bridge collapse. To the story of the Mothman. Why will no one talk about any of this?"

"I don't know . . ." I begin, but I can't finish the sentence. I don't even know what I don't know, other than that I don't know what to say.

"Do you know I'm completely obsessed with the Mothman? That I used to have nightmares?"

"I didn't know you knew anything about any of this," I bluff. I knew, at least, that she had been watching the movie one night, when I'd heard the snippet of dialogue issuing from her room.

"How could I grow up in this house and not know?"

"We never talked about it."

"Quod erat demonstrandum! That's precisely the problem."

"I had no idea . . ."

"Good grief, Mom. I even have a tattoo."

"You have a tattoo? I never gave you permission to get a tattoo! We talked about this!"

"Okay, that's totally not the point. We talked about it when I was a kid. I'm nineteen now. I didn't need permission."

"What's the tattoo?" I ask, hoping it's not something to do with her long-term high school boyfriend, a bro of a hockey player who drank too much, and whom I never especially liked. Mercifully, he wound up going to college in Scotland and they seem to have drifted apart.

"You're really not following, Mom. The tattoo is of the moth."

"You have a tattoo of the moth? Can I see?" I'm a mix of contradictory emotions: angry, fascinated, and deeply moved.

She pulls up the sleeve of her t-shirt, and on her left shoulder I see a tiny, beautiful moth. It's a purplish color, rich in detail, a thing of art that is neither menacing nor cartoonish.

"I love that, Vera," I say, surprising myself. "I'm even a little jealous."

"You should get one too," she says. "I'll go with you."

"Ha! As if." I'm too old and timid to get a tattoo, plus it was ingrained in me as a child that this is not something I should ever do for religious reasons—not that I was ever especially religious, but the prohibition lodged in my mind nonetheless.

"You know I've watched *The Mothman Prophecies* about a thousand times," she says.

"Um, no. I did not know that."

"It's kind of weird, how Dad looks like that character who also happens to work at the *Washington Post*. I'm guessing you've seen the movie."

"I have. And I know, right?"

"I asked Olivia about it once. She freaked out and told me not to talk about it around you. She said it was too triggering."

"That's completely untrue, Vera. I'm so sorry she said that.

I need to talk to Olivia about all of this. She's the one who's been keeping secrets, more so than I ever knew. I learned some pretty life-changing things on this trip that I need to talk to you about at the right time. I'm still piecing it together myself. But for now, I'm sorry it's trickled down to you and possibly inflicted some whole intergenerational trauma thing on you too."

"You were in West Virginia, right? Maybe I can go there with you sometime? I'd like to see the bridge. The new bridge, I mean."

"That would be great. I'm going back in two weeks. I need to pick up my car. It's a long story. Do you want to come?"

"I can't. A bunch of us might go skiing in Pennsylvania over MLK weekend."

Does it make me a terrible mother to say I'm mildly relieved she can't come? I'm looking forward to time with Ingram but would without question prioritize a road trip with Vera over that.

"I'd love to go with you. Spring break road trip?"

"Yeah, maybe. Although I might go to New York with some friends. I'll get back to you about that. But I do want to go. I want to see the museum. And the gift shop. I bought a few things from there online."

"You did? Why have I never seen any of it?"

"Well, like Olivia said, I didn't want to *trigger* you."

"Please. It takes more than whatever you might buy in a gift shop to trigger me. Can I see some of the things?"

She goes over to her dresser, digs around, and produces a t-shirt featuring a cuddly-looking Mothman set against the backdrop of what might or might not be a bridge. She has a hooded sweatshirt, too, with a slightly less campy version of the moth.

"I like that one! I saw it in the shop. I would have bought more stuff for you, but I didn't have time . . . We had to go to lunch with Cynthia, and then . . . Well, you wouldn't believe it if I told you the whole story. It's a long one. But I'd rather see what else you have."

"You will not believe what I just got. Guess what it is."

"I can't begin to guess."

Vera walks into the bathroom and returns with a plastic case of . . . something. Hopefully not Mexican jumping beans. Or retainers. Maybe I *am* easily triggered.

"What even is that?"

She hands it to me, and I see an adorable looking she-moth adorning the cover of the plastic case. She looks coquettish, somehow, with those bright red eyes. She clasps a can of something between her wings.

"It's eyeshadow, Mom. This is called the Mothman Palette."

She opens the lid, and I see a spectrum of shimmering colors.

"Those are really pretty!" I say, surprised.

"Yeah, listen to the names—this one is called Moth Bunz. Get it, Mom? Like moth behinds."

"I got it. Cute. What's that one?" I point to a shade of orangey pink.

"You don't want to know. Some of these are sort of suggestive."

"I can handle it."

"Okay, that one says MILF."

"Seriously?"

"Yes, but it stands for Mothman I'd Like to Find."

"All right then. What's that one? The silvery one?"

"Premonitions."

"Oh, that's pretty rich."

"It's many things, the moth. I'm thinking I might want to write about it sometime, maybe for the sociology class I'm taking next semester."

"What about, do you think?"

"Maybe something about the sociology of consumption. Like how society can take a tragic event and turn it into a shopping opportunity."

"Well, that's America for you. Or capitalism. Or human nature, as people who like to excuse that kind of thing say. What do I know? But you're not wrong about that."

"I do have one question, Mom."

"Ask me anything."

"Do you believe any of it is true? I mean the Mothman part? Obviously the bridge collapsed."

"I believe people believe it is true. That's all I need to know."

"But do you believe it?"

"Truly, that's my answer. Disappointing as it is. Not everything can be explained. But that's what makes life a wonder."

"That's a kind of milquetoast answer."

"It's a terrible answer. I'm still working on a better answer."

"Okay, no offense, Mom, but can we talk later? I need to get back to work."

"Sure, sure, but . . . I have something else I need to talk to you about. It's important."

"What? You and Dad are . . ." She makes an overly dramatic slashing gesture across the throat.

"Did he tell you already?"

"No. We don't really talk about stuff. Only about the weather. And now his book. That's all he wants to talk about since I got home. His book *this*, his book *that*. But I just figured."

"Are you okay, honey? I mean . . . I haven't prepared a big speech or anything. It all feels very sudden, and I know this is a big deal. But I want you to know nothing will change between us. And he'll still be your dad. And . . ."

"Mom, please. I'm a big girl. It's been over for a long time. I'm glad you can finally see that—I was starting to worry about you. You'll be okay. I know you will. We can talk more about it later. I need another couple of hours to work on this paper."

And with that, I am dismissed.

CHAPTER 38

Reckoning, 4

ALTHOUGH MY OLD pair of glasses is a touch behind prescription-wise, it's nice to be able to see again even if, fashion-wise, these oversized black-rimmed spectacles make me look part owl. I'm reminded of the first time Olivia took me for glasses, when I was twelve. I'd been telling her for a few months that I was having trouble seeing the chalkboard at school, but she thought I was just whining and insisted that everyone in the family has perfect vision. When a routine vision test at school validated my claims, she finally took me to the optician. I remember putting on my first pair of glasses, looking up at the sky, and for the first time I could recall, seeing stars.

⋈　　⋈　　⋈

I have arranged to meet Olivia this afternoon in the NPR studio, where she is popping by to pick up some mail and catch up with colleagues in person. I keep forgetting that I'm walking around with a bandaged head until I see people staring at me, but I succeed in getting a security badge and finding my way to her tiny office without having to field any questions. I settle into a seat in the corner of her dusty, windowless pod. It's like a little slice of heaven in here. Not the West Virginia kind of outdoor heaven but the indoor, bookish kind. There are so many volumes that at some point, inevitably, the shelves will crack and collapse onto themselves, unleashing a book avalanche, or a book tsunami—it doesn't matter which, since either is a fitting way for Olivia to transition from this messy corner of self-made heaven to heaven proper, living up to the inscription on the white marble headstone that will surely read: *Here lies Olivia Oliver, by the weight of stories eternally crushed.*

I wait some twenty minutes, by which time I complete *Wordle* and get to "Nice" in *Spelling Bee*, then start to wonder if she has forgotten about our impromptu meeting. Just when I'm thinking of shifting to plan B, Olivia sweeps in, her voice booming, laughing as she winds down her conversation with a young man who is saying something about getting an actress whom I have never heard of on the show. The actress in question has apparently written a juicy memoir that includes tales of her literary agent father sleeping with several of her friends.

All these people and all their books. This office and these books. It makes my head hurt in an existential, as opposed to physical, way.

There are a number of close calls where it seems like they are done talking—the young man even begins to back away—but then Olivia switches conversational gears. She knows how to keep people talking just as well as she knows how to shut people down.

They finish, finally, and he leaves. She shuts the door, and I have her attention at last.

I have a brief delusional moment where I think she is going to say something warm, maternal, the sort of thing I need to hear, even if I don't quite know what that is myself.

"What the hell, Cassie?" she says instead. "We were worried sick about you!"

"You didn't look all that worried last night," I say, thinking of her sitting at my dining room table, laughing, talking to Elaine.

"Well, I was worried, truly. Why do you think Harry and I drove into town? To be with Vera. And to see what I could figure out about your whereabouts without alarming her. I had no idea Richard had news. We were kind of accidentally sucked into the celebration of his forthcoming book product with your friend Elaine."

"She's no friend of mine," I say. "Not anymore."

I assume Olivia has no knowledge of Elaine's relationship with Richard, but she's not big on domestic drama, and she lets my comment slide.

"Well, I tried to leave when I realized I'd walked into . . . whatever I'd walked into. Your friend, or your not-friend, Elaine, had just arrived with a cake and champagne, and it was awkward to leave. So there we were."

It occurs to me that Richard might want to stay on Olivia's good side, that already he is plying her with cake, quietly lobbying to show up as a guest on her program. The thought is almost more horrifying than the idea of the comeback strategy book itself.

"I find it all kinds of depressing," I say, "that he is going to be paid—*well* paid—to turn his debacle into a book."

"On this we are in complete agreement. But such is publishing. The public loves a good redemption story. They gobble them up."

"Publishing is a form of alchemy. Have you thought of that?"

"Yes, dear—making gold out of crap."

"Plus, he hasn't redeemed himself yet, your Richard, my future-former."

"That's not really the point." She lets my announcement of the impending split slide. Is she surprised? Disappointed? Or simply doing what she usually does—that is, pretending anything unpleasant away?

There is a knock at the door and a woman with an iPad looks in, studies me briefly, then apologizes: "Sorry, I didn't know you were in a meeting."

"No problem. Just give us a few minutes and I'll meet you in the studio. And do me a favor and close the door again?"

I take a deep breath.

"Why didn't you tell me?" I ask. We both know what I mean.

"You went to West Virginia. I saw the bag you gave to Vera," she replies, ignoring my question.

"I did. It was surprisingly instructive. And easy. The universe—or the town of Point Pleasant, West Virginia, at least—seemed to want me to know my story. I talked to a bunch of people, including another survivor."

Does Olivia's expression change when I use this word, *survivor*, to describe myself? It's hard to say.

"She said something about seeing a blue plastic ball, a Hoppity, on the riverbank."

Olivia starts to fiddle with her hair.

"And I talked to a doctor. He told me about how he'd stitched up a young girl who had sustained some horrific injuries. They were able to save her life."

Olivia starts to cry, which is deeply unsettling, something I've not previously ever seen her do. I didn't even know she had functioning tear ducts. She puts her head in her hands, doubles over. Her body shakes.

I press on. I need to let it all out, lest she leave and slam the door. "The doctor said my stitches were not consistent with a child who had fallen into a tomato cage."

"For the record, you did fall into a tomato cage. And you needed stitches. In pretty much the same spot. So that story is not untrue."

I'm not sure what to do with this piece of information, but I file it away.

"And then I talked to a dog breeder," I continue. "He told me about some heroic dog who saved a child's life."

Now Olivia is in full breakdown mode. Her head falls to the desk. She's sobbing audibly. There is a knock on the door. Yet another put-together young woman looks in, glances at Olivia, assesses me, nods, lingers an instant, and leaves.

"I'm so sorry, Cassie," she says. This is the first time I've heard words to this effect. "I didn't know what to do. It was a different era. They had a different approach to trauma, physical and psychological, back then. I talked to a psychiatrist who said you were too young to remember anyway, so it would be better to scrub that memory, free you from growing up with it. And you know me . . . I'm not so good with these things anyway. I'm not one of those oversharing types. I don't drink tea, or do bubble baths or yoga . . ."

I don't know what tea, bubble baths, or yoga have to do with anything, but I give her a pass.

"And I was in my own state of shock. Your mother and I were very close. I lost my best friend. And I loved your dad, even though I'd only known him a few years."

"How did I even get out?"

"Out?"

"Of the car. It's one of the tiny details I keep turning over in my head."

"We'll never really know, but no one was big on seatbelts back then, so you were probably bouncing around in the back, playing with your new dog. The car was a convertible, so it's possible the roof popped open—the clasps that attach the ragtop to the top of a windshield are weak, deliberately perhaps—and you and the dog must have floated out. You held on to the dog's collar, they guessed. The Hoppity followed you. Sometimes I think it did that to make sure. I'm not a touchy-feely type, but I do believe that good toys do that.

"The police held on to the dog and to Hoppity. It took a while for them to reach us, and it took us a while to reach them— we heard about the accident and started calling, and once we learned what happened, we rushed to West Virginia to get you.

"Fortunately you were not that far from shore when the car plunged. Otherwise, you would never have made it with the cold. Even so, they all said it was a miracle. We waited a few days until you could travel. I remember the three of you on the back seat, that wonderful hero dog. The blue Hoppity, who I think commanded your rescue, and you, flat on your tummy, asleep. Your back hurt a lot, but they had you on painkillers, so you slept most of the way."

"But why . . . Once I was old enough, why didn't anyone tell me?"

"It became harder and harder. Once you begin to tell a story, it's hard to dial it back. You want to make it make sense. You know that, you're a writer."

Am I? I'm tempted to ask. But that's hardly the point.

"I was in so deep by the time you were older, I didn't even know where to begin. There came this moment when it was easier to keep embellishing. So I started piling on the details. Harry and I argued about this, but in the end he went along."

"Like telling me about the wedding for the nonexistent cousins in Toledo?"

"Right. Although who knows. It's a big family. If you go on Ancestry, or 23andMe, or what have you—"

"Not the point! You wouldn't answer my questions. You made me feel bad for asking. I can't even find any pictures except the one downstairs. What happened to all of their *stuff*?"

"It was wrong. I know. But it exists. It's in storage back in DC. I can give you the code. Honestly, I couldn't bear to have it in the house, and I didn't want to traumatize you with it either.

"I do love you, Cassie. I probably don't say that enough. This was wrong. Absolutely. I can see that now, but I was trying to protect you. And like I said, Harry wanted me to tell you from the start. He said I was behaving like his parents, who refused to talk about the Holocaust once they arrived in America, and he wasn't wrong. But then it all seemed so unhealthy, the way you became obsessed, always reading that book, then going on the internet, looking up that nonsense about the moth. No good could come from any of that."

"How can you, of all people, say that? You're a storyteller. And you've been shutting me out of my own story my entire life."

"Cassie, I'm guilty of everything you say. I think there's only one way for you to fix this. Well, not fix it. It's done, and it's not fixable. But you can own it now, stake it out, like a land claim—your place in the world. That's at least one form of amends."

"What do you mean by 'own it'?"

"I mean, write that book you've been not writing your entire life. Make some sense of all of this."

"I don't have any idea how to do that."

"Why don't you go back to Delaware for a week or two? Harry and I are going to hang out in the city for a bit and catch up with friends. You can have the beach house to yourself. Turn it into a little writing retreat."

"I wouldn't even know where to begin."

"That's easy. Begin with the bridge."

CHAPTER 39

Flight, Cont.

IT'S A PERFECT winter's day, with no storms in the forecast. Now that my relationship to weather has been given some air, I did the responsible thing and checked my app before setting out, just to be safe. The bright sun turns the bay a cerulean blue, and for a moment it is possible to imagine we are elsewhere, on the French Riviera perhaps, although there's no denying I am most decidedly here, suspended nearly two hundred feet over the Chesapeake Bay on a bridge, and I am okay with that.

My vision is so clear that I can see the details on the fishing boat that's about to pass beneath us. People are scurrying on the deck, bottles of wine being poured even though it is midday.

"It's like I have megavision now," I tell Vera. "I can make out the expressions of the seagulls flying overhead."

"Get a grip, Mom," she says. "It's called getting an updated prescription and new glasses."

Vera has agreed to come with me to Delaware, where we will spend the weekend walking Luna along the chilly beach, eating crabs and fries on the boardwalk, and otherwise catching up.

Then, on Sunday, Vera will drive back to school in her car and leave me in Rehoboth to write until Ingram picks me up to take me to West Virginia.

We've done a lot of talking these past few days, but it is not until we are safely on the other side of the bay that I tell Vera about my incident on the bridge. About the moth in the car. About Luna barking and lunging at the moth, about my fear that she might eat it. I tell her I had been listening to a song involving a dog that had just stopped barking at the same time Luna's barking began. Weirdly, the song had mentioned West Virginia.

I tell her the whole long story about hitting my head, about Olivia's Hoppity disclosure, about the newspaper's advertising supplement: "If Bridges Could Talk." I explain how all this set me in motion. I leave out the part about her father, about Elaine and the nightguard on my bedside table; she doesn't need this level of detail. Let her figure out which part of this matters on her own.

At the end of the story, she has one question.

"What was the song?"

"Which song?"

"The one about the barking dog."

I tell her the title: "The Skin of My Yellow Country Teeth."

"What a terrible name, Mom!"

"Not denying it." I hand her my phone, and she locates it on Spotify. We listen to the infectious, catchy beat, the goofy lyrics, the scratchy, yearning voice of the lead singer. She says she loves it despite the title, then plays it again, this time louder.

"This is my new favorite song," she says when it ends, and plays it again.

And again and again.

"It makes me want to dance," she says.

By now we are winding through rural Maryland roads dotted with farm stands, all closed for winter.

"It's, like, the happiest song I've ever heard. Let's dance when we get to the beach."

"I'm not sure I remember how to dance."

"Oh please. Just jump up and down and flap your arms. Like you're flying. Or you're on a pogo stick."

"Like I'm a moth. Or a bluebird."

"Sure. Choose whatever creature you like. Also, let's watch the movie."

"Which movie?"

"The Mothman movie."

"Seriously?"

"Yes. Let's make a big bowl of popcorn and throw pieces at the screen whenever something ridiculous happens. Or maybe every time the guy who looks like Dad appears. No offense to Dad. It's just for fun."

"That will take a lot of popcorn!"

"It will. We can eat some of it too."

"This sounds like it might be the most fun weekend of my life."

✠   ✠   ✠

Once Vera leaves for school, I'm stranded without a vehicle, and there is nothing to do but take long walks, then stare out at the winter sea, and write.

Each morning, before I sit at my desk, I spend a few minutes thinking about what I will find in the storage locker when I

return: the unfinished stories of my parents' lives, not unlike the threads of my students' stories that have all been left
dangling. Before I write, I say a silent prayer for those characters in distress: the soccer goalie, the nanny, the philanthropist,
the Marrano, the man whose family perished in the back of a
coyote's van. A new class will begin as soon as I return from
Point Pleasant. New stories will accumulate, then join the others
clamoring in my head.

For now, I focus on my own story. And I write and write
and write. Then I delete everything I've just written and begin
to write again. I take more long walks on the beach, return to
the computer, make strong coffee, then stare at the screen in
despair.

Two weeks go by in a flash, and from that turmoil, a strong
beginning has emerged: It has to do with a woman who finds
herself on a bridge. Traffic comes to a standstill. In the car are
a puppy and a moth.

I play with the tense, changing it from present to past, from
past to present, again and again, before deciding to leave it in
the past, because I am determined, finally, to look ahead. I
sense it's pointed in the right direction, but even if it isn't, I'm
not going to give up.

Luna begins to bark as I'm puzzling over a scene involving a
child running for a ball, falling backward into a tomato patch.
Does she land on the rusty wire cage protecting the plant? Does
her back gets badly torn up, requiring stiches? Do those stitches
join the network of scar tissue formed from stitches that were
already there? Is this story to be believed, and does it even
matter? This is fiction, after all.

A car has pulled into the driveway, and there is a scratching at the door. I swing it open and little Bernie jumps excitedly at my leg, then runs past me to pounce on Luna. They jump on the couch, they jump off the couch, and the puppy mayhem begins.

Ingram is standing in the doorway watching the dogs, waiting to be formally invited in. He looks different and he looks the same. Gone is the cryptozoologist costume and the cryptozoologist vibe. He has lost the beard. He wears even thicker-framed, nerdier glasses than before, a newish-looking Irish fisherman's sweater—a holiday present, perhaps—and his hair looks freshly cut. He looks like the academic that he is. I get that this is not only a bit of snobbery—my snobbery—at work, but also what Harry would call confirmation bias: I'm processing information about Ingram that is consistent with what I already know.

Shyly, we embrace, causing the dogs to once again bark. *None of this in front of us*, they seem to say. I invite him in, make some tea, and we spend hours talking. Between us we have two lifetimes on which to catch up.

We will leave for West Virginia in the morning, and then return to our separate cities, but already we are hinting about ways to make the geography work. After my recent marital turmoil, I'm in no particular rush.

The dogs grow restless, having clearly had enough of this conversation. Right now, what they seem to want is a walk along the beach.

⋈　　⋈　　⋈

It's a cold, clear winter's day, and bundled in our parkas, we draw a little too close to the surf, our shoes getting wet in the foam. Half a mile down the shore, we come across an enormous sandcastle, its turrets, moats, and complicated network of waterways still visible despite some erosion. As we marvel at the craftsmanship, a small creature scurries through one of the castle's doorways.

"A crab!" I say, startled.

Ingram squats and studies it more closely. "I think it's a ghost crab."

"A *ghost* crab? Is that different from a sand crab?"

"Not my area of expertise, stranger, but ghost crabs are generally nocturnal. I don't know what it's doing here in daylight."

"I thought you knew everything," I chide him.

"There are more things I don't understand than those I do understand, or ever will. That's the nature of my job. And of the universe, I might add."

"I'm not sure I understand much of anything," I say. "But at least I've figured out a lot these last couple of weeks. And it led me to this," I say, opening my arms wide, gesturing, to what, I'm not sure—the sand, the sky, the ghost crab, my fresh outlook on life, and to this lovely man. "At the risk of being cheesy, it led me to you."

"I love cheesy," he says, turning toward me. My hair is blowing in the wind, probably tangling itself into knots. Ingram gathers it into a ponytail, then presses his lips to mine.

Our picturesque moment is interrupted, unsurprisingly, by a dog. Luna bolts, running so far up the beach I can no longer see her. Panicked, I run ahead. I assume she is chasing a seagull, but when I draw closer, I can see she has met up with another dog, another family. I walk a few more feet and see it's the men we met at the beach a few weeks ago, Olivia and Harry's new neighbors, Damian and Leon, in their lime-green parkas, with their overweight dachshund, Patrice.

As I continue to run toward them, looking out onto the expanse of grey-blue water, I feel a lightness, and think I might, at long last, achieve flight.

THE END

Notes and Acknowledgments

I AM GRATEFUL to the DC Commission on the Arts and Humanities for their support of this project.

This is a work of fiction, and I have taken some small liberties with the details of the 1967 Silver Bridge collapse, with West Virginia geography, with the names of Point Pleasant establishments, and with reports concerning the sightings of a giant creature—part man, part moth—prior to the catastrophe.

The book *The Silver Bridge Disaster of 1967* was a primary source for details, as was the archive at the Mothman Museum. Many other sources directly or indirectly fed into this narrative, including the movie *The Mothman Prophecies*, the *Astonishing Legends* podcast, and an advertising supplement that fell out of my morning newspaper called *West Virginia, Explore Mountaineer Country*.

On the weather front, thank you to my meteorologist cousin, Sam Coplin, and to everyone's favorite DC meteorologist, Matthew Cappucci, both of whom gave me ideas about the ways a person might blow up a career. Any mistakes in describing meteorological conditions are entirely on me.

Thank you to everyone on the Harper Muse team for giving me a forum in which to further explore this story, which has haunted me for many years. My editor, Kimberly Carlton, is one of a kind—insightful, supportive, and wise, and she helped me to better understand my own book.

Once again, Jocelyn Bailey saved me from errors large and small. I am fortunate to work with everyone on the HM team including Amanda Bostic, Savannah Breedlove, Nekasha Pratt, Margaret Kercher, Colleen Lacey, Kerri Potts, Taylor Ward, and many, many others. Thank you to Halie Cotton for yet another excellent cover. And endless thanks for the ongoing support and great editorial feedback from my agent, Josh Getzler, as well as Jonathan Cobb and everyone at HG Literary.

And who knew about the intersection of booksellers and Mothman enthusiasts? Thank you to Morgan Harding for telling me about the Mothman Palette, and thank you to Andrew Pettis for pointing me in the direction of the excellent and very helpful *Astonishing Legends* podcast. Thanks to Anton Bogomazov for sending me inspiring Mothman ephemera over the last couple of years. Thanks, too, to Wendy Wasserman for allowing me to model Luna, the Lab-husky mix in the novel, on Annie.

And to Lynda Goldberg for sending the WVPB transmitter map, and to Katie Goldberg for the frequent and amusing Mothman DMs.

And thank you to my friends and family for reading drafts of this book in progress, including Michelle Brafman, Ally Coll,

Molly McCloskey, Lisa Zeidner, and the members of my 2021 Novel Year class who agreed to look at a (terrible) early draft of chapter one: Holly Piper, Amy Tercek, Sarah Williams, Varun Gauri, Daniel Knowlton, Suzanne Aro, Tamar Shapiro, and Nick Manning.

My children are the absolute best: thank you to Ally, Emma, and Max Coll, and to Sarah and Katie Goldberg, for their on-going support.

And most of all, thank you to my husband, Paul Goldberg, who read many, many, many drafts, weighed in with always smart suggestions, drove with me to Point Pleasant, West Virginia, introduced me to deep-fried Oreos, and would not let me give up on this book.

Discussion Questions

1. Like Cassie, have you ever uncovered a family secret? How long did you suspect something was amiss, and what was the fallout of your discovery?
2. Describe Cassie's marriage to Richard. Would you be able to tolerate her situation? Why do you think she stays with him as long as she does?
3. Would you describe Cassie's road trip as a "midlife crisis"? What about the period of midlife makes us prone to drastic changes or actions?
4. Why do you think Cassie is so preoccupied with her students' stories? Is this preoccupation at all related to the fact that she seems to be a blocked writer?
5. By the end of the story, what were your thoughts about the Mothman? Do you believe in such supernatural occurrences? What conspiracies or urban legends do you find most interesting (if any)?
6. Why do certain myths and legends tend to last for so long in the public imagination? What purpose do they

serve? And what does our belief or interest in them say about us?

7. Cassie's adventure is spurred on by a combination of frustration and instinct. What else causes her to hit the road? Does your assessment of her change from the beginning of the novel to the end?

8. Have you, like Cassie, had family members who made you feel nuts? Describe Harry and Olivia's behavior: What about it is odd? What about it can you understand? What obvious mistakes have they made?

9. What do you make of Ingram's work as a philosophy professor, researcher, and writer? What sort of observations might he make about people who believe in the Mothman or other cryptids?

10. Why do you think Cassie is finally able to put pen to paper in the end? What have her discoveries unlocked for her writing and her life moving forward?

About the Author

Photo by Marvin Joseph

Real Life and Other Fictions is Susan Coll's seventh novel. Her previous books include *Bookish People*; *The Stager*, a *New York Times* and *Chicago Tribune* Editor's Choice; and *Acceptance*, which was made into a television movie starring Joan Cusack. Her work has appeared in publications including the *New York Times Book Review*, the *Washington Post*, *Washingtonian Magazine*, *Moment Magazine*, NPR.org, and Atlantic.com. She is the events advisor at Politics and Prose Bookstore in Washington, DC, and was the president of the PEN/Faulkner Foundation for five years.

✻   ✻   ✻

Visit Susan online at susancoll.com
Instagram: @susan_keselenko_coll
Twitter: @Susan_Coll
Pinterest: @susancollauthor